THERE GOES MY HEART

The Maine Sullivans

Rory Sullivan and Zara Mirren

Bella Andre

THERE GOES MY HEART

The Maine Sullivans

Rory Sullivan and Zara Mirren

© 2019 Bella Andre

Sign up for Bella's New Release Newsletter

www.BellaAndre.com/newsletter

bella@bellaandre.com

www.BellaAndre.com

Bella on Twitter: @bellaandre

Bella on Facebook: facebook.com/bellaandrefans

Rory Sullivan, a renowned artisan woodworker, has no plans to fall in love anytime soon. Especially not with Zara Mirren, who shares a converted warehouse space with him in Bar Harbor, Maine. While she is a brilliant maker—the eyeglasses frames she designs are practically works of art—everything else about her drives him bonkers. The way she's always whistling cheesy pop songs off-key. The way her half-finished cups of coffee litter every available countertop. And especially the way he can't take his eyes off her whenever she enters a room...or stop thinking about her after she leaves.

Zara loves everything about her career—designing and manufacturing bright, fun glasses frames fulfills both the creative and technical sides of her brain. The only downside to coming to work is bumping into irritating, far-too-handsome-for-his-own-good Rory Sullivan...even if she secretly enjoys the zingers they throw at each other. On the plus side, thinking up new ways to torment Rory on a daily basis has helped Zara stop dwelling on the fact that her ex-boyfriend cheated on her with her stepsister.

But when Zara learns that her ex and her stepsister have just become engaged, she's doubly stunned by Rory's suggestion that he go to the engagement party as her pretend boyfriend, in a one-night truce where they'll be a team rather than adversaries. Only, when it turns out that the sparks between them disguise a deeper passion—and a bigger emotional connection—than either has ever known, will both Rory and Zara end up losing their hearts to the last person they could have imagined?

A note from Bella

There Goes My Heart is dedicated to girls with glasses!

I have been wearing glasses since I was nine years old. I might not have looked cool in the oversized brown frames, but it meant that I could play tennis, read the chalkboard in class, and not trip over things when I walked.

I've long wanted to write about a heroine who wears glasses—and a hero who thinks she's even more beautiful while wearing them.

Rory Sullivan is the perfect man for Zara Mirren. And not just because he loves chocolate cake as much as she does, but because when Zara needs him, he'll do whatever he can to bring her joy.

I hope you absolutely love Rory and Zara's romance, set in beautiful Bar Harbor, Maine.

If this is your first time reading about the Sullivans, you can easily read each book as a stand-alone—and there is a Sullivan family tree available on my website (www.bellaandre.com/sullivan-family-tree) so you can see how the books are connected!

Happy reading,
Bella Andre

P.S. More stories about the Maine Sullivans are coming soon! Please be sure to sign up for my newsletter (bellaandre.com/newsletter) so that you don't miss out on any new book announcements.

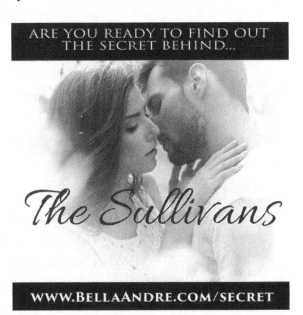

CHAPTER ONE

Zara Mirren couldn't stop laughing. It was either that or cry. Or, better yet, not give a damn what her stepsister and ex-boyfriend did.

Like, say, get engaged.

Zara poured herself another glass of bubbly. So what if it was just before nine in the morning in Bar Harbor, Maine? It would soon be five p.m. in Helsinki, and that was good enough for her.

She gulped her second drink so quickly that the bubbles barely had time to fizz on her tongue. Normally, she wasn't much of a drinker and would have nursed a glass of Prosecco for a good hour. Today, however, she was glad to be a lightweight. The sooner she got flat-out drunk, the better.

"Celebrating something?"

Zara looked up to see Rory Sullivan leaning against the door frame of the communal kitchen. In his white T-shirt and well-worn jeans, he resembled a modern-day James Dean.

It was just her luck that Rory would be here bright

and early on a Friday morning to find her drowning her sorrows in a leftover bottle of bubbly from the open house their artists' collective had held the previous weekend.

Together with six other makers, Zara and Rory rented space in a converted warehouse a few miles outside of downtown. Zara got along well with everyone else in the building. Only Rory drove her crazy.

She was pretty sure she drove him even crazier.

Smiling at the thought, she topped up her glass, then brought it to her lips for another long glug. After she'd emptied it, she replied, "It's another day in paradise. What's not to celebrate?"

Still leaning against the door frame, he looked out the window. "Blue skies and sunshine are definitely nice after all the rain we've been having," he agreed before turning his gaze back to her. "Why don't we go take a walk and enjoy it?"

She snorted her response to this ridiculous question—the two of them had never willingly spent time alone together, unless they were arguing. The gesture knocked her glasses slightly askew, but she didn't bother to right her specs. She was okay with everything going a little blurry today. "No, thanks." She refilled her glass, lifting it toward him in a quasi-toast. "I'm happy here."

He moved closer, and unfortunately, she wasn't drunk enough yet not to notice how good he smelled. Like fresh cedar wood. During the year she'd been working here, she'd found that no matter how sweaty he got while working in his furniture workshop, he never smelled bad. What's more, his work was always brilliant.

Damn him.

He poured himself a cup of coffee and pulled a chair up to the table. "Care to share what you're so over the moon about?"

She got the sense he was choosing his words carefully, something he'd never done with her. With everyone else, he was charm personified. But when the two of them were talking—sparring, more likely—he took great pleasure in acting the devil.

And if more often than not, he made her want to laugh...well, she wasn't about to admit that anytime soon.

Perhaps if her head hadn't started to feel like it was going to lift up off her neck and float away, she might have been able to come up with a brilliant answer to his question. Instead, she found her mouth shaping the words, "My news is going to make your day."

He gave her a small smile, one that made her stomach feel fluttery. No, that had to be due to the Prosecco. Still, it didn't help that he was sitting close enough for her to see the flecks of green in his blue eyes.

"I can't wait to hear it," he said.

Again, it seemed wisest to take another drink before speaking. When she put the empty glass down, it wobbled on its base and started to tip. Before she could get her hand to obey her brain's instructions to reach for it, Rory had righted the glass.

"My stepsister just got engaged," she said. He raised an eyebrow, obviously waiting for her to explain why this wasn't fantastic news. "To my ex-boyfriend." His other eyebrow went up, but he remained silent, as though he knew instinctively that wasn't the end of the story. "I found them in bed together a year ago."

That was when she had decided to leave Camden and move to Bar Harbor. Camden was too small a town—she kept running into the happy couple in the grocery store, and the coffee shop, and while filling her car with gas. Two weeks after she'd discovered their affair, she'd packed up her things and headed north.

Rory didn't look like he pitied her, thankfully, though he did note, "That sucks."

It did. Of course it did. But Zara had been down similar roads with her stepsister for fifteen years now, albeit on a less grand scale. She didn't blame Brittany for being beautiful and fashionable and irresistible to all men everywhere. Instead, Zara tried to tell herself she was grateful that Brittany had helped her see Cameron's true colors before she got in too deep. Now her stepsister was stuck with him. Good riddance.

Besides, she'd been through far worse things than this. Her stepsister and her ex getting married would be a walk in the park compared to the loss of her mom when she was fourteen.

Zara shrugged. "They're good together. Better than he and I ever were. It's no big deal." At least, it wouldn't be once she'd had more to drink.

She reached for the bottle and turned it upside down over her glass. Her aim was no longer great, however, and were it not for the fact that the bottle was nearly empty, she would have drenched the table. She put it down and swiped her fingers through the small pool of sweet bubbles, licked them off, then held up her phone and waved it at Rory.

"I got her text a few minutes before you showed up." She squinted at the screen, rereading her stepsister's words. "There's a party too. Just a small gathering." Zara almost laughed again. Nothing Brittany did was small. Apart from her waistline.

"When is it?"

Zara rested her chin on her hands. She couldn't remember the last time her head had felt so heavy, like it was twice as big as it should be. *What had Rory just asked?* Oh yeah, the party details. "Tomorrow. They're so excited, she said they can't wait to celebrate with everyone." Her stepsister had sent a selfie of Cameron kissing her while she held up a massive diamond ring to the camera.

"Tomorrow works for me," Rory told her.

Zara's eyes had been closing, but when his words finally sank into her brain, she goggled at him. "What do your Saturday plans have to do with me?"

"I'm free to go with you."

Had he lost his mind? "I didn't ask you to go with me."

He reached for the roll of paper towels on the counter behind him, his T-shirt riding up to expose a couple of inches of tanned skin, along with abdominal muscles that only made her goggle more.

Gently, he lifted her arms, wiped up the Prosecco puddle beneath them, then said, "Going with me has got to be better than going alone."

On any normal day, she would have scoffed at that statement. But on one that had begun so awfully, she found herself seriously considering his proposition. She stared at him. "I suppose some people might think you're attractive."

That got a low laugh out of him. "I've had my share of compliments over the years."

She rolled her eyes at his fake modesty. "And you're not at *all* egotistical." Her words dripped sarcasm.

"Can't blame a guy for letting you know you're on the right track."

This time, she was the one huffing out a laugh. "Whatever." She suddenly felt so loose-limbed and numb that she didn't see the point in prolonging their conversation. "If you really want to come, I guess you'll do." She could barely keep her eyes open, but there was one more thing she needed him to know before she gave in to the urge to close them. "You're going to like my stepsister. Everyone does. Brittany is really pretty. And perfect."

With that, Zara laid her head on the table and let sleep take her.

CHAPTER TWO

What the heck had he just done?

Rory reached out to take Zara's bright green glasses off, but though he had to nudge her to get the side of the frame out from between her cheek and arms, she just kept snoring.

They'd worked together for a year, but he wouldn't have said they were friends. On the contrary, most days they were barely civil.

Case in point: He'd come to the kitchen to give her grief for parking in his space *again*. Having worked in the building the longest, Rory figured he'd earned the parking spot outside his workshop door. Plus, as a furniture maker, he usually had the heaviest supplies and tools to cart in and out of the building.

Everyone else played by the rules, but Zara never seemed happier than when she was thwarting them—and especially *him*.

The last thing he'd expected was to find her getting bombed on bubbly at nine in the morning. If someone had asked him for a one-word description of Zara

Mirren, he would have said *bulletproof*.

Today, she seemed anything but.

The bare bones of her story were bad enough. He couldn't imagine stealing one of his brothers' girlfriends. The sibling code was crystal clear—if he, Brandon, Turner, or Hudson so much as *looked* at a woman, she was off-limits to the others. Family came first.

Zara's stepsister obviously didn't feel the same way, not only having no compunction about cheating with Zara's boyfriend—but about agreeing to marry him too. He supposed some people might somehow think that because they were now headed to the altar, "true love" had won out in the end and that all wrongs were now made right. But Rory didn't see it like that at all.

If anything, it only made their betrayal cut Zara deeper.

It was why he'd impulsively offered to go with her to the engagement party. He didn't have to be Zara's best friend to hate the thought of a colleague wading into *that* shark tank on her own.

And, not to toot his own horn, but he had it on good authority that he scrubbed up pretty well. It wouldn't hurt to make her ex a little jealous after the nonsense the jerk had put Zara through—not only cheating on her, but with her *stepsister*.

If some guy did something like this to one of Rory's sisters...

His hand fisted on the handle of his mug. No one deserved to be treated like dirt.

Even if Zara was a total pain in the butt.

And snored like a vacuum cleaner.

A car door slammed in the parking lot as the other artists who rented space in the warehouse started to arrive. Rory might not be Zara's bestie, but he knew enough to be absolutely certain that she would *hate* anyone else in the building seeing her like this. She didn't just come across as bulletproof, she was also fiercely proud.

What's more, he would never forgive himself if something happened to her while she was drunk. Especially after what had happened with Chelsea last year...

Forcing the thought back into the dark recesses of his mind, he put his hand on Zara's shoulder and jostled her gently. "Hey there, sleepyhead. Why don't I take you home so you can dry out in bed?"

She opened one eye. "I always knew you wanted to get into my pants."

Her words were slurred enough that he almost couldn't make them out. Nor could he hold back his laughter. "In your dreams."

"I *was* dreaming," she grumbled, "until you woke

me up."

Still laughing at the idea of wanting to get into her pants—the fact that he had been turned on when she'd licked bubbly off her fingers was surely down to his year of abstinence, rather than the fact that it was Zara doing the licking—he put one of her arms around his shoulders, slid his arm around her waist, and hoisted her up from the table.

"Where do you live?" he asked.

"None of your business."

Even when she was only half there, she was still a stubborn pain in the rear. It was pretty impressive, to be honest.

"Then my place it is," he said.

He waited for her to exclaim in horror, but at this point she really was down for the count. He slid her glasses into his pocket, then lifted her into his arms to carry her out to his truck before anyone could catch sight of them.

Thankfully, she woke up just enough to help him lift her into the passenger seat and buckle her in. But by the time he reversed out of the lot, she was leaning fully against him. Not wanting her to slide into the footwell, he put his arm around her and held her close as he headed toward his house.

In a million years, he never would have seen any of this coming. Zara, he'd noticed at various warehouse events, wasn't much of a drinker. It was how he'd known something must be wrong this morning. Had Zara truly been celebrating, it was far more likely she would have asked his sister Cassie to bring her those marmalade candies she loved so much. His sister was a marvel with sugar—but even he couldn't stomach marmalades. Only someone as weird as Zara would like an equally weird candy.

His house was on the shore, a lighthouse that had been in such a state of disrepair the State of Maine had nearly demolished it. Last year, his brother Brandon had mentioned it during Friday night dinner with the family, and Rory had known instantly he had to buy it. He'd needed to move somewhere he could be alone, where no one was close enough to drop by and ask him if he was okay when he felt like standing in the high tower and staring out into the rugged, swirling sea for hours on end.

Since moving in, he'd been renovating the living quarters in his spare time. Though he wasn't done, thus far he'd made good progress in the living room, kitchen, master bedroom, and bath. He'd also done the necessary work to make the lighthouse fully operational again—and he'd done operator training with the state, as well—so whenever a strong storm blew in, he stood watch in the tower the way a true lighthouse keeper would have.

Rory had loved growing up in Bar Harbor, and though he'd traveled extensively after college, he'd always planned to come back to the small town in northern Maine. His family was here, his friends were here, and the woods and ocean that inspired his furniture were here too.

Zara woke as he lifted her out of the truck. "Why are you carrying me?"

"It's what knights in shining armor do." Even when she was having one hell of a morning, he couldn't resist teasing her.

He thought he saw her lips curve up slightly before she buried her face against his chest. "You smell nice." She inhaled, loud enough that he could hear it. "I wish you didn't." And then she fell asleep again.

She smelled good too. A little like the Prosecco she'd dripped on herself, but mostly like lavender-scented shampoo.

Again, he told himself his attraction to her must be due to the long, cold year he'd had without female companionship. No sex, and no dates either. Not since the horrible night of Chelsea's accident.

His family, he knew, was still worried about him, though none of them had outright said anything in recent months. They didn't have to speak their concerns out loud when their glances spoke volumes.

Stepping inside his house, he decided that though

Zara would surely be more comfortable sleeping off the booze in a bed, he didn't want her to wake up later and worry that anything might have happened between them. It was far more likely that lightning would strike through his roof out of the bright blue sky than that they'd ever sleep together. Nonetheless, he got how iffy waking up in his bed would feel for her.

He laid her on the leather couch, propping two pillows behind her head and covering her with a blanket he'd purchased from the fiber artist in their building. Half the contents of his home had been sourced from Bar Harbor artists. He appreciated the local support he'd received from the start and was happy to give back to the maker community, especially when they were all so talented.

Zara was one of the most talented among them. Rory didn't need glasses, but the frames she designed and manufactured sometimes made him wish he did. He had bought a handful of pairs for his cousins on the West Coast, and he'd been glad to hear that they liked them enough to pass the word on to their friends, who had subsequently also bought frames via her online sales portal.

Rory knew how hard it was to set up shop for yourself—to find the money to pay for materials, shipping, and warehouse space ninety days before your invoices were paid. In the early years, every sale counted more than your customers knew.

Keeping an eye on Zara to make sure she was doing okay, he walked into his open-plan kitchen and poured ground coffee into the machine. She'd be desperate for a cup when she woke up, and she growled at him enough on a good day for him to guess how loud her growl would be on a bad one.

Though there were hours of work waiting for him in his workshop, he mentally pushed his to-do list aside and pulled out a sketchbook. Might as well take advantage of the quiet time to get some new ideas for a bench down in black and white.

Right then, Zara's snores ramped up. Okay, so it wasn't exactly quiet in his house. But, even if she wasn't someone he'd ever envisioned hanging out with, he was surprised to realize it was nice to share his home with another person. For a year, he'd kept everyone at arm's length, until he'd had no choice but to bring the last woman on earth he'd ever thought would need his arms around her into his house.

An hour of snores turned into two. And then, abruptly, she sat up.

Her hair was sticking out on the side of her head, her cheek had an imprint of the pillow on it, and yet Rory was still struck by just how pretty she was. She was even more striking when wearing her glasses, actually. He'd noticed her beautiful features right away, but after their opening swipes at each other on her first day in the warehouse, when she'd parked in his spot and refused to move her car—and then he'd decided her expensive artisan coffee was fair game, much to her incensed chagrin—he'd done his best to ignore her looks.

"Where am I?" She squinted around the room, then at him. "And why are *you* here?"

CHAPTER THREE

Zara's head spun like a retro turntable as Rory walked across the room and held out her glasses. It was a relief to put them on so that she could see more than fuzzy shapes. But while things might now be visually clear, nothing else seemed to be.

Yes, she remembered drinking most of a bottle of Prosecco. But even then, she couldn't imagine agreeing to spend the morning chez Rory, if that was in fact where they were.

The house was gorgeous, with wood beams and dark floors and natural light spilling in from the floor-to-ceiling windows.

And *wow*, was that an attached lighthouse?

They were perched on the edge of the shore. The seas were calm today, but she could imagine how raw and intense it must feel to be here in the middle of a storm. It was the home of her dreams, especially when filled with his brilliantly conceived and crafted furniture.

"I couldn't leave you snoring in the communal

kitchen," he said, finally answering her questions, "so when you wouldn't share your address, I brought you to my house instead." His voice sounded so loud she had to cover her ears. "Hopefully, this will help prevent a nasty hangover." He put two aspirin, a glass of water, and a cup of coffee on the table in front of the couch.

"Too late," she ground out, then swallowed the pills and drank every last drop of liquid.

When she was done, he pointed to his left. "The bathroom is that way if you want to…" He scanned her head to toe. "Freshen up."

Normally, she'd come back at him with something witty and barbed, but she needed to wash the grit from her eyes and tongue first. She stood up, then when she belatedly realized her legs weren't anywhere near close to steady, she plopped down hard on the couch again. Which made her head throb like the dickens times two.

He offered a hand to help her up, and she was about to bat it away when she realized her standard responses to Rory weren't quite fair anymore. Not after he'd saved her from making a complete ass of herself in front of their six colleagues at the warehouse.

Clasping his hand with her own, she let him haul her to her feet and hold her steady.

"Okay?" he asked, looking genuinely concerned.

She nodded. It wasn't lying if she was simply answering his question about how her legs were doing supporting her weight.

It was everything else that wasn't okay. Not only that her stepsister and ex were taking the next step toward their forever—but also that she wasn't absolutely hating Rory's touch.

On the contrary, judging by the thrill bumps popping up over her skin, a part of her *loved* it.

The shock of that realization should have had her yanking her hand from his. But it was so much easier to lean on him as he led her toward the bathroom than it would have been trying to grit it out on her own. She was stubborn, but she wasn't stupid.

Once they reached the threshold, she said, "I've got it from here." Her voice sounded like she'd been swallowing sandpaper all morning.

After locking the door, she caught sight of herself in the mirror above the sink and nearly groaned aloud. She wasn't sure which was worse—the drool that had dried on her cheek or that her hair had Medusa-fied while she'd slept.

Not that Rory would ever mistake her for a beauty queen. And not that she would want him to. But still. She had some standards, and right now she was falling *far* short of them.

It was utter bliss to splash cold water over her face. She put her glasses back on, then finger-combed her hair as best she could, and used some toothpaste on the tip of her finger to freshen up. With that taken care of, she took a deep breath and left the bathroom to deal with the complications of her big drunk mouth.

Rory was standing by the living room window, looking out at the ocean. It wasn't just the house of her dreams—this view was also one of the best she'd ever seen. She could so easily imagine wild swimming in the ocean at sunrise, or beneath a full moon.

"Thanks for looking after me this morning." It was far easier than she'd expected to express gratitude to Rory. No question, he had done her a solid by whisking her out of the warehouse before the others showed up and got an eyeful of her emotional breakdown.

"No problem."

Amazing. She would have expected him to hold this incident over her for all eternity. Not to shrug off her thanks as though this was all in a day's work for a highly in-demand furniture maker.

He must really feel sorry for her.

Certain there were few things worse than being the object of Rory's pity, she said, "I'm really sorry to have taken you away from your work for so many hours, but I'm good to head back to the warehouse now."

"No worries, and no rush on my part. I've been getting plenty done here." He pointed to the kitchen table, where his sketchbook was open to a black-and-white drawing. Even from across the room, she could see that he was designing yet another gorgeous piece of furniture. "I've been wanting to get these ideas down for a while now. Your snoring was the perfect sound-track."

Ah, there it was. A snarky comment. Her rapidly beating heart settled. He must not pity her *too* much if he was game for teasing her the way he always did.

"You should have recorded them for instant play-back," she retorted.

"Who says I didn't?" She hoped he was joking as he handed her another cup of coffee. "Probably best if you drink this before we head back."

Though she felt almost completely sober now, she could use the caffeine infusion. Not to mention a little more time to get her head around things before facing everyone at work with a smile. Plus, one whiff from the mug told her that he stocked fantastic coffee, possibly even the same artisan brand that he'd stolen from her on her first day at the warehouse.

As she drank, she forced her brain to rewind the morning. First, the text with the news. Then, the selfie of the ring. Then, drowning her sorrows in a bottle of Prosecco. Then, Rory had arrived and—

Wait. No. He couldn't have offered to go to the engagement party with her, could he?

And she couldn't have reciprocated by accusing

him of wanting to get into her pants, had she?

She couldn't hold back her groan. This would teach a lightweight to drink. Next time she was upset, she was going to sprint around the block to work off her angst, or go to one of those places where you could throw plates against a wall, instead of getting hammered.

"Of course you're off the hook for tomorrow," she told him. "It was nice of you to offer to go with me to the engagement party, but it will be better if I go alone."

"Are you sure about that?" With one eyebrow raised, he looked insufferably sexy. "To my way of thinking, showing up with me would go a long way to convincing both of them that you don't give a damn what they do."

"I love my stepsister," she protested. It was a tiny bit harder to force out the words, "I'm happy for her."

"Then she's lucky to have you. But being supportive of her doesn't mean being her doormat."

"I'm not Brittany's doormat!" Although hadn't she had thoughts along those lines once or twice in the past? "Anyway, you'd be bored stiff at her party."

"One thing I can say for you, Zara, is that I've never been bored when we're together."

Unable to figure him out, she asked point-blank, "Why are you so hell-bent on going with me?"

"You've met my sisters."

Cassie was a regular visitor to the warehouse, making frequent candy deliveries to the makers in the building. Ashley had also been by for a couple of openings, as had a couple of Rory's brothers. "I've met two of them," she said, "and they're great. But what do they have to do with anything?"

"I hate the thought of one of my sisters being in your position."

Zara was about to protest that the engagement party was nothing she couldn't handle, but she decided not to waste her voice when Rory already knew it had been bad enough to lead to Prosecco-guzzling and a two-hour morning nap on his couch.

"Okay, maybe going with a plus-one would play better," she conceded. "But I don't want you to go unless you're absolutely certain that you won't hate every second of it. Especially since it's all the way in Camden."

"I like Camden." He was like a bull in her china shop. "What time does the party start?"

She just blinked at him. Even had her brain been working at top capacity, she would have had trouble making sense of his behavior. "At six, so I was planning to leave no later than four. But we can just meet there."

"No way." He outright rejected that idea. "We

want them to think I'm besotted."

"Besotted?" She couldn't believe that word was in his vocabulary. "Just being seen together will be more than enough."

"I disagree. In fact, I think we should dig a little deeper to make it really believable. Learn each other's favorite colors and whatever else a couple does."

Couple? He wanted to pretend they were a *couple*?

This day was going from bad to worse.

Rory Sullivan being this into pretending to be her boyfriend was clearly karmic punishment for something she'd done in the past.

Long-buried shame for her past misdeeds rose up to hit her hard in the solar plexus, and it took every ounce of self-control she had to shove the shame back down deep. So deep that she could pretend it wasn't there if she tried hard enough.

That was when she realized he was smirking at her—a look Rory Sullivan had likely patented at birth—which meant this wasn't karma. No, far more likely it was payback for stealing his parking space. "You're loving this, aren't you? Winding me up with all this pretend-boyfriend stuff?"

He didn't bother to hold in his laughter. "You should see your face. The more I say, the greener you get."

She breathed a sigh of relief. "So you don't actually

want to pretend to be a—" She could hardly bring herself to say it. "Couple?"

No was the right response. *Of course not* would be even better.

"Actually, we probably should," was the wrong answer on every single level. But one he gave anyway.

If only she hadn't drunk so much earlier. More synapses might have been firing, and she would have done better than saying, "No one would ever believe it."

"Sure they would." He looked far too confident as he moved toward her. "Two single makers sharing a workspace all these months." He was barely a foot from her when he stopped. "Plenty of people have probably wondered what we're getting up to all those late nights when we're the only ones left in the building."

"Working!" She was horrified by any other possibility, particularly when the truth was that she'd had more than one secret fantasy after seeing Rory use his saws and drills and sanders without a shirt during a few particularly hot nights. "We've both been working. Separately!"

"You and I know that. But your stepsister and your ex don't." She couldn't miss the naughty glint in his eyes. "All they're going to see is that we can't keep our hands off each other."

This time, she was the one laughing. "We touched

for the first time five minutes ago. I can't even *imagine* what it would feel like to put my hands all over you."

It wasn't until the words were out of her mouth that she realized what she'd just done. With a handful of words, she'd thrown down the gauntlet. Firmly and undeniably in front of the man who had driven her crazier during the past year than anyone else ever had. And who would surely *never* let her walk out of here without taking up the challenge.

No surprise, then, that he responded by holding his arms wide. "Go ahead. Put your hands on me."

Did his voice suddenly sound a little hoarse? Or was it simply that she had completely lost her grip on reality?

She had to lick suddenly dry lips before responding. "It won't be a big deal if I do." She forced a shrug. "You're just a guy I work with, doing me a favor. Which," she made sure to point out, "I will owe you for big-time to make us even."

He lifted his arms slightly. "I'm still waiting for you to get over your revulsion to touching me. Better to face it now in private than tomorrow night in front of everyone."

That was just the problem. She was anything *but* revolted.

CHAPTER FOUR

Zara had vowed to get over her fatal flaw of falling for guys who always ended up wishing they were with Brittany. At first, each of the guys had been so convincing. They told her how much they admired what she was doing with her business and how they liked that she didn't dress or act like other women they'd known—only to inevitably fall head over heels for her stepsister, who ticked every "perfect girlfriend" box with her swishy blonde hair, her job in PR, and her fashionable clothes.

Zara's ex was a paler, smaller, less-built version of Rory. Which only reinforced that she would have to be an utter fool to let herself give in to these strange new feelings for Rory.

Okay, then. It was time to buck up and touch him and prove that she felt nothing. Yes, that was her new mantra. She was going to *feel nothing*.

She gave him no warning before slapping her hands on his chest. The sound was loud enough to reverberate through the room.

"Sorry." She winced as she added a white lie. "I don't think I've fully got my balance back."

"I'm tough enough to take it."

Good thing one of them was. Because now that she could feel his warmth seeping through his shirt to her palms…now that she knew exactly how hard and well-built his pecs were…now that she was getting a lungful of that delicious wood-chip/cedar scent he had going…

She suddenly felt more wobbly on her feet than she had when she was drunk.

"Losing the grimace might help," he suggested.

She worked to school her face into a smile. "How's this?"

"If you want everyone to think you're having a bad case of heartburn, it's perfect."

She made herself think of puppies and butterflies and every single person in the state of Maine wearing a pair of her glasses.

"Much more believable," he said. "Although it would be better if you looked into my eyes, instead of at my shoulder."

Shoot. She'd been hoping to get away with that. Because she really, *really* didn't want to lift her gaze to his. Not when she was afraid he'd see the budding attraction that she was hell-bent on hiding.

Slowly, she raised her eyes to meet his, all the while chanting her mantra in her head. *Feel nothing. Feel nothing. Feel nothing.*

Of course, he had to choose that exact moment to smile at her. Between the crinkles at the sides of his mouth and the light in his eyes, she couldn't have felt nothing if she'd been anesthetized.

"No problems here." It took everything she had to sound unaffected. "Any issues for you?"

He held her gaze for a long moment. "Nope, everything's good for me too."

She lowered her hands and stepped back, relief coursing through her that she'd made it through one of the hardest tests of her life. "Great. Then we're good to go for tomorrow."

"Not quite."

She frowned. "What now?"

"You've gotten used to touching me, but I still don't know how it feels to touch you, beyond helping you off the couch."

Plenty of sexier things had been said to her over the years. Rory's sentence clearly wasn't meant to be at all seductive. And yet, her body had never responded this way to a couple of sentences strung together. As though she were a firework, and he a match.

"You're really taking this seriously, aren't you?"

"If we're going to do this, we should do it right," he countered. "Flinching at my slightest touch would blow the whole thing."

Darn it, he was right. Only, it had taken everything she had to stay stoic while touching him. She wasn't sure she had anything left to fight her next reaction. Clearly, she was going to have to dig deep.

"Fine." She scowled. "Whenever you're ready, go ahead."

But instead of moving closer, he suddenly stepped back. "You know what? I'm being an ass. I shouldn't have forced your hand with any of this. If you don't want me to go with you to the party, I need to respect that." He was clearly upset with himself as he said, "I'm really sorry I'm trying to convince you to let me touch you. My mother would rake me over the coals for my behavior." He was careful not to touch her as he took her mug over to the sink and rinsed it out, along with his.

Zara was surprised by how disappointed she suddenly felt at the thought of his *not* coming with her, especially when she'd belatedly realized that he was right about her making an I'm-not-a-doormat statement to Brittany and Cameron.

"You have nothing to apologize for," she told him. "It's just that I've never done something like pretending to be in a relationship. That's why I'm a little prickly." Normally, he would have made a cutting comment about how she was far more than a *little* prickly. The fact that he didn't razz her was testament to his concern that he'd been acting inappropriately. "You're in no way forcing me to do anything," she insisted. "It might not have been my idea for you to come with me tomorrow night, but if I didn't want you there, I wouldn't have agreed. So…" She couldn't believe how nervous she felt as she asked, "Are we still on?"

He dried his hands on a dish towel before replying. "We are. But I want you to promise me something from here on out. If I do or say anything that makes you uncomfortable—even if I'm just joking around like I was earlier—you need to tell me."

"You won't."

"Promise me, Zara."

His low, slightly demanding tone sent more thrill bumps racing over her skin. "I promise. But only if you promise me something too."

"What's that?"

"That you won't worry I'm made of porcelain." She held out her arms the way he had before. "I might have had a stumble this morning, but I'm tough."

"I know you are."

For the first time today, she felt like smiling. "In that case, why don't you get that touching-me thing over with before we head back to the office?"

"Are you sure you want that?"

She raised an eyebrow. "Tough, remember? And,"

she added in a teasing tone, "simply *longing* for your touch."

He didn't laugh, however. Instead, he stared at her for a moment, before reaching out to brush a wisp of hair back from her face and behind her ear. "How was that?"

She hoped he couldn't tell she was practically gasping for oxygen. "Fine."

"Good." He brushed the backs of his knuckles over her cheek. "What about this?"

Praying her face hadn't flushed red and given her away, she nodded. "Still fine. Should we move on to our get-to-know-each-other lists?"

His hand lingered on her skin a beat longer before he lowered it. "My favorite color is green."

"Mine's orange."

"I'm one of seven kids," he said. "My mother's Irish, and my father met her in the town of Cong nearly forty years ago, then convinced her to marry him and move to Bar Harbor."

"I grew up in Kennebunkport as an only child," she said. "Then when my mother passed away, my dad married my stepmother when I was fifteen. We moved to Camden to live with her and Brittany, who is one month younger than me. I lived there until I moved here a year ago."

He frowned. "After Brittany and your ex cheated."

She'd been worried he would ask how her mother died. It was a relief that he'd focused, instead, on Brittany and Cameron. "Breakups in a small town are never good."

"You're right, they're not," he agreed. An expression that looked like a combination of guilt and remorse crossed his face, then disappeared so quickly she almost wasn't sure she'd seen it. "Anything else I should know?"

"I'm allergic to cats. I'll swim in any body of water I can get into, even if it's freezing. And I have a borderline unhealthy obsession with your sister's candy—and chocolate cake. What about you?"

"I was never going to let you know this," he said, "but I've bought a half dozen of your frames over the past several months to ship off to my cousins on the West Coast and New York."

"Seriously?"

"You're great at what you do, Zara. You and I might not see eye to eye on many things, but you don't need me to tell you that your frames are brilliant."

"Thank you." She met his olive branch with one of her own. "I might secretly covet your furniture once my financial ship comes in and I can afford it."

"I won't tell anyone if you won't," he said.

She grinned. "Who would have thought the two of us would ever agree on anything?"

"I'm just as amazed as you are," he said, grinning right back. "What do you think? Will we be able to convince your stepsister and ex that we're the real deal?"

"You know what?" Rory was the least-likely co-conspirator she could ever have imagined. And yet... "I think we just might."

CHAPTER FIVE

Making furniture was the kind of work that gave you a lot of time to think. Which was precisely why, during the past year, Rory kept heavy metal music blaring in his workshop. Anything that could bash away his dark thoughts was welcome.

For the first time in a long time, however, it wasn't guilty memories of the aftermath of his breakup with Chelsea that plagued him. Instead, as he worked to finish a custom table on Friday afternoon and Saturday morning, Zara occupied the bulk of his thoughts. He'd even bowed out of his usual Friday night dinner with his family. If they found out that he and Zara were attending her stepsister's engagement party together, his siblings and parents were bound to ask questions. Questions he had no desire whatsoever to answer.

What's more, he kept circling back to how Zara had almost breezily dropped into the conversation the fact that her mother had died. When a friend in high school had lost his mom, the guy had gone off the rails—drinking, drugs, unsafe sex. While Rory couldn't imagine Zara reacting in any of those ways, he also didn't think she could have come away without scars. And though the two of them hadn't had the greatest start this past year, he hoped she'd feel that she could talk openly to him about her mother if the conversation ever went that way again.

Now, as he stood outside Zara's front door at a few minutes before four in the afternoon, his heart was pounding harder than usual. Not because he was nervous—on the contrary, he was looking forward to tonight more than he'd expected to.

He was simply acting the part of Zara's date so that her stepsister and ex wouldn't think they'd crushed her spirit. Nothing more.

And yet…

When he'd touched her yesterday morning, with just the barest sweep of his fingertips over her skin as he'd brushed back her hair, it had felt like *more*.

Which was crazy. Rory couldn't imagine actually being with Zara any more than she could imagine being with him. They would do each other in within the hour.

All the more reason to have fun with tonight's charade. Pretending something so wrong was right was bound to be a kick for both of them.

He was smiling as he rang her doorbell, and when she opened it, a sassy comment immediately fell from her tongue, as expected.

"You're grinning like a dog who just snuck a bag of treats out from under his owner's nose."

"And you look like…" He stopped to take in her outfit. Head-to-toe black. Voluminous fabric without a hint of a shape beneath. Even her glasses were framed in black, which was odd when she normally wore vibrant hues on her face. "You're headed to a funeral."

She sighed as she let him inside. "Everything else I tried on seemed like I was trying too hard."

"You are." Her eyes widened at his blunt statement. He knew firsthand how bad pity felt when it was directed at you. He would help her, but he wouldn't coddle her. "It's like you've wrapped yourself in an I-don't-care flag, which only shows how much you *do* care."

"Tell it like it is, why don't you?" she muttered. "I suppose you think I should change?"

"Only if you want to." Having grown up with three sisters, he knew better than to tell a woman what she should do with her clothing. "I'm cool with standing beside you holding a hanky for you to weep into all night, if that's the look you're aiming for."

"Fine," she said with a roll of her eyes. "I'll go change. But just in case I forget to tell you this later, I had a *really* annoying time with you tonight."

"Right back at you," he called as she headed into

her bedroom.

Alone in the living room, he took in her space. She'd made the cottage her own with bright colors across every surface, from the artwork on the walls, to the throws over the couch, to the rugs on the hardwood floor. Her home felt eclectic, yet perfectly representative of the colorful, bold, fascinating woman who lived there. For as much grief as he'd given her over the past year, the truth was that she'd impressed him from the start with her determination, focus, and talent.

"Okay, let's go." She marched across the room to grab her purse and overnight bag. "And whatever you've got to say about my new outfit, I don't want to hear it."

She had changed into a flowing, semi-translucent purple top with a lace-up V-neck and black bra underneath, black leather pants, dark boots with thick soles, and bright purple glasses. The outfit wouldn't have worked on anyone else, but on Zara, it looked exactly right.

"Okay," he said as they headed out to his car. "I'm perfectly happy not telling you that I think you look great."

The pleased smile she couldn't contain had him grinning again. At times like this, he could almost forget he'd spent so many months gritting his teeth around her. As long as she didn't start whistling, which she knew drove him crazy, they might be able to rub along okay for the next few hours.

"So," she said once they were in the car and off to Camden, "I was thinking—"

"Uh-oh." He couldn't resist. Just as she couldn't resist thwacking him on the arm.

"As I was saying, we should make sure we have our story straight before we get to the party. I know we've got favorite colors figured out, but people are probably going to want to know how we met."

He could barely keep a straight face as he said, "You should tell them that you took one look at me and fell head over heels in love."

"That would be a great story if we wanted them all to think I've gone *insane*." She barely let the dig land before continuing. "In any case, since I haven't lost my mind, I'm thinking that keeping our story as close to the truth as possible will be the best way to stave off getting caught out in a lie."

"No problem," he agreed. "I'll tell anyone who wants to know how much your whistling drives me crazy."

She whistled a few bars of his favorite Metallica song, sending his teeth back into grinding mode. "And I'll tell them that one day I'm going to take the speakers you're always blaring heavy metal on in your woodshop and toss them into the river to sink into the mud."

He didn't let on that he'd seen her rocking out to his music when she hadn't thought he was looking. "Telling them it was mutual dislike at first sight is a smart move. Everyone loves an enemies-turned-lovers story, don't they?" The *lovers* part shouldn't have sounded nearly so appealing.

"Exactly. Hating-you-to-dating-you can be our schtick."

"Instead of a meet-cute, we had a meet-puke."

The laugh that burst from her made him feel like he'd just won a prize. "Maybe keep that one to yourself," she suggested, but she was grinning. "The only issue I can see is that someone at the party might want details on how we came to stop being so irritated by each other and fell in *looooove*." The word *love* dripped with sarcasm from her lips. Lips that looked far too tempting for his peace of mind.

"Hmmm," he said, playing the moment for all it was worth. "That *is* a hard one. Good thing we have the whole drive to Camden to think of reasons they'll believe."

"I'm going to punch you again, if you're not careful."

Despite her bravado, he detected a hint of self-deprecation in her tone that he didn't care for. For all their teasing, his intention was never to make her feel bad. It was more that he hadn't had this much fun sparring with someone in a very long time. Particularly during the past year, when everyone had been walking on eggshells around him.

Zara didn't know his damage, so the only eggshells that would come from her were the ones she might decide to throw at him. Whatever happened tonight, he didn't like the thought of losing their zing-y relationship. It would be far less fun to come into work if he couldn't go a few verbal rounds with her.

"Just to be clear," he said in a serious voice, "despite the fact that we're always bantering and teasing each other, I've *never* felt we were actually enemies, or that we hated each other, or that you in any way have ever made me want to puke."

"I haven't either." But before they could get too gooey, she added, "Although you do really irritate me sometimes."

"Likewise."

Perhaps it shouldn't have made sense that they were grinning at each other after declaring their mutual irritation. But it did.

"Now that we've got that clear," she said in her back-to-business voice, "let's make a list of the things we can't resist about each other. I'd say three reasons each should suffice. I'll go first. You're really talented, and I love your furniture. Reason two is that you obviously care about your family a great deal. And for my third reason…"

She scrunched up her face, clearly thinking hard. He might have felt a little insulted by how long it was taking her to come up with a third reason, if she didn't constantly make him want to laugh out loud. He'd never met anyone like her, female or male. Zara said exactly what was on her mind, no matter the consequences. Plus, he wasn't going to deny that he was pleased by her first two reasons for fake-falling for him—his work and his family were two of the most important things in his life.

"I've got it!" She snapped her fingers. "Your lightning-quick comebacks during our bantering sessions prove how quickly your mind works. What woman doesn't love a man with a brain who isn't afraid to use it?" She looked extremely pleased with herself for filling out her list. "Your turn."

"You stole my first reason—that you're a hell of a designer and manufacturer."

"Mutual respect for each other's work sounds good to me, as long as your next two reasons stand apart from mine."

Rory was surprised to realize it wasn't at all difficult to come up with his second reason for fake-falling for her. "I didn't know anything about your family until yesterday, so I can't copy you on that one. But I have noticed how supportive you are of other artists. You're the loudest to cheer another maker's success, the first to volunteer to help, and the last to leave their side when there is still work to be done."

She looked surprised by his comment. "We all know how hard it can be to get a business off the ground, especially in the arts. Of course I'm happy to help."

"Not everyone is."

Though his eyes were still on the road, he could feel her gaze trained on him. "Did something bad happen to you when you were starting out?"

"It's not something I talk about much."

"It won't leave this car," she promised.

Though they hadn't exactly been friends up until now, he realized he trusted her not to break her promise. "It was a few years back. Another furniture maker, a guy I really respected, accused me of copying his work."

"You would *never* do that!"

Rory appreciated Zara's conviction more than she could know. "No, I wouldn't. I don't know if he felt threatened in some way, or if he was having a hard time in his personal life and thought he'd take it out on me, or if he was just burned out. Whatever the reason, when I called him on it, he backed off, but it left a bad taste in my mouth."

"Is he still in the area?"

Rory shot her a look. "Why do you ask?"

"Because I'd be *more* than happy to give him a piece of my mind. I don't care how many years it's been since he pulled that crap, or what his reasons were for doing it. You're far too compassionate and forgiving for your own good."

"There's a fourth good thing to add to your list."

She thwacked him on the arm again. "I'm being serious. You're the one who told me it's okay to fight for myself by not being such a doormat. Now I'm telling you that it's okay to do the same with your art, especially when someone tries to attack or take away what you've worked so hard to build."

"You've just illustrated the third reason on my list." For once, he was glad for a minor traffic jam so that he could turn away from the road to look into her eyes. "You're fierce, Zara. Fierce in your determination to pursue your dreams and not let anyone get in your way. Especially," he said with a smile, "some jerk who happens to work in the same building."

"You're not *always* a jerk," she conceded, with a smile of her own.

"Yet another point for your list. Five reasons to fall for me so far."

He expected another arm thwack and would have

been disappointed had it not come.

"Okay," she said as traffic picked up again, "we've got our how-we-met stories straight, our why-we-fell-in-*looove* lists, and I'm no longer dressed like I'm headed to the morgue. Anything else you think we need to check off our list before we're good to go?"

"Only one thing left I can think of."

"What's that?"

"Let's have a damn good time."

He couldn't see her smile, but he knew it would be just the right side of wicked as she turned off Metallica on his car stereo without asking, then found a pop station and cranked a boy band to ear-splitting levels. "The best time *ever*."

CHAPTER SIX

Zara didn't care for her pounding heart and her sweating palms as they stood at the entrance to the country club where the newly engaged couple were having their party.

She'd had a year to get over Brittany and Cameron's relationship. Then again, now that the couple was going to make it a forever thing, Zara was in for a lifetime of family gatherings where everyone would expect her to take one for the "true love" team.

She couldn't wait.

Not.

Zara was so lost in her thoughts that she didn't realize Rory had reached for her hand until he had it in his grasp. "I haven't felt a palm this damp since my first middle-school dance," he noted.

His comment had the desired effect, spurring her to give the romantic performance of a lifetime. Head held high, she walked into the building hand in hand with Rory.

She wasn't surprised when every head turned to

take in their procession. And not simply because everyone had surely been waiting for her arrival in the hopes that sparks would fly between stepsisters—but because Rory Sullivan was a truly magnificent-looking man.

Where previously it would have galled Zara to admit just how handsome he was, tonight she wanted to give a fist bump at the way everyone was swooning over him from the barest glance.

Knowing they were all watching, she leaned in to whisper in his ear, "I'm thinking some next-level touching would be good here, if it's okay with you."

"Definitely okay." He put his arm around her waist and pulled her in close.

Wow. If she'd thought holding hands with Rory was a shock to her system, it had *nothing* on being held in his arms.

This close, she could no longer deny his impressive strength. His delicious scent. And the fact that he exuded sex appeal from the top of his head, to the tips of his toes.

Amazingly, though, the sensations coursing through her were about more than attraction or pheromones. For the first time in a very long time, she felt safe.

Like nothing could hurt her ever again as long as Rory was by her side.

When she turned her gaze to his and realized how he was looking at her, she had to wonder if he could feel it too.

Zara's stepsister and her ex were both forgotten as she silently scrambled to corral her crazy feelings. But it felt like she was attempting to herd wild mustang horses back into their pen after finally giving them a heady taste of roaming wild and free.

An impossible task, if ever there was one.

"Well, hello there."

Brittany's purr broke Zara out of her careening thoughts. She'd been dreading the moment when she came face-to-face with her stepsister at her engagement party. Now, however, she was thrilled that Brittany had broken the spell Rory was casting over her, regardless of how awkward this conversation was bound to be.

Her stepsister enveloped her in an expensively perfumed embrace, during which Rory continued to hold tight to Zara's waist, proving it was going to take far more than this to shake him free.

"I'm so glad you could come on such short notice, Z." Brittany let Zara go, then offered her hand to Rory. "It's lovely to meet you. I'm Brittany, and this is Cameron." She nodded toward Zara's ex, who was standing at Brittany's side, looking more than a little gobsmacked by Zara's date.

"I'm Rory Sullivan." He gave Brittany's hand a firm shake and then did the same with Cameron.

Zara had to stifle a smile at the slight wince on Cameron's part when he took his hand back. Her ex's handshake had always been a little soft. Whereas there was *nothing* soft about any part of Rory, especially his big woodworking hands.

"I'm glad to finally meet you both," Rory said. "I had hoped to meet you at Zara's last product launch, but better late than never."

He let the subtle rebuke dangle in the air as he turned to gently stroke the back of his hand across Zara's cheek. She allowed an instinctive shiver at his touch, figuring it would help make their ruse look completely above board.

He gazed at her, adoration in his eyes. "I'm so proud of you, baby."

She nearly laughed. *Baby* was a little overkill, but since they had agreed to have fun with this tonight, she gave him her own over-the-top admiring look. "Not nearly as proud as I always am of you."

From the corner of her eye, Zara could see both Brittany and Cameron gaping at them.

+1 for Team Zara and Rory.

Sensing that Rory was working just as hard to keep his laughter in, and that any further antics were likely to send both of them over the edge, she turned back to her stepsister and ex. "Congratulations on your engagement."

Brittany slid her arm through Cameron's and rested her head on his shoulder. "We knew from the start that it was true love." She batted her eyelids at her fiancé. "Didn't we, darling?"

He kissed her forehead. "From the first moment I set eyes on you, I knew we belonged together, my angel."

Darling? Angel? Bile rose in Zara's throat.

She felt Rory's arm tighten around her as he said to Cameron, "The first time you set eyes on Brittany, weren't you dating Zara?"

It belatedly occurred to Zara that she should have set the ground rules with Rory more carefully. No going for the jugular. No shooting poison arrows. Though she had been hurt like hell to find Brittany and Cameron cheating on her, when their parents and friends—and pretty much everyone else she knew— were immediately supportive of Brittany and Cameron's new relationship, Zara had decided it wasn't worth fighting a losing battle to remind everyone that she had, in fact, been there first.

Brittany was the first to recover from Rory's question. "Don't be silly. None of us would call a couple of dinners together and maybe a movie *dating*." She pinned her bright gaze on Zara, imploring her to agree.

"Right, Z?"

For a moment, Zara was tempted to point out that she and Cameron had had a good two dozen dinners, movies, and nights during the two months they'd been seeing each other—which met even the most stringent definition of *dating*.

But she couldn't bring herself to ruin her stepsister's celebration. Though Brittany didn't always look at things from all angles before she spoke and acted, at her core she was a good person. The big difference between the two of them was that Brittany's misdeeds were on the surface, whereas Zara kept hers buried as deep as they could go.

In any case, as she worked to shake the painful thought away, she didn't need to make a scene. Not when she had Rory at her side acting the part of the sentry, rather than simply the charmer she had assumed he would play tonight.

She couldn't stand to lie, though. So instead of nodding, she went with, "I'm really glad things have worked out so well for both of you. You make a perfect pair."

Brittany's face lit with another smile. The same smile that had lured all of Zara's previous crushes her way. "We do, don't we?"

"Zara, honey!" Her father's booming greeting was accompanied by a hug. "You look great. So healthy and happy. Doesn't she, Margie?"

Zara stepped forward for her stepmother's air kisses on each cheek. "You certainly do, darling." Margie turned her gaze to Rory and gave him a thorough once-over. "Very well, indeed."

"Dad, Margie, this is Rory Sullivan."

"Very nice to meet you." Her father robustly pumped Rory's hand, clearly pleased by this proof that his daughter wasn't moping over losing her boyfriend to her stepsister. "How long have you two been an item?"

Rory spoke before Zara could reply. "The first time I met Zara, she caught my eye."

Zara almost laughed out loud, remembering the argument they'd had on her first day at the warehouse. Yup, she'd *definitely* caught his eye.

Rory continued, "I consider myself a very lucky guy that she finally agreed to go out with me."

"Where did you meet?" Margie asked, looking as surprised as the rest of them at the idea of magnificent Rory Sullivan chasing Zara.

Thankful that they'd gotten their story straight beforehand, Zara said, "We work in the same building. Rory designs and builds furniture. His pieces are exceptional." At the last second, she realized she should add in some lovey-dovey stuff. Turning to him with a heated look, she said, "*Everything* about you is exceptional."

To his credit, instead of looking horrified by her terrible excuse for flirting, he rolled with it by pulling her closer.

Only, somewhere in there, he decided to roll with it too far.

Way too far.

Because the next thing she knew, he was leaning toward her, his mouth barely a breath away—

And then his lips were pressed to hers in a kiss unlike any she'd ever known.

Soft.

Sweet.

And yet ripe with sensuality.

Somewhere in the back of her brain, Zara knew this wasn't part of the plan. They hadn't agreed to kiss. Heck, they had barely agreed to hold hands as they walked inside.

But she couldn't pull back.

Not when Rory's kiss felt more *right* than anything else ever had.

CHAPTER SEVEN

Only when Zara's father—or maybe it was Cameron—cleared his throat did they finally release each other. Even with their audience, however, Zara still couldn't bring herself to look away from Rory's face.

Had he felt it too?

Like the earth had stopped spinning?

And diving in for another kiss was the only thing that mattered?

Unfortunately, she couldn't read what she saw in his eyes. And even if she could, how would she have been able to trust it when he would likely have just been playing his part? How could she trust *anything* that happened between them tonight when it was all predicated on a lie?

"Young love," her stepmother sighed, looking more than a little flushed by the kiss she'd witnessed. "Is there anything else like it?"

Good thing no one seemed to expect Zara to speak. Because she couldn't wrap her head around what had just happened. By what she had just *felt*.

Her *feel nothing* mantra was more useless than ever. Still, she had to pull it together—and quickly—before Brittany or Cameron realized anything was amiss. The last thing she wanted was for the two of them to figure out that she and Rory were just putting on a show. That would only make her look more ridiculous and pathetic.

"I'm starved," she said.

"I'll take you over to the buffet," Brittany said, grabbing Zara's free arm to yank her away from Rory.

For a few moments, Zara was the rope in a tug-of-war, with both of them holding tight to her. After she shot a quick look to Rory—*it's okay, you should go have a well-earned drink*—he let her go.

"Well, aren't you a dark horse?" Brittany grabbed two glasses of champagne from a passing waiter and handed one to Zara. "I can't believe you've kept that gorgeous specimen of a man a secret for so long." She paused to take a tiny sip of her drink, her eyes narrowing fractionally. "How long have you been seeing him, exactly?"

"We flirted with each other for the better part of the past year," Zara said in an easy voice, "before I finally gave in and went out with him."

"So it's really true that *he* was pursuing *you* this whole time?"

Zara knew Brittany wasn't being mean. Her stepsister always wanted to know every single detail. It was why she was great at PR—she rarely overlooked any of the particulars, whether a style of shoe or dress, or a casually dropped name or location.

"I've never seen a man so determined." Zara smiled at her fib as she sipped from her glass. "The chase was fun, but at a certain point, I couldn't hold out any longer."

Her stepsister turned to look at Rory, now standing by the bar with Zara's father and Cameron. Rory looked perfectly comfortable as he talked with them. Brittany's fiancé, on the other hand, seemed to be gulping his wine rather desperately.

"What woman could resist a man like that?" Brittany murmured.

Jealousy speared Zara in the center of her chest, just from her stepsisters looking at Rory like she wanted to lick him from head to toe. Which didn't make sense when Zara and Rory were not actually a couple, and she had no claim on him in any way other than as her co-conspirator for the night.

"Now it's your turn to tell me everything," Zara said, planting a bright smile on her face. "How did Cameron propose?"

Zara had expected Brittany to relish giving her every last detail of the proposal, but her stepsister barely seemed to hear the question. She hadn't yet taken her eyes off Rory. "His name and face are so familiar, but I would have remembered if I'd met him before…" She snapped her fingers. "I remember now! My colleague shot him for a piece a client did in conjunction with Maine makers earlier this year. I wasn't able to attend the shoot, but I will admit to drooling a bit over the pictures."

Zara was used to biting her tongue around her stepsister. But she couldn't keep from saying, "You did a piece on makers in Maine…and you didn't ask me to be a part of it?"

Brittany finally dragged her gaze away from Rory to frown at Zara. "You make glasses, Z. That doesn't count as art."

Zara swallowed hard. Maybe she'd been too hasty when she'd decided not to make a scene tonight. Yes, her work had a very practical application—but that didn't mean it wasn't also art. Just as with Rory's tables or chairs or benches, the use of her glasses frames on a daily basis didn't make them any less beautiful.

Rory's arms slipping around her waist distracted her from her sudden burst of anger. When had he moved from the bar?

And why did her brain go completely to mush whenever he touched her?

"This is my favorite song," he said. "Let's dance."

"*Glory of Love* by Peter Cetera is your favorite

song?"

Instead of replying to her, he turned to Brittany. "You don't mind if I steal Zara away, do you?"

Brittany flashed him her most sparkly smile. One that had made every other man she'd given it to fall at her feet in supplication. Rory, however, didn't seem to notice in the least that she was sparkling.

"Of course not," Brittany said. "You two lovebirds should dance and have fun. That's the mark of a great party, after all."

Rory practically dragged Zara onto the dance floor. "If you want to put your arms around my neck and lean in a little while we sway to an oldie but goodie," he suggested, "that might be best."

Knowing he was right, she snapped back into her role as his besotted lover and wound herself around him.

"You looked like you were going to carve out a piece of her heart," he murmured as they moved together on the dance floor. "Did I get you out of there in time?"

Zara sighed, letting herself relax into Rory's body. *Relax* was a relative word, of course, given the heat of his body against hers. If only he wasn't so well built, so strong, so all-around perfect.

"Just barely." He was tall enough that even with her high-heeled boots, she could lean her head against his chest as they danced. "It's not that I don't love Brittany, because I do. It's just that sometimes I wish she'd think before she speaks. And acts."

"Did she say something about Cameron that upset you?"

"No." Zara let herself nuzzle into him a bit more. What was the harm when he smelled so good—and it would only make their ruse more believable? "I actually think I'm starting to get over that."

"I'm very glad to hear it," he said. And then, "What was it that upset you, then?"

"If I tell you, are you going to go charging back over to call her out for pistols at dawn?"

"Even though I know you're not made of porcelain and can protect yourself, I have a hard time not wanting to protect you." He didn't sound at all apologetic. "And when your ex said their first meeting had been perfect, I couldn't take the high road. But I think I understand why you did. Letting them have their big night—even after the way things went down between the three of you—is really kind."

"Actually—" She held on tighter. "It's nice to have someone leap to my defense for once."

"I'm surprised your father isn't already doing that."

"Don't be too hard on him. From the start, I think my dad and stepmom were so afraid that their two fifteen-year-old daughters wouldn't get along that they would have said or done anything to keep the peace. Even all these years later, my father wants so badly for me to be okay with Brittany and Cameron getting together that I don't have the heart to disappoint him."

"And here you called me the compassionate one," Rory said.

"Yeah, that's us, two Mother Teresas lying to everyone about our relationship to get back at my stepsister and ex."

"I'd do it again in a heartbeat, if you needed me."

A pang landed in the middle of her heart, simply from knowing that Rory didn't only have her back tonight, but would for as long as she needed him.

She wasn't used to letting herself need people. Not when she couldn't push away the thought that there were far more deserving people than herself out there. And not when she knew all too well the pain of losing someone you loved.

"Thank you," she finally replied. "Anyway, what pushed my buttons was when Brittany mentioned a piece about local Maine makers that she promoted earlier this year. She said you looked familiar, because you were profiled in the story. Until tonight, I had no idea she was involved with that story at all." Zara swallowed hard. "Or that she deliberately left my name off the makers list they submitted for the piece. Because I just make glasses, not *art*."

The sound that reverberated up from his chest was not far from a growl. "She's jealous."

"Jealous?" Zara wouldn't have been more surprised if he'd grown two heads. "No." She shook her head, hard enough that she had to right her glasses on the bridge of her nose. "No way. Brittany is *definitely* not jealous of me."

"She is. Trust me on this. It doesn't make things right, but at the very least, I hope it will help you remember that her behavior doesn't have a single thing to do with how great you are. Cameron went with her because he's weak. And your name likely didn't end up on the list for the makers story because she knew you'd outshine everyone else. Especially her."

"You've been amazing tonight, Rory, but whatever you're seeing…I just can't. She was the first one picked for every team at school and voted class president. She had her choice of top-flight universities. She got an amazing job right after graduation. And she always looks fantastic. I promise you, the very last thing she wants is to be like me."

"That's quite a list." But he still didn't look impressed. "Now tell me yours."

"Mine?" She made a face. "I was a mediocre high school student. I went to a midlevel college. I didn't get picked for the best jobs. And as you know from earlier tonight, my fashion choices often need help."

He smiled at that before saying, "You forgot a few things. First, that you love what you do. Don't you?"

"You know I do."

"Second, that you get to stretch your creative muscles and be your own boss every day, right?"

"Again, you know the answer is yes."

"And third, that you don't want to look like anyone else, otherwise you wouldn't have turned your creative passion into creating funky, bright, unique glasses that are most definitely art."

Had he always made her want to smile this much?

"Who *wouldn't* want to be like you? Especially," he added with that wicked glimmer in his eyes, "when out of all the women here, you're the one who gets the privilege of dancing with me?"

She couldn't hold back a laugh. "You're really something, aren't you?"

"Something great?"

"If it will help you sleep better at night, let's go with that." But she couldn't hold back the truth. "You have been really, really great here tonight. Thank you for coming."

"Don't thank me yet." He looked more wicked than ever. "The night is still young."

CHAPTER EIGHT

When Rory was a kid, his parents had made him take ballroom dance lessons. He'd been a terrible trouble-maker in class, but he'd gotten away with it because he'd been a natural dancer. Though he enjoyed dancing at family events with his cousin Lori, who was a professional dancer, he rarely got the chance to bust a move with anyone else who knew what they were doing.

It was one heck of a surprise to learn that Zara knew how to get down.

Her movements weren't trained, or practiced, but her innate grace—and exuberance—mattered far more. During the months that they'd worked together at the warehouse, she'd never seemed to care the slightest bit what anyone thought of her. She brought that same energy to the dance floor. She clearly danced for joy, rather than to impress.

And as he spun and twirled her, bringing her close then letting her go again before reeling her back in, he couldn't help but wonder what it would be like to do a different dance together…in his bed.

He could already guess how it would be to make love to her. Their one short kiss—a kiss he'd been driven to give Zara in the face of her stepsister's obstinate refusal to admit that she'd done anything wrong—had shocked him.

He was blown away by the heat they generated. By Zara's delicious taste.

And, most of all, by his sudden desire to claim so much more from her than just one kiss.

Wanting nothing more than to crush her mouth beneath his, in a bid to regain his sanity, he spun her around the dance floor instead. Yesterday morning, when he'd stumbled upon her solo descent into oblivion, he hadn't seen the potential danger in offering to be her wingman tonight. Of course, even if he had, he wouldn't have made a different decision—not when he felt strongly that she needed someone to have her back.

He just hadn't expected to like her so much. To relish the fact that she was funny. Irreverent. Witty.

And far kinder than her stepsister and ex deserved.

What's more, tonight didn't feel like any date he'd ever been on. Granted, he'd never pretended to be half of a fake couple before. But though their relationship status wasn't real, their conversation in the car had flowed easily. Kissing her had lit a match inside of the coldest parts of him. He'd never been so in sync while dancing with anyone else.

And perhaps the most damning thing of all?

Every sign seemed to point to Zara feeling all the same things.

He'd been sure that neither of them would ever be here, in a place where sparks were flying like they'd lit a bonfire. He hadn't yet stopped reliving Chelsea's accident—and his part in it. As for Zara, no woman had ever seemed *less* interested in him before tonight.

All his life, Rory had been flirted with and fawned over. His ego had been stroked. Women had bent over backward to be with him. Zara had been the only holdout, not only utterly immune to his charms, but also determined to provoke him as often as possible.

Two days ago, he would have bet the house on the two of them forever remaining in their separate corners. Tonight, however, he wouldn't touch that bet with a ten-foot pole.

Not when he could think of few things he wanted more than to join Zara in her corner. The smaller the space, the better, if it meant getting to be close to her.

"Earth to Rory." Zara was standing before him, waving her hand in front of his eyes. "Where'd you go?"

"You don't want to know."

"That sounds serious," she said as they walked off

the dance floor and headed for a corner of the room that wasn't heaving with people. "If you've got five cents, I'll be Lucy van Pelt, and you can be Charlie Brown. The doctor is in."

Despite himself, he laughed. "You'd love to pull a football out from under me right before I kick it, wouldn't you?"

She looked shocked that he would even ask. "It would be the *greatest thing ever.*"

"Remind me not to leave you alone with my brother Brandon."

"Does he like torturing you too?" She looked so hopeful he nearly lost control and kissed her again.

It wasn't easy to concentrate on talking about his brother, rather than the way his pulse leaped whenever Zara got close. "We're closest in age and have been pranking each other since we were kids."

"Who's currently in the lead?"

"I am." He said it with pride. "Brandon is often on the road, opening and managing his hotels, so when he launched his latest location, I sent him a gift basket full of his least-favorite things during the press event. He not only had to look happy about it, he had to take a bite of one of the fancy marzipan candies that I asked Cassie to make him in the shape of his new hotel. I'm sure he's cooking up one heck of a prank to get me back for that one."

"You might look like a man, but you're still a ten-year-old boy on the inside, aren't you?"

"My ten-year-old nephew is *far* more mature than I am."

She was still laughing when the sound of a spoon clinking against glass turned their attention toward the newly engaged couple. Waiters circulated with glasses of champagne. After they'd each taken one, Rory gave Zara's free hand a squeeze.

"Thank you *so much* for coming to celebrate with us tonight," Brittany said to the crowd. "It means everything to Cameron and me to share our excitement over our engagement with our close family and friends." She beamed as everyone applauded.

Brittany was obviously born for the spotlight, given how much she enjoyed being the center of attention. Zara, on the other hand, never seemed the least bit comfortable being anyone's focus. Even during the launch party for her new glasses line, she'd remained on the sidelines instead of lapping up people's admiration for her work.

"We know we need to save our vows for our wedding day," Brittany continued, "but we couldn't resist the chance to share some of our feelings with you tonight." As she took both of Cameron's hands in hers, her expression was almost comically earnest. "Cameron, you are the love of my life, the yin to my yang, the peanut butter to my jelly, the macaroni to my cheese."

Rory was only just barely keeping from laughing. Due to the size of his extended family, he'd been to plenty of engagement parties and weddings, but he'd never heard anything so cheesy.

Unfortunately, Zara didn't seem to be finding the situation anywhere near as humorous. It wasn't that she looked like she was about to storm the mini-stage the couple was standing on, or throw one of the small jade plants dotting the tables at them. She had even managed a small smile. But he knew what her real smile looked like—and this one didn't come into her eyes.

He pulled her closer as Brittany continued to gush over Cameron.

"Our relationship has been wonderful from the start," her stepsister was saying, "and I can't wait for it to become even more wonderful as husband and wife."

When the engaged couple kissed, the cheers came again. Zara, to her credit, put down her drink to clap, even after Brittany's blatant misrepresentation of how wonderful, and blameless, her "start" with Cameron had been.

Rory wasn't nearly as big of a person, however. At the moment, he was silently hoping lightning would strike down Cameron before he could open his mouth and make things worse. Which he surely would, because he was a tool.

No luck on the indoor storm, unfortunately. Because the jerk had already started flapping his lips.

"Brittany, I never dreamed a woman like you would so much as look at me—let alone agree to be my wife."

Cameron was sweating beneath the lights, his cheeks sporting red blotches. Objectively, Rory could understand why some people might find the guy attractive. But all Rory could see was a slimy weasel.

"You're my angel," Cameron continued, "my *raison d'être*, my endless love."

"It's like listening to a poet," Brittany responded in a stage whisper that was clearly meant for everyone to hear.

As they leaned in to kiss again, Rory pulled Zara toward the bar. "I need a drink. Hopefully, the bartender will make it strong enough to wash their speeches out of my brain."

Despite the concerns that he had been grappling with on the dance floor—namely, wanting Zara when they were just supposed to be a pretend couple—he was more glad than ever that he'd come tonight.

The thought of her alone in this viper's den made his stomach twist.

"Give us the strongest drinks you've got," he said to the bartender.

"Two Long Island Iced Teas coming up, sir."

Rory certainly didn't advocate getting drunk every time Zara's stepsister drove her to the edge of sanity. Given what he'd seen of Brittany so far, that was a one-way ticket to disaster. Especially since it was clear that, despite everything, Zara loved her. But at this exact moment, if a mix of gin, vodka, tequila, and rum would take the edge off the nonsense they'd just heard, then Rory was all for doing whatever it took to help Zara forget.

The bartender handed them their drinks, and Rory directed them toward a private corner of the room. "Bottoms up." He was about to clink his glass against Zara's when she put it down on a nearby table.

"I don't want to get drunk again."

He put his glass down too. "Tell me what you want, and I swear I'll do whatever I can to make it happen for you."

"For one night," she said in an impassioned voice, "I want to go home with the grand prize instead of the ribbon for second place. I know I have my career, and I love that." She shot a glance at her stepsister and ex, who were standing with their arms around each other as they accepted everyone's congratulations. "But I don't have anyone to hold my hand and say how much he adores me." She turned her gaze back to him. "I want that, Rory. I want to know how it feels to be wanted. Truly wanted for *me* and not just as a stepping stone to *her*. Even if I don't deserve to be given what I want, that's how I feel right now."

"Of course you deserve it." Regardless of how many times they'd been at each other's throats during the past year, he couldn't understand how Zara could think she was at all undeserving of happiness. He cupped her cheek with his hand. "Any guy who ever used you as a stepping stone was an idiot." He nodded toward her ex. "Especially him."

That almost got a smile out of her. But then she shook her head. "You know what? Forget everything I just said. We should go now. I've done my duty to support Brittany—and you've gone above and beyond in playing the part of my besotted lover."

She began to move away, but he reached for her hand before she could. "Who says it's just a part I'm playing?"

She seemed stunned by his question. "Of course it is. I mean, I know we kissed, but—"

"I want to kiss you again, Zara. I've been wanting to kiss you again and again and again since the moment my lips left yours."

"Are you feeling all right?" She tried to say it in her usual sassy voice, but her words came out all breathy. "Last thing I knew, we couldn't stand each other. More kisses... More everything... It would be crazy."

"I'll tell you what's crazy. Here with you tonight—I can't think of the last time I've enjoyed being with anyone as much. And when we kissed, the whole goddamned earth moved."

"That should have sounded cheesy." It was almost as though she was talking to herself. *"Why didn't that sound cheesy?"*

"Because I have a feeling this is where we've been headed all along. To one night." He paused to let her take it in. And to make sure he'd wrapped his own head around it before he took things any deeper. "Together."

"One night?" She whispered the words in a shocked tone. *"Together?"*

He didn't move, didn't speak, didn't push her to agree. He might have put the crazy idea out there, but it had to be her decision.

He didn't know how long she thought it over. It could have been five seconds or five minutes. Finally, she nodded. "One night. That's all it will be."

He wanted to drag her out of the cocktail bar, run down the street to the hotel they'd checked into earlier, and toss her onto the bed so that he could taste every inch of her from head to toe, then back again.

Instead, he made sure to heed the voice in his head telling him to make absolutely sure she wanted this. "I don't want you to wake up tomorrow and regret anything that happens tonight."

"I won't if you won't." He knew her stubborn look well. It was the one she'd worn during every one of their previous sparring sessions. "Kiss me, Rory. Show me what it feels like to truly be wanted."

A man could take only so much temptation and still hold on to his control. His was done for as he slid his hands into her hair and crushed his mouth to hers.

★ ★ ★

Listening to Brittany and Cameron gushing over each other, Zara had been stunned that they still behaved as though she hadn't been a part of their beginning—and that they hadn't both cheated on her. For the first time, she truly had felt like a doormat.

Fortunately, Rory had come through for her again, getting her out of the bad situation before anyone else noticed her reaction. And then he'd gone one better and offered her a lifeline.

Himself.

This had all started with simply wanting to get through Brittany and Cameron's engagement celebration in one piece. But the longer Zara spent in Rory's arms, the less tonight had to do with her stepsister and ex.

Now, it had to do only with Rory.

She wanted him. And not because she knew going

back to the hotel and making love with him would stick in Brittany and Cameron's craw.

Forget about their engagement. Forget wanting to prove something to them. Forget gunning for the big prize.

Suddenly, all that mattered was how much Zara had come to like Rory. How safe she felt with him. How hot he made her.

She didn't want to share him with anyone else. At least for this one night.

She made herself stop kissing him long enough to say, "What do you say we take this to the hotel?"

As though he couldn't keep from touching her, he brushed the pad of his thumb over her lower lip before giving her a truly wicked smile. "I say, *hell yes.*"

CHAPTER NINE

Thank God the oceanfront hotel where they had booked rooms for the night was only around the corner. If she'd had to wait any longer to tear off Rory's clothes and have her wicked way with him, she might very well have combusted.

She'd never been afraid or ashamed of her sexuality, but the truth was that none of her partners had ever truly plumbed the depths of it. Given how delicious Rory's kisses were—not to mention how heady the feel of his large hands caressing her curves were—not only was he going to be able to keep up with her, but she had a feeling she might learn a thing or two from him tonight.

Half a block from their hotel, he proved her right by pressing her up against a brick wall, threading his fingers with hers, and lifting her arms above her head so that he could hold her captive for the crush of his mouth over hers.

She was so damned happy about it that she grinned against his mouth as she lifted one leg to wrap it around his hips and urge him closer.

He lifted his mouth from hers. "You like this?"

Where another man might have taken her obvious attraction and passion as a green light, she appreciated how Rory went a step further and asked for words too.

"I *love* it."

He grinned back. "If you think *this* is good, just wait…"

She laughed as they headed, hand in hand, for the front door of the hotel. "Nice to know that a few kisses haven't made you any less cocky."

He raised an eyebrow. "*Cocky.* Now that's a perfect word for tonight if ever I've heard one."

She was still laughing as they walked inside. They had checked in before the party so that they could change, which meant that Zara's things were in her room and Rory's were in his. She didn't care which room they used, and he must have felt the same way, because without any discussion, they made a beeline for hers on the lower floor of the building.

Somehow, they managed to keep their hands off each other long enough to get inside. Once the door was locked behind them, she tossed her bag and key onto a nearby counter and got ready to tear his clothes off. They could start with sex on the plush carpet, then move to the couch, then the bathtub, and then, when they were finally starting to get tired, the bed.

Instead, Rory captured her hands in his and simply stared at her. "You're beautiful, Zara."

She paused, suddenly off-kilter. "You don't have to say that."

"I can't tell you the truth?"

"In case you haven't noticed, I'm a sure thing here. You don't have to give me a bunch of pretty words, or flatter me, to get into my pants."

He scowled. "When have I *ever* given you a bunch of pretty words?"

"Never."

He still looked upset, however, as he said, "I know you've been with some pretty big jerks, but that's not how I roll."

"Okay." She squeezed his hands. "Sorry. I was just trying to say that—" She broke off, realizing she had several hard questions to ask herself.

What *had* she been trying to say with that knee-jerk reaction to his compliment? Why couldn't she just believe it? Especially when Rory had never lied to her with pretty words. It wasn't his style. He preferred blunt, straightforward, even stark.

"Say it again, Rory. Please."

"You're beautiful, Zara."

This time, she smiled and replied, "Thank you. You're quite a sight to behold too."

"Such a way with words," he murmured as he

drew her closer. "Now…let's see what I can do to make you forgot how to use the English language entirely."

Her breath hitched in her chest at his sexy intention. "Is that a dare?"

"No." He gave her another wicked grin. "It's a promise."

By that point, she'd nearly forgotten how to breathe, so she supposed he already had her part of the way to forgetting how to speak. And all while she was still wearing her clothes.

Impressive…

"I remember what you were wearing the first time we met." He moved his hands from hers to slide the zipper of her sheer top down the center of her back as he spoke. She laid her hands flat against his broad chest to steady herself against the onslaught of sensation as his fingertips trailed, featherlight, over her spine. "You had on a little blue tank top, oversized jeans hitched up with a big belt, flip-flops, and glasses the bright blue of a parrot's wings."

Though fashion and clothes had never been at the top of her priority list—apart from her glasses frames, of course—she remembered her outfit from that day too. Just as she remembered the flash of heat in Rory's eyes when he'd looked at her. Heat she'd attributed to the fact that she'd managed to infuriate him within five minutes of entering the building.

"I wasn't wearing a bra."

"You most certainly were not," he agreed in a low voice that caressed her skin the same way his fingers were. Ever so lightly, but with sinful intention. "Do you have any idea how hard it was not to touch you the way I am now?"

"Maybe." She weighed the wisdom of admitting the truth before deciding to be just as honest. "I felt the same way. But then, you were so irritating that it didn't matter how hot you were. If I had only realized you were pulling my pigtails on the playground because you had the hots for me—"

"You would never have let me live it down." He lifted her gauzy blouse over her head as he finished her sentence. "Thank God I can stare as long as I like tonight."

Though she was still wearing a black bra and leather pants, as Rory drank her in, she felt naked. No one had ever looked at her like this before. Like she was a work of art. Like she was absolutely perfect. Like she was the most wonderful gift.

And even though she knew she wasn't, for one night she wanted to pretend that she was.

When he feathered his fingers through the hair at the nape of her neck, she shivered in response. "You're going to torture me by taking your sweet time getting

me to the finish line, aren't you?" Her words came out
breathless. Borderline desperate.

"You'd be disappointed if I didn't." He slid a hand
over the bare skin of her back. "And you should know I
intend for you to cross the finish line over and over
again."

"Rather confident of your sexual prowess, aren't
you?"

His answer came by way of a kiss that was at once
wonderfully filthy and breathtakingly romantic. "I
know better than to bring anything but my A game
tonight. You'd taunt me endlessly at work otherwise."

She slid her fingers through his surprisingly silky
hair. "And you'd be disappointed if *I* didn't do just
that."

"I would. Although I can already guarantee *nothing*
about tonight is going to disappoint me. No matter
how much we do or don't do, I'm already a very happy
man." She appreciated that he was giving her time
once more to make sure she was fully on board. "So
before I strip you down completely and run my tongue
over every inch of your gorgeous skin, I need to know
your limits—anything that isn't on the table."

"I don't have a lot of rules for tonight," she said.
Especially when it came to his tongue and her skin. In
fact, she couldn't remember ever wanting anything
quite so badly. "Only that neither of us gets to act

weird when it's over."

"Works for me."

"Good. And for every piece of clothing you strip from me," she added, "you'll lose one too." To make her point, she slipped her hands beneath the lapels of his jacket and pushed it off his shoulders.

"I always did think strip poker would be better played without cards," he murmured as he played his fingers over her abdomen. "And I'll have you know that you're my full-on teenage dream in those leather pants. Especially the part where I'm about to take them off."

Was there anything hotter than watching Rory use his big, brilliant hands to pull down her zipper? She'd never be able to watch him work again without remembering this heat flooding her body and the mouthwatering anticipation of just where he was going to put his hands next.

"Well, well, well..." His heated gaze caught on her lingerie. "Aren't you full of surprises?"

Zara had never been a girly girl, but she couldn't resist soft, pretty things against her skin. She'd chosen a simple black bra to wear beneath her translucent shirt tonight, but there was nothing simple about the lace and silk she was wearing beneath the leather.

Rory knelt before her as he unzipped her boots and took them off, then slid her pants down her legs and helped her step free of them. Once she was standing in only a bra and panties, he stopped to stare again.

"My God..." With his callused fingertips, he traced the extremely thin, extremely small strip of material that covered mere inches of her hips.

He wrapped his hands around her hips to press a kiss to the fabric that still covered her, and she couldn't hold back a low moan of pleasure. If he was making her feel this good already, how was she going to survive his hands, his mouth, on her bare skin?

He looked up her body from where he was kneeling on the floor. "Please tell me you normally wear big cotton briefs beneath your clothes when you're working."

The touch of his hands and mouth, and his nearness to the center of her arousal, made her feel weak in the knees. Tonight was a first on so many levels—no man had ever made her legs feel shaky enough to collapse. "You don't want me to lie, do you?"

"No," he said. "Always tell me the truth, even if I don't want to hear it."

"In that case," she informed him with relish, "the truth is that the baggier and more shapeless my clothes, the prettier and more sexy I like my lingerie."

He groaned. "I'm never going to get another damned thing done in my workshop. All I'm going to do is sit there and wonder what you've got on under your overalls."

"If you ask really nicely," she said, "I just might let you take a peek every now and again. Especially if you don't mind me drooling as I stare at your big, brawny hands while you work."

He held up said hands. "Got any ideas what you want me to do with them now?"

Another thrill of anticipation ran up her spine. "Absolutely *anything* you want."

CHAPTER TEN

In Rory's wildest dreams, he hadn't known to dream of Zara.

Now he suspected he'd dream of little else.

She was beyond gorgeous, with curves that filled his hands just right. That wasn't the only thing that was right, though. He'd never been a big talker during sex, but it made perfect sense that with Zara, verbal sparring should be part of even their most intimate moments.

The hotel room overlooked the sea, and though it was night, the sound of the crashing waves provided a backdrop to their lovemaking. With the moonlight shining over the sea, it wasn't too different from the view he had from his lighthouse home. He wanted to take Zara there again, wanted to carry her into his bedroom with its floor-to-ceiling glass, where on a stormy night you almost felt as though you were out there riding the waves.

One night only meant he couldn't do that, however. Not unless he could convince her to go for more.

Here they were, barely into their first night together, and he was already longing for more. So much more…

Starting with running his hands over every inch of Zara's beautiful skin.

He'd often seen her head out for a run in the middle of the day and not return for over an hour, so he knew she was in great shape. But as she waited for him to make his next move, her breath was coming faster and faster.

He leaned forward to press a kiss to her stomach. She made only the slightest sound, a sudden intake of breath, but he was so attuned to her every move that he couldn't miss it.

"Wait," she said, and instantly he went on high alert, expecting her to back away and say she must have lost her mind to be here doing this with him tonight. "It's my turn to take off something of yours."

Relief whooshed from his lungs. "What do you want off?"

"Hmm…" She took her sweet time perusing him. "I'll play fair, for now at least, and say your belt." She licked her lips. "What do you say to a little striptease? You still on your knees before me, undressing for my pleasure?"

"Anything for you." And he meant every word as he slowly undid the buckle, then slid the leather from one belt loop to the next and then the next.

"Ooooh…you're *good*." Her eyes were lit with both heat and humor. "Are you sure you haven't moonlighted as a stripper?"

She always made him laugh, even now when there was barely any blood left in his brain. "Not yet. But if you ask nicely," he offered, just as she had before, "I might be willing to put on a show just for you sometime."

"I'd like that," she said in a husky voice. "Both of us doing a little secret show-and-tell for each other at work."

The thought alone was nearly more than he could take. Hell, after what felt like a year long tease of being near Zara without having her, he couldn't wait another second to unsnap the front hook of her bra so that her gorgeous breasts sprang free, then slide his thumbs into the sides of her panties and pull them down too.

That was when one of the strongest women he'd ever met…whimpered.

And he hadn't even put his hands—or mouth—on her yet.

He got it, though. Because he was on the verge of whimpering himself. That was how badly he wanted her. How much he wanted to pick her up and toss her onto the bed and claim her as his.

"That was two pieces of clothing," she said, her

words raw with desire. "It's my turn now to take two pieces off you."

Considering she was still able to string so many words together, he obviously needed to do a better job of making her incoherent with pleasure. At the same time, he didn't want to make the mistake of ignoring either of her two rules.

She moved her hands to his tie. He hadn't noticed how elegant her fingers were, or how erotic, until she loosened the knot at his neck. Sweet Lord...she might as well be stroking him for as hard as this made him.

Finally, she tossed the blue striped fabric to the side. "Now it's time for your shirt to go. But don't stand." She gave him a wonderfully naughty smile as she put her hands on his shoulders to keep him on the floor. "I like having you on your knees."

"Don't get used to it." He was doing his damnedest to speak normally when he was the one losing his grip of the English language with Zara standing naked in front of him. All he wanted to do was touch and kiss and stroke and *have*. But a deal was a deal—he just hoped she would be quick about getting his shirt off.

So of course she took her sweet time, moving agonizingly slowly as she undid one button at a time, sneaking in the brush of a fingertip here, the light scratch of a nail there.

Rory couldn't remember ever being this aroused.

To the point where the lightest brush of her breasts against his face as she dawdled over the second-to-last button had him momentarily losing control and ripping his shirt open so that he could shove it off and throw it across the room.

"Looks like someone's getting antsy," she said, laughter underscoring her words.

"Antsy was ten minutes ago. I'm straight-up frenzied now." Still on his knees, he rose high enough to rub his five-o'clock shadow over her breasts.

"*Rory...*"

His name on her lips was more breath than sound. And when he turned his face the other way to caress her again with the bristles over his jaw, her whole body shuddered. His hands, his mouth, were greedier than ever by now, and she wasn't the only one feeling a little shaky when he cupped her full breasts.

How had he never guessed that her strong surface hid such softness?

All Rory's life, he'd used his hands to carve, to shape, to draw out the beauty of the wood he was working with. But he'd never before held so much passion, so much exquisiteness, with his bare hands.

He could spend the rest of his life touching Zara and never get enough.

Moving slowly to imprint every sensation into his memory, he ran his hands from her breasts to her waist, then over the swell of her hips. He didn't blink, barely breathed, as he slid one hand between her legs…then over her sex.

She was so hot. So wet.

So damned perfect.

Breath whooshed from her lungs. "I was starting to wonder if you were *ever* going to get there."

"You mean here?" He barely allowed time for his words to register before sliding one finger into her.

Her head fell back, and her fingers tightened in his hair. *"Yes. There."*

She writhed against his hand, urging him to move deeper, faster, rougher. All the things he wanted too. All the things he *needed* as he took the tip of one breast into his mouth and then the other.

Her inner muscles clenched over his fingers as he laved her soft skin, then gently ran the edge of his teeth over the taut peaks. Never in his life had he felt a bigger rush than taking Zara to the brink of climax. Wanting to prolong the beautiful moment as long as he could, he stilled his hand to breathe her in.

A growl of frustration rippled from her throat. Her glasses were slightly askew on her nose. And she had never looked sexier as she said, "Stop now and you'll forever pay the price."

Though he was just as caught in the grip of desire, he laughed. How could he not when she was this gloriously fierce in her passion, in her insistence on pleasure? And when he pressed his mouth to her sex, she was so damned sweet on his tongue that he couldn't get enough of her.

At last, she lost hold of her command of the English language, the sounds coming from her lips a random mixture of vowels and consonants.

He wanted to take her this way—wanted to make her feel this good—every night, wanted to feel her skin damp and flushed beneath his hands, wanted to hear her breath come hard and fast, wanted to feel her limbs trembling from the aftershocks of her climax.

How the hell was one night with Zara ever going to be enough?

CHAPTER ELEVEN

As Rory scooped Zara into his arms and carried her to the bed, pleasure continued to radiate through every inch of her, from his hands roving over her skin...his mouth on her breasts...the play of his fingers, his tongue, between her thighs...

He crawled over her as she lay sprawled on her back on the bed, her limbs feeling buttery and loose. "You look good enough to eat." He paused as though for impact, before adding, "Again."

Though she'd never felt more relaxed, she owed it to him to come back with, "A teenage boy could have done better than that."

"I blame your orgasm for blowing my mind into a million little pieces."

She laughed as she summoned the energy to reach up and lay her hand on his bare chest. "Just as long as the rest of the equipment is in good working order, all is well."

"Don't worry, baby, all is *definitely* well."

"Baby." She snorted out the word as she ran her

hand down the deep ridges of his abdominal muscles until she reached the top edge of his suit pants. "You should have warned me you were going to call me *baby* in front of my family. It took everything I had to keep a straight face." Before he could reply, she said, "Sorry, I didn't mean to bring them up. Especially when you're still left hanging here."

"If you want to talk about your family—or anything else—we'll hit the pause button and talk as long as you want. Hell, even if you decide to kick me out right now, I'll go."

She wasn't sure she'd ever been with a man so attuned to making sure a woman felt not only safe, but in charge. Was this due to a great upbringing and having so many sisters?

Or was it simply that Rory Sullivan was one of the good ones?

"I don't want to talk about my family," she assured him. "And I *definitely* don't want you to leave."

He blew out a comically relieved breath. "That was going to be one hell of a cold shower."

She moved her hand lower, cupping his erection—as much of it as she could fit in her palm. "Wasting this on a cold shower would be a travesty. In fact..." The few minutes' rest had refueled her to the point that she was strong enough to surprise him by flipping them over on the bed. Straddling his hips while he lay on his back, she said, "I'm thinking it's long past time for me to see if the reality lives up to the hype."

"There's *hype* about my junk?"

"You really are a teenage boy on the inside, aren't you, calling your penis *junk*?" She couldn't think of the last time anyone had made her laugh so much. "And yes, given the way women follow you around at the warehouse shows, your junk practically comes with its own publicity team. Not that I'm judging you for the sex you have," she clarified. "All I care about is tonight. What you did before and what you'll do after is all good."

His expression turned suddenly serious. "I haven't been with anyone for a year."

Wow, she hadn't been expecting that. Although if she stopped to think about it, she hadn't actually seen him go home with any of his groupies. It was just that he was such a spectacular-looking man, not to mention successful, it didn't make sense for him to be single.

But this wasn't the place or time to dig deeper into the hows and whys of Rory's celibacy or lack of a romantic relationship. All she needed to say for tonight was, "I haven't either." She smiled as a lovely thought hit her. "You're my fresh start."

He smiled back as he cupped her breasts and stroked them so softly it almost made her crazy. "And you're mine."

"I always did love the first day of each new school year," she murmured as she reached for the zipper of his slacks. "The sense that anything was possible. That I might become passionate about a new subject." She felt giddy with anticipation as she added, "Although I'm pretty sure I never felt quite as passionate about school as I'm feeling right now."

Rory looked like he might have laughed had he not been clenching his jaw in an obvious effort to keep control as she slowly drew his zipper down. And when she moved the final layers of fabric away, he did *not* disappoint.

In fact, she was stunned speechless for a long moment. "One night with you is going to ruin me for other men."

"Good."

She looked at him in surprise. He sounded far too happy about her dry streak continuing forever after the sun rose on their one-night blip in reality. Well, two could play that game. If he wanted her to spend the rest of her days longing for a repeat of tonight, she would damn well make sure he left feeling exactly the same way.

But when she wrapped her fingers around him, she forgot everything but how good he felt. So big. So hot.

So ready to rock her world in ways it'd never been rocked before.

Tightening her grip, she moved her hand up and down his rock-hard shaft. It wasn't enough just to touch him, though, she needed to kiss him too. She leaned forward to press her lips to his at the same time that he threaded his fingers into her hair and dragged her mouth to his.

The kiss he gave her was incendiary. How the hotel room didn't go up in flames, she'd never know.

Still, she forced herself to pull her mouth from his so that she could run kisses over his face, his shoulders, his chest, his abs. And all the while, she stroked him, loving how he grew bigger and harder with every kiss, every caress.

She couldn't let her hand have all the fun, though, and moments later she pressed her lips to his erection. But that wasn't enough either—she needed to taste him, needed to know just what her tongue sliding across his skin would do to him.

Zara soon learned the answer: It would drive him absolutely *wild*.

As his hips bucked up, she opened her mouth wide to take him in. It was beyond heady to know that she could do this to him, make him feel so much, make him desire her so fiercely that he lost control.

Only, as she soon learned, he had enough control left to maneuver them so that she was beneath him on the bed again, while he levered over her. Her glasses had finally fallen off, lying beside the pillow.

"Please tell me you pack condoms even when you're with the last guy you'd ever think to sleep with."

Though it wasn't at all handy that they were currently condom-free, she was still pleased to know he had no condoms with him either. Yet another mark in his favor, that he wasn't the kind of guy who always expected to score.

"No luck there." He was doing such seriously potent stuff with his mouth on her earlobe that she only barely managed to get the words out. "But I am on birth control to regulate my period."

He lifted his head and looked at her as though she'd just presented him with the Furniture Design of the Year award in London. "I'm clean, I swear. And I would never do, never suggest, anything to hurt you."

"I'm clean too," she said. "And I hope we never hurt each other, Rory." She put her hand on his cheek. "Because as much as it pains me to admit it, I've fallen quite into like with you over the past couple of days."

They shared a smile.

And then things got *real*.

Especially when she leaned up to whisper in his ear, "Be as rough as you want. I can take it. In fact…I *insist* on it."

His low-uttered curse came a beat before he captured her mouth in an intense kiss. Then he moved his big hands to cup her hips, she wrapped her legs around his waist, and the next thing she knew, she was his as he moved inside her.

Entirely, completely, wholly *his*.

She could happily spend the rest of her life like this, captured in his arms, their bodies entwined into one, his mouth against hers, their hearts beating the same hard-driving pace…

She was so overwhelmed by her feelings that she had to tell him, "I really, really, really, really like you."

"*Zara.*" He gripped her hips even tighter, and she could feel him throbbing huge and hard inside her. "You have *no idea* how much I like you."

"Show me." No matter how she had meant the words to sound, they came out as a desperate plea.

And when he covered her mouth with his again, what she felt went beyond mere passion, resonating far closer to the center of her chest than she could have anticipated. Much closer to her heart than she was sure she could possibly deal with.

But then, thought spun out of her head as he took her even higher with his kisses, and caresses, and the wonderfully deep thrust of his body into hers.

So high that her world grew impossibly bright, filled with more colors than she'd known existed and sensation so sharp and sweet that when she hit the peak, she didn't simply break apart, didn't just shatter into a million pieces—she detonated, crying out his name as the waves of pleasure went on and on and on.

Moments later, Rory followed her over the edge, her name on his lips between kisses. And every part of him inside and out was so strong and beautiful and surprisingly likable that she began to crest again.

"Please," she outright begged him this time. "I still need you."

"I'm here, Zara." His hands, his body over hers, his deep voice, were the only things still tethering her to the earth. "Let me feel you go over again, sweetheart."

So much about tonight had been crazy. But nothing was crazier than the impact of hearing Rory call her *sweetheart*.

The endearment sent her into a third orgasm, one that was even bigger, even more breathless, even brighter and sweeter than the two that he'd already given her.

And when pleasure finally let her out of its grip, a combination of pure exhaustion and unexpected emotion meant she couldn't do anything more than snuggle in against Rory's broad chest and fall asleep.

CHAPTER TWELVE

Rory was wide awake. Only a fool would sleep and miss relishing a single second of Zara naked and warm in his arms.

It had been a year since he'd gone to bed with a woman, but that wasn't why it felt so good to hold her close, to feel her breathe softly and evenly against him, to lightly stroke the strands of dark hair that lay across her shoulders.

After what had happened with Chelsea last year, he wasn't sure if—or when—he'd ever feel fully alive again. But every moment he'd spent with Zara since Friday morning had been a revelation.

Speaking of revelations…

He drew her more firmly against him, and when one of her legs slid over his, he was reminded all over again of how being with her had been nothing short of mind-blowing.

Now that he knew how hot they burned together, he could look back and see clear signs of the sparks that had been between them from the start. Sparks he'd been mostly blind to, lost inside the dark twists and turns of his head and heart this past year.

There was another reason he wasn't sleeping, though. The deal they'd made before they'd gotten naked had been for one night only—and no getting weird afterward. He would never have agreed to only one night if he'd known how much he would end up regretting how quickly it had passed.

Having been fairly wild in his twenties, Rory was no stranger to mutually beneficial one-night stands. He'd never before had trouble walking away in the morning, and he'd always stuck to protocol—namely, no asking for a second night. With other women, he'd never been tempted.

With Zara, however, he wasn't looking forward to walking away come sunup. Not at all. He wasn't actually sure he would be able to do it, if he were being totally honest with himself.

Was it fair to ask her for more than just one night, though, when all he had to offer was great sex, rather than any kind of real relationship? He didn't trust himself with those anymore, didn't trust himself not to end up hurting a woman. It wasn't just Chelsea with whom things had gone wrong, it was every woman he'd ever been with.

At the end of the day, he was the common denominator. And the equation always added up the same way: with Rory getting a 0 out of 100 at relationships.

Besides, when he tried to imagine what Zara would say if he asked her for a repeat of tonight, it was all too easy to envision her spitting out a string of blazing-fast retorts. Even in sleep, her expression held a touch of mutiny.

Who would have thought he'd find obstinacy so damned sexy...

Two hours passed before she stirred. Still draped across him, she began to stretch, then stiffened against him as she realized she wasn't alone in the bed.

"Rory?"

Even just the sound of her voice aroused him, especially when she was saying his name in a slightly husky, sleep-filled voice. "The one and only."

Her eyes went big as she abruptly scooted away from him. She felt around on the side table for her glasses, which he'd been careful to move off the mattress as soon as she fell asleep. Once she had them on, she said, "I liked everything we did tonight—loved it all, actually—up until the point where you had to go and screw everything up by calling me *sweetheart*." She looked mutinous. "You shouldn't have said it."

The entire time she'd been speaking, he'd been working like hell to keep from reaching for her and pulling her back against him. Were it not for the fact that she'd inadvertently hit the nail on the head by

accusing him of screwing everything up, he might have
given in to his urges and done just that.

Instead, he kept his hands to himself. "*Sweetheart*
just slipped out."

"Look, I get it." Fully awake now, she got up,
walked over to the minibar, and grabbed two sodas.
Still gloriously naked, she popped the tops off the
bottles, handed him one, then downed hers. Clearly,
she'd worked up a wicked thirst over the past few
hours, with help from him. "The sex was *hot*. And
humans are stupidly hardwired to think it means more
than that. But you and me—we know it doesn't.
Right?"

He knew the correct answer. The answer they'd
agreed on before they'd launched into their "one night
only" plan. But Rory hadn't just been wild in his youth,
he'd been rebellious. Still was. So instead of giving her
the answer she was waiting for, he decided to tell her
the truth. "When I called you *sweetheart*, it felt like
more."

She leveled a *you've got to be kidding me* look at him.
"Like I said, it's perfectly natural to get caught up in the
heat of the moment. But that doesn't mean either of us
should read more into it."

Neither of them was used to backing down. What's
more, Rory didn't care for the way she was outright
dismissing him. "I've gotten caught up in the heat of

the moment before. What happened tonight felt like a hell of a lot more than that. Are you honestly going to stand there and tell me you didn't feel it too?"

Though she scowled and her cheeks were flushing with irritation, he was glad she didn't keep trying to deny that she had felt something beyond just physical pleasure with him. Instead, she said, "You promised we weren't going to be weird afterward."

"I'm not being weird," he countered. "I'm being honest. And the honest truth is that despite all rational reasons to the contrary, I can't sit here and say I want things to end for you and me after tonight." Case in point: Her skin had flushed in this same way when she'd been writhing in ecstasy beneath him. She hadn't been irritated then, had she?

"You want us to *date*?" Clearly aghast, she grabbed the sheet and pulled it around her like a cape. "Or are you talking about being friends with benefits?"

He probably should keep things easy and simple by signing up for a friends-with-benefits plan. But when had his relationship with Zara ever been *easy*? Even now, he found he couldn't lie to her and tell her that was all he wanted.

"These past couple of days, I've realized that I like you and like being with you. It also turns out that sex with you is epic. And when you were asleep in my arms, it felt good. Good enough that I'm not convinced friends with benefits will be enough." He ran his hands through his hair. This was where things got sticky, when he knew just how little he had to offer her. "But there are reasons I haven't dated anyone for the past year. Reasons that make me a bad bet for anything long-term."

"Ditto to all of the above. The only difference right now is that while you met two of the reasons for my damage tonight, I know nothing about your reasons. Before I can make any decisions about your...proposition, I guess we can call it...it would help for me to know what happened to turn you off relationships."

Rory had never thought he'd be naked with Zara in a hotel in Camden, the surf crashing outside the window while he got ready to confess his sins to her. The strangest part of it all, however, was that sometime during the engagement party, he'd started to feel like one half of a really great team. One he wasn't ready to quit anytime soon.

Still, it wasn't at all easy to tell her, "My last girlfriend got hurt really badly because of me."

Zara didn't gasp. Her eyes didn't widen in horror. Instead, she said, "That can't be true. Tell me exactly what happened."

"Chelsea and I were together for two years. Everyone assumed we were the real deal, when the truth was that I had realized fairly early on that I couldn't see spending the rest of my life with her. The magic my parents found with each other—we didn't have that."

"If you stayed with her for two years," Zara said as she sat on the bed, "you must have had a reason."

He appreciated her blunt comment. It would have been far worse if she'd pussyfooted around him. "Chelsea's background was pretty rough," he confirmed. "She wasn't close to her family, and I knew how much it meant to her that my family took her in." Realizing how that might come across, he said, "I'm not trying to say I was some sort of saint—"

"I wouldn't believe it even if you had said it," Zara put in, just as she might have during one of their normal verbal sparring sessions. But since this conversation wasn't anywhere close to normal, she followed it with, "I take it you broke up with her and it didn't go well?"

"I tried to end it several times before, but every time she got so upset that I couldn't see it through." If he closed his eyes, he was back there on that night, reliving Chelsea's sobs, her pleas to give her another chance, her repeated vows of undying love, that she would do whatever it took to change into someone who would make him happy. "She thought I was going to propose to her that night. She somehow believed that's where we were headed—to wedding dresses and vows of forever." His gut churned. "I hurt her with the things I said to make it clear that it was never going to happen. It doesn't matter that I didn't want to be cruel. I was. I thought it was the only way to get her to finally accept that we were through, so I didn't hold back."

Every time he thought about that night, he felt sick. If only he could rewind time and do it differently. Explain to Chelsea that it wasn't about her not being good enough for him. That someone else was out there for her who would be a much better fit.

Zara scooted closer, then took both his hands in hers. "You can be a real pain in the butt sometimes, not to mention utterly full of yourself, but I can't see you ever aiming to wound." She squeezed his hands. "Whatever you tell me next, I'm not going to blame you."

"I should never have let her leave my place on her own," he said. "Not when I knew she would head straight to the nearest bar and end up drunk—a target for some creep to take advantage of. I didn't stop her, though. Didn't follow her either, in case it would have given her false hope." He grimaced as he admitted, "This wasn't my first relationship to go bad. Where I let things linger too long, where—just as you so rightly put it—I screwed everything up."

"Rory—"

"I'm not knocking you for seeing the situation so

clearly and saying that. Not at all. In fact, maybe if Chelsea had seen things more clearly, they could have worked out differently for her." He released a heavy breath. "You won't be surprised to hear that it took me far too long that night to realize I was being an idiot by not watching out for her. Unfortunately, I was too late to keep her from getting hurt. She was walking out of a bar when she tripped and hit her head on the curb. The paramedics got there at the same time I did. Somehow, I knew to follow the sound of the sirens, that they had to be for her. She was in the hospital for a week. Thank God she was okay. She wouldn't let me in to see her, though. Wouldn't talk to me again either. Her best friend came out from California to take care of her." He had a hard time swallowing past the huge lump in his throat. "Her friend told me flat out that I had nearly killed Chelsea, that she was going to take her to California so that I could never hurt her again, and that I should stay away from her for good."

Zara's expression had grown more and more stormy with every word. Finally, her response thundered out. "I'm sorry your ex-girlfriend had a horrible accident and that you had to go through the fear of worrying about her. And I'm really glad that she recovered from her fall. But it isn't your fault that after your breakup she ended up getting drunk in a bar and falling—no matter what her friend said. Just like it isn't

your fault that she wasn't your one and only love."
Zara's words shook with passion. "You can't force
yourself to love someone any more than they can force
you to love them back. Surely I can't be the first person
to tell you this. Because from what I've seen, your
family doesn't seem shy about giving their opinions.
And I know they'd be the first ones to defend you to
the ends of the earth."

"You're right. They all told me it wasn't my fault.
But how can I see it any other way when I knew damn
well that for all of Chelsea's life she hadn't felt good
enough, hadn't felt like anyone's first choice? All I did
by breaking up with her was prove her right."

"Rory, you're not the one who raised her! You're
not the one who taught her about love!" Zara was
practically yelling at him now. "All you did was see if
you could give your heart to her. And when you
realized you couldn't, you did the only thing you
could. You broke up with her so that she could find the
person who would be a perfect fit." She inhaled a deep
breath in an obvious bid to calm down. "Look, I'm not
saying breakups are always rational. That's obvious,
given that we've just pretended to be a couple tonight
so that I could save face in front of my ex. But while we
certainly have every right to be upset when someone
dumps us—I for one had a great time making a dart
board out of a blown-up picture of Cameron's face—at

the end of the day, I don't think it's fair to blame other people for our unhappiness. We have to take responsibility for our *own* happiness, even if sometimes it seems impossible."

"Is that why you haven't lashed out at your stepsister or your ex?" he asked. "Why you kept holding back tonight, even when most people would think that they deserve your fury? Because you think it isn't fair to blame them for hurting you with their cheating?"

"I might not like the way they found love," she replied, "but I can also see that they're happy with each other. Taking their joy away wouldn't make me any happier. Trying to crush them under a mountain of guilt wouldn't either."

"But what if facing up to the harm they caused you is exactly what they need to do? What if it's their big chance to finally redeem themselves and correct their behavior?"

"You mean like how you've decided that if you ever let a woman get close to you again, you're bound to hurt her? So now you think you need to steer clear of relationships forevermore?" She didn't wait for him to reply. "And I'll bet you wish you could turn back time so that you could do the whole breakup scene differently, don't you? Maybe you even think it would have been better to have stayed with her, because then she wouldn't have gotten drunk and hit her head?"

When he didn't deny any of the above, she let out a frustrated growl.

"Even if you could turn back time, even if you could have kept Chelsea from drinking and falling, she was *never* going to be your true love." She glared at him like an angry schoolteacher. A gloriously naked one. "In fact, if you could open your eyes for just one tiny little second, you'd see that staying together would have been the worst-possible choice, because then you would *for sure* have been consigning her to a loveless life." She put her hands on his shoulders and shook him. "What is it going to take for you to see that you *had* to let her go so that she could find her real Prince Charming, you big numbskull? Do I need to make it my life's mission to help you see the light so that you'll give a real relationship another try?"

All his life, Rory had been surrounded by his supportive family. Someone standing up for him wasn't new, wasn't out of the ordinary. But Zara was downright *ferocious* in her determination to make him see the light.

Then again, even if he was bound to fail, he'd never been able to resist one of Zara's challenges. "Are you one hundred percent sure you're right?"

"One *million* percent sure! You're irritating and insufferable and far too cocky for your own good, but at your core, you're not a bad guy. And there are plenty of women out there who would be able to survive dating you perfectly well, without falling apart."

"Are you willing to prove it?"

"Did you hear anything I just said? Of course I'm willing to prove it."

"Okay, then." Did she realize he'd just effectively boxed her into a more-than-one-night corner? "Scratch everything I said earlier about not dating. Let's do this for real. Let's be boyfriend and girlfriend."

Her eyebrows rose so high they nearly flew off her face. "Excuse me?" Her tone had pitched up nearly an octave. "How did our conversation just spin from you getting over what happened with Chelsea to the two of us becoming a for-real couple? What the heck has gotten into you?"

He barely resisted the urge to play with the double entendre that *he'd* just gotten into her. Mostly because he knew she wouldn't just smack his shoulder, she'd likely knock his head right off his neck.

"If you're right that what happened with Chelsea and my previous girlfriends was the exception instead of the rule," he explained, "then it stands to reason that you and I should be able to date for long enough to know for sure if we are, or aren't, feeling magic. If we aren't, we'll prove that we can go through a breakup without experiencing any problems or hurt feelings at the end. If you're wrong, however, and the whole thing goes pear-shaped…"

"I'm not wrong. In fact," she said as she thought more about what he'd just said, "it's quite possible that you're not just a pretty face after all."

"Don't hold back," he muttered. "Tell me what you really think."

"Seriously, your idea is genius! This is the *perfect* way for both of us to prove to each other that relationships don't always have to go down ugly at the end. We'll have fun dating, and then, when we can no longer hide from the fact that we don't have the magic that your parents do—I'm thinking one week should do it, so we could make our official breakup date Saturday—we'll happily call it quits, no harm, no foul. I won't cry or beg or get drunk like your previous girlfriends. And you won't sleep with my stepsister like my previous boyfriends." She held out her hand. "Let's shake on it."

Though their deal sounded good on paper, Rory had to wonder if there was any chance that a week as a couple could possibly end up that cut-and-dried. Especially when he'd never forgive himself if he hurt Zara.

Good thing she was the most resilient person he'd ever met. He had to trust that she wouldn't make this agreement with him if she wasn't sure she could handle it.

Before he shook on it, however, he needed to clari-fy one thing. "Officially dating doesn't mean stepping back on the sex, does it?"

She rolled her eyes. "Of course not. Sex is *definitely* still on the menu. So do we have a deal? Are we going to do our darnedest to prove to ourselves that dating and breaking up doesn't have to be ugly?"

"Deal." He gave her hand a firm pump. "And now that we're officially on our first date, I have to say…" He took in her naked body. "So far, you're the girl-friend of my dreams."

She laughed. "Hurry up and make me come again so that I can say the same thing about you."

He didn't hurry…

But the look in her eyes was *extremely* dreamy by the time the sun came up.

CHAPTER THIRTEEN

"Make it stop."

There should be a law against phones ringing in the middle of the night. Zara squeezed her eyes shut and tried to block out the annoying sound. But it wasn't just her cell buzzing on the bedside table—a land line was ringing too.

Wait. She didn't have a land line at her house.

At last, she pried open an eye...and realized from the sunlight pouring in the window that not only was it *not* the middle of the night, but she was also lying across a man's bare chest.

The very well built, shockingly sexy bare chest of Rory Sullivan—her onetime nemesis, now one-week-only lover.

Was this going to happen *every* time she woke up? Was she always going to be taken aback by how tightly her arms were wrapped around him? Or at some point during the next six days, would it fully sink in that the two of them were together in the most intimate of ways, however temporarily?

After being adversaries for the past year, she supposed the new terms of their relationship would throw anyone off. And she couldn't help but think that if waking up in bed with Rory could send her reeling this hard, just imagine how messed up she'd be if she fell in love with him...and then had to let him go.

No, she *definitely* wouldn't make that mistake.

She relinquished her hold on him enough to look up into his sleeping face. How on earth he managed to stay asleep through the annoyingly insistent ringing and buzzing, she had no idea. But since he wasn't able to see her mooning over him, she couldn't stop a little sigh of pleasure at the memory of all the delicious things they'd done together.

When a man was *that* good at sex, a person couldn't fault herself for being only human and appreciating it.

Reluctantly, she rolled over to pick up both the hotel phone and her cell at the same time, one at each ear. "This is Zara." Though it was nearly noon, according to the clock on the bedside table—Rory had given her one glorious orgasm after another until nearly sunrise—she still wasn't happy about being woken up.

"Hey, sis!" Brittany's voice was extra perky, especially coming through two phone lines at once. "I had hoped you, me, Cameron, and Rory could all have brunch together this morning, but I've been calling your cell since ten a.m. with no answer." Perky gave way to pouty as she added, "I finally had the hotel also call your room to make sure you were there, even though it's now so late that we have another engagement to head to soon."

Yet again, Zara gave silent thanks that Rory had worn her out enough with his brilliant moves in the sack that they had both slept through the buzzing of her phone and breakfast. "Rory and I were up late last night." She was glad to be able to insert a little truth this morning into her lies from the night before. "He's still sleeping."

The big hand moving across her hip let her know that Rory was now wide awake. With a gentle tug, he drew her back into the bed so that her back was flush against his front. His very aroused front.

Mmmm. Zara nearly hung up both phones. After all, she could talk to Brittany anytime, but the clock was ticking down on six days of what had to be the best lovemaking on the planet.

"Wow, that must have been some night," Brittany said, sounding strangely subdued. "I was really hoping to see you this morning, even if just for five minutes."

That was all it took for Zara to give up on a few more sexy minutes with Rory. She had never been able to resist Brittany's requests to spend time together. How could she, when as teenagers they had been each other's only lifelines after each losing a parent and finding themselves plopped into a new family?

"If you give me ten minutes to get dressed," Zara said, "I'll come down to see you two off."

"Yay!" The smile was back in her stepsister's voice. "We don't have to leave for a half hour, so I'll order coffee for the four of us."

As soon as Zara hung up, Rory spoke from behind her. "If you can get dressed in one minute," he said, obviously having figured out the pertinent details from her side of the conversation with Brittany, "that means we still have nine minutes to have some fun before we go downstairs."

Despite the pressure weighing on her chest at knowing she was going to have to make small talk with Brittany and Cameron again, Zara was glad to know she wasn't going to have to endure them alone.

She rolled over to face him. "As tempted as I am to see what tricks you can pull out of your hat with a nine-minute deadline, I should probably throw myself into the shower. And since we're supposed to check out by noon, you should do the same."

"Nine minutes with you in a shower?" He gave her a very wicked grin. "Consider yourself done."

She laughed again, even as she made herself slide from the bed and head for the bathroom. "If you actually manage to make me see fireworks in the next..." She looked at the digital clock beside the bed. "Eight minutes, I'll be very impressed."

She was turning on the water and stepping into the shower enclosure when she felt his lips on the back of her neck and his naked body pressed against hers. Though the water was warm, she shivered.

"Let's get you under the water." He moved them both under the spray, his hands roving over her breasts as he separated her legs with his thigh.

She'd never been this responsive to a man's touch before, never felt like she was already on the edge with the barest whisper of his lips and hands over her. Barely sixty seconds in the shower with Rory, and all it took was one large, callused hand slipping slowly over her skin, from her breasts to her stomach, then finally between her thighs, for her to nearly come apart.

"You have no idea how much I want you," he murmured against her earlobe as he slid one finger, and then a second, into her more-than-ready body.

"If it's as much as I want you," she whispered back as her inner muscles clenched against him, "I do."

The next thing she knew, he had taken his hand away and thrust into her. He felt so hard and hot and *perfect* that she sobbed out his name, the sound reverberating inside the tile-and-glass enclosure. She pressed her hands flat on the tile as she arched her hips against his, wanting more, needing everything he could give her.

One hand came around her hips for leverage, while the other cupped her face. The gentle way he turned her cheek so that he could look into her eyes was a surprising counterpoint to the wonderfully rough way he was taking the rest of her. *Exactly* the way she wanted to be taken.

And when he kissed her, though he hadn't spoken, she could swear he was calling her *sweetheart*, this time with the passionate brush of his lips over hers. Yet again, it sent her straight to heaven, with Rory's mouth, hands, and body urging her pleasure on and on and on.

As he let himself go, his groan of pleasure sounded like a roar in the small room. It was the same roar of victory she would have made herself if she could have found the breath for it.

She was still panting when she felt his hands in her hair, massaging in shampoo.

"Good?"

She turned in his arms to face him. "Amazing." She reached up to gather some excess suds from her hair, then mirrored his movements as she washed his hair. She couldn't resist giving him a slightly snarky look as she said, "I think I'll call you Mr. Speedy from now on."

"And here I thought for sure you were finally going to give me a compliment." He followed up his words by dunking her head beneath the water.

She was sputtering when she came up for air, but he had already danced out of her way to rinse off. "I'll get you back for that, you know," she warned him.

He had the nerve to grin. "I'm counting on it."

And damn him, she was grinning too as she soaped up, rinsed off, then stepped out onto the bath mat to grab a towel.

"Not so fast." He took the towel from her and began running it over her curves to dry her off. "How many minutes do we have left?"

She was sorely tempted by the heat—and the promise of even more pleasure—in his eyes. But she couldn't forget how sad Brittany had seemed about not seeing her this morning to say good-bye. "Not enough even for Mr. Speedy," she teased.

He waggled his eyebrows. "Want to bet?"

Yes! But she made herself say, "We really should get dressed and head downstairs." That was when it hit her. "Your clothes are in your room. If they see you wearing the same thing as last night, they'll wonder why you didn't already have your clothes in my room."

"Don't worry." Now that she was dry, he rubbed the towel over his own wet skin. Skin she was dying to wet all over again with her tongue. "It won't take me more than a couple of minutes to run upstairs, grab my bag, and change."

While she rummaged in her overnight bag for jeans and a top, he quickly put on yesterday's clothes.

"I'll be right back," he said, then drew her close and kissed her before grabbing her room key and heading for the door.

She stared at the door for several long seconds after he left. No question, the hot sex had scrambled her brain. But it was his kiss—the kind of kiss people who were *actually* together gave each other when they were about to leave a room—that truly had her head spinning.

It must have been an accident. The two of them having hot shower sex in a hotel room had probably made him forget for a second that what they were doing wasn't real.

That they didn't have a future.

That they were together only temporarily...until they most decidedly were *not* together anymore come Saturday.

CHAPTER FOURTEEN

True to his word, Rory was back inside of two minutes, changed into jeans and a T-shirt. Seriously, there couldn't be another man alive who wore jeans better.

Noting she was still naked, her clothes in her hands, he said, "Not that I'm at all averse to you not wearing clothes, but are you sure you're up for seeing Brittany and Cameron again this morning?"

He'd never believe her if she told him that his kiss had made her forget all about them for a few minutes. Pushing away her unease, Zara said, "I'm cool." And as she put on her clothes and shoes, she was relieved to realize it was mostly true. Courtesy of Rory's brilliant distraction methods.

She gathered up her clothes from where he'd tossed them on the floor the night before and shoved everything into her bag. "Here's my secret sign if I need you to make an excuse so that we can escape." She crossed her eyes and stuck out her tongue.

He was laughing as he said, "They'll never guess

your secret code. Or mine." And then he crossed his eyes and stuck out his tongue too.

Of course, she had to pretend to bite it. Which ended in yet another kiss—one that meant her cheeks and lips were still flushed by the time they finally made it downstairs just past the ten-minute mark.

"I was about to ask the manager to let me into your room so I could make sure you were okay," Brittany said when she saw them. "You always answer your phone and are never normally late." She sent a borderline accusing glance in Rory's direction, as though he was clearly the problem.

"I'm great," Zara said as she gave her stepsister a hug, trying to hide her blush at the thought of what Brittany would have walked in on in if she'd come up to Zara's hotel room five minutes ago.

Her stepsister studied her face. "Are you sure you're feeling okay? Your cheeks are a little flushed."

"It was a little hot in our room." Talk about an understatement. Zara could have been in the Arctic and as long as Rory was there too, she would have overheated.

Brittany reached into her purse. "Here's some gloss for your chapped lips."

Zara made herself smile as she took the gloss, reminding herself that her stepsister was only trying to look out for her as she applied a light coat to her lips, which were in fact slightly chapped due to all the kissing she'd been doing.

With Brittany's birthday a month before Zara's, she took her responsibilities as "older" sister seriously. At times like this, when Zara was tempted to be irritated with her, all she had to do was remember the many nights her stepsister had held her while she sobbed over her mom. Though Brittany had been tougher on the surface, Zara knew how devastated she'd been over losing her father.

Cameron was looking worse for the wear this morning as he led them over to the facing couches and coffee table where four cups were waiting. Her ex had always been a little on the delicate side, too cold or too hot or needing more sleep.

As Rory put his hand on the small of her back while they walked across the room, Zara couldn't imagine anyone *ever* calling *him* delicate. And as he sat beside her on the small love seat, then put his arm around her waist and tugged her closer, for once she couldn't have been happier that he was inclined to hog most of the cushion. If only for the excuse to sit practically in his lap.

They all picked up their coffee and drank, and when neither man spoke and Brittany frowned into her cup, Zara decided it was up to her to lead the conversation. "Have you decided where you're going to get married?"

"We're still working out those details," Cameron said, "but we have picked our honeymoon destination. Haven't we, honey?" He gave Brittany's hand a squeeze.

She looked up from her cup and finally smiled. "Harbour Island, Bahamas. I read about it in a magazine recently—a British woman who is related to the royals has a place right on the pink sand beach. We're renting one of her guest houses."

Given Brittany's impeccable taste, it was sure to be a five-star wonder. "I'm sure you'll both have a fantastic time." Even though Cameron tended to turn red like a lobster when he sat out in the sun too long.

"Have you been to the Bahamas before?" Brittany asked Rory.

"One of my cousins has a place on Eleuthera, the island just over from Harbour." He gave Zara a lazy smile, one that sent her heart racing as though he were doing far more than just smiling at her. "Anyone who loves wild swimming needs to experience diving into the warm, crystal-clear water. Promise you'll let me take you sometime."

She knew she shouldn't be making Rory any promises beyond Saturday, but when he was holding her this close and looking at her with this much heat, it was impossible to do anything but nod. And when he dipped his head to kiss her, it felt so good that she nearly forgot where they were—and who they were with.

Blushing even harder now, she turned back to the other couple. "I'm sure your mom has plenty of ideas for where she'd like you to hold the ceremony."

Brittany nodded, but she was frowning as she said, "She's been trying to convince us to have it at the yacht club."

Zara nearly gasped at the suggestion. Brittany's father had died of a sudden heart attack on the club's golf course. As long as Zara had known her stepsister, she'd never been comfortable there. "Do you need me to talk to her about it? I'm sure I can find a way to convince her that there are at least a dozen better options in the area."

"The library amphitheater would be an *incredible* place for our wedding."

Zara had never spent much time thinking about her own wedding—why would she, when she'd never truly been in love?—but if she had to pick her favorite place in Camden, it would be the large lawn behind the library that overlooked the sailboats in the bay. "I can't see how Margie could object to that. Do you have a date yet? We should check to make sure the library has rental availability before going full-court press on your mom."

"We?" Brittany beamed at her. "Does this mean you're offering to help me plan the wedding?"

We had been a slip of the tongue. Given that Zara hadn't even been sure she'd be able to deal with having coffee with the couple, helping plan their wedding was a major stretch. But she wasn't sure how to back out of the messy spot—or even that she should, considering how unwavering Brittany's support had been when they were teenagers.

"With your new product launch coming up," Rory said before Brittany could pressure her to agree right then and there, "are you sure you have the bandwidth to fit anything else in?"

She hadn't realized he knew her release calendar so well, not when it had always felt like whatever she said to him went in one ear and out the other. But he was right. Hopefully, she was going to be slammed with orders once her new line launched.

Still, this was her stepsister's wedding. Even if Brittany had come by her fiancé in less than ideal circumstances, Zara didn't feel right about bowing out completely. "For now, you can definitely count on me to step in with your mom and bring her around to having the ceremony at the amphitheater," she told Brittany. "Let's talk again later this week to see if there's anything else that you're getting stuck on. After all," Zara reminded her, "you're the master party planner. I'm sure you'll easily be able to put on the wedding of the century."

The alarm on Cameron's phone went off. "We need to head out now, honey, or we'll be late to Jeff's house."

"Cameron's friend is throwing us a small garden celebration this afternoon," Brittany explained. "Why don't you guys come with us? Jeff always has enough food and wine to feed an army."

Zara kept her expression bland. Jeff was her least-favorite of Cameron's friends. A smarmy financial analyst, he wore too much cologne and had wandering hands. "Thank you for the invitation," she said, "but we really should get on the road back to Bar Harbor. You know how bad Sunday afternoon traffic can be if we leave too late."

Zara almost laughed at the relief on Cameron's face. Clearly, he wasn't enjoying her being pulled into the middle of their engagement celebrations and wedding planning any more than she was.

When they stood, Brittany threw her arms around both Zara and Rory. "Thank you *so* much for coming to our little celebration. It wouldn't have been nearly as wonderful without you both there—and I hope we see *lots* more of the two of you in the near future. I don't think I've ever seen Z so blissfully happy."

Zara couldn't read Rory's expression when Brittany

finally let him move away to shake Cameron's hand. In any case, she wasn't sure she wanted to know what he thought about Brittany's *blissfully happy* proclamation. Surely he would think it was simply down to the hot sex…

After waving Brittany and Cameron off, Zara collapsed onto the couch cushions, closing her eyes as exhaustion took over. "I need sugar. And fat. And butter. And carbohydrates. And lots more caffeine." She held out her arm. "If you could hook me up to an IV drip with all of those things, that'd be great."

"You eat too much junk food," Rory admonished, albeit in a gentle voice. But then he offered, "I'll see what I can rustle up from the diner down the street."

If he brought her a kale and tofu salad, she was going to punch him. That was, if she could muster up the energy when it felt like things had just spiraled even more out of control. Last night, after spending time with Brittany and Cameron, Zara had ended up in bed with Rory. And then this morning, fifteen minutes with the happy couple was all it took for her to nearly sign on the dotted line to be their official wedding planner. If she wasn't careful, Brittany would be scheduling Zara to work as her personal maid on her honeymoon in the Bahamas.

She must have dozed off in the hotel lobby, because the next thing she knew, she was waking up to the tantalizing smell of bacon and coffee. Though she was still sleep-deprived, her two favorite things went a long way to temporarily reviving her.

She opened one of the to-go boxes and shoved an entire piece of crispy bacon into her mouth. "You're an angel." Actually, given that she was also wolfing down a massive bite of a waffle, it came out much closer to *murf an afuel.*

Shaking his head at her food choices, Rory pulled the top off a container of oatmeal and didn't even coat it with brown sugar before digging a spoon into it.

"No." She had to stop eating long enough to make sure he understood precisely how she felt. "Oatmeal does not count as food." She made a mental note to put it on their breakup list for Saturday. A junk-food fiend and a health nut could never make it as a couple long-term.

"You're right about this," he said as he shot a grim look at the gruel on his spoon, "but when Mom makes Irish oatmeal?" His face broke out in a rapturous smile. "It's one of the best damn things you'll ever eat. I'll ask her to make it for you sometime."

"Every meal I've had at your family's café has been great." Though Zara knew Rory's mom ran the kitchen at Sullivan Café, she had never been on-site when Zara had eaten there. "What was it like growing up in a town where your family is such a big part of things?"

"It was great...unless we were getting in trouble. All the cops in town, the teachers, the other store owners, knew my parents. I honestly have no idea how many times we were hauled into the café with our tails between our legs."

"Somehow, I can't picture you ever having your tail between your legs, regardless of what you did."

"You haven't heard my mom yell. When you meet her, don't be fooled by her outwardly sweet demeanor. Beth Sullivan is a badass. And all of us live a little in fear of disappointing her." It was clear he had an infinite amount of respect for his mother.

Zara wished she could tell her mom how much she respected her. Especially given that in their last moments, she had been anything but respectful.

The food that had been so good minutes before now tasted like sawdust as it settled like a rock in her twisting stomach. She closed the lids abruptly, picked up the containers, and shoved them into the garbage can. "We should go before traffic picks up too much."

If Rory thought her sudden mood change was at all strange, he didn't comment on it as they checked out, then he grabbed their bags and headed out to the car. Normally, she would have made it a point to carry her own luggage, but in the aftermath of her Brittany/Cameron anxiety, an all-night sexfest, and her sudden renewed grief over her mother, it was all she could do just to drag herself over to Rory's car and climb into the passenger seat.

Of course, as soon as he turned on the ignition, the radio came on, tuned to a heavy metal station. "You have no taste in music," she mumbled as she bundled up her sweater to use as a pillow against the window. She made another mental note to put *hate each other's music* on their breakup list for Saturday.

The last thing she heard him say was, "Have a nice nap, Backstreet Girl," in an obvious bid to take down her appreciation for boy bands.

She dreamed of a boy band where every member was Rory. All five were singing a pop version of the classic Nat King Cole song *There Goes My Heart*.

And they were singing right to her.

CHAPTER FIFTEEN

Two hours later, Rory pulled into his driveway and turned off the car. Zara had been sleeping soundly for the entire drive—he'd even turned off the heavy metal for her—but as soon as they stopped moving, she stirred.

She pulled off her glasses, rubbed a hand over her eyes, then slipped her glasses back on and looked up at the lighthouse in surprise. "Why are we at your house? I thought for sure you'd have had enough of me for one day."

Three days ago, he would have been certain of that too. Now, however? He wasn't anywhere close to having enough of her. "I'm in the final stages of making a chess board for one of my cousin's movies and just remembered that I need to throw another coat of varnish on it right away if I want to get it to him on time. Once I've done that, I'll take you home, if that's what you want to do."

"Actually…" She opened the car door and stepped outside, taking a deep breath of the ocean air. "Since I woke up on your couch on Friday, I haven't been able to stop dreaming about doing some wild swimming here."

"If you can wait fifteen minutes, I'll join you."

She shot him a look. "We might have just found something we agree on." She blushed slightly as she added, "Apart from all the awesome sex."

Just talking about the awesome sex made him want to grab her, instead of his bag. But she was already heading up the walk to his front door, so he took his bag out of the trunk and followed. After unlocking the door, he let her inside. "Have at anything in my fridge."

She surprised him by picking an apple out of the bowl on the kitchen island. "Can I watch you varnish?"

Rory had never found anything about woodworking to be sexual. Not until Zara said *varnish* in a slightly husky, just-woke-up voice. With Zara watching him brush on the varnish, the entire process was going to feel like one big act of foreplay.

"You can help if you want."

She shook her head. "No way. I'd never forgive myself if I ruined your creation at the eleventh hour."

"I've seen you put together your eyeglasses frames. You have very steady, precise hands." And last night she'd given him even more proof of just how good she was with her hands. "I have a feeling you'd be a brilliant woodworker if you ever wanted to learn."

"Funny you should say that, because after seeing some of your furniture designs, I've often thought you would create some really great frames."

Interesting. Twice in the past five minutes, they'd been in complete agreement with each other, first over going for a wild ocean swim and then over each other's maker skills. Sure, their food and music choices weren't similar, but how much did those things really matter in the end? Especially if they respected each other where it counted.

Rory knew better than to say any of this aloud, however. Not when they'd agreed on Saturday as their do-or-die breakup date. And not when he still wasn't convinced that he had anything real to offer her in the long term, when he'd been such crap at relationships until now. For the past year, he'd stuck fast to one relationship rule: If there wasn't magic from the outset, there wasn't *ever* going to be magic, so it wasn't fair to string a woman along.

Only, when it came to Zara, while there hadn't been *obvious* magic from the beginning, there couldn't be a better word for the night they'd just spent together.

Last night had been magic from start to finish.

They were both lost in their thoughts as he took her across his property to the auxiliary workshop in the barn.

Zara looked around the room with obvious appreciation. "What a fantastic space. Why don't you work here all the time, where no one can bother you?"

"That's exactly why." He got out the can of varnish. "Growing up with six siblings, I got used to living and working in the middle of noise and chaos. All this quiet is great when I need to wind down, but Monday through Friday, heading into the office and being surrounded by other creative people helps keep my own creative juices flowing."

She nodded. "I never felt like I fit in until I met other makers."

He imagined growing up with a stepsister who epitomized *bubbly, blonde,* and *by the book* hadn't made things any easier for the decidedly *not* by-the-book woman in his barn. Which was why he had to ask, "You're not seriously considering helping to plan Brittany and Cameron's wedding, are you?"

"I know how things look on the outside, but our history isn't as simple as it seems."

"How so?"

She didn't reply right away as she moved to run her hands over a wooden canoe that he'd been working on in his spare time. "We were both pretty messed up at fifteen, when we were suddenly thrown together." It was as close as she'd come yet to referencing her emotional response to losing her mother. "I know we seem really different—and I'm not saying we aren't—but Brittany was there for me when I needed her most." When he looked up from his work, he saw a bleakness in her eyes that made him want to put his arms around her and never let go. Obviously, she was still grieving the loss of her mother—just as he knew he would be, even after fifteen-plus years. "I know she has her faults, just like I do, but at the core, she's my sister, no matter what."

"I get it." And he truly did. Family wasn't always easy, or straightforward. But no matter how hard you had to fight for it, it was worth it. "Though I still don't like the thought of you getting hurt again by Brittany or Cameron, even if that isn't what they intend."

Zara waved away his concern. "I'm sure she'll find a top-notch, must-have wedding planner and forget all about me."

Rory wasn't nearly as certain about that. Which was why he decided that even after Saturday, he was going to look out for Zara, to make sure her sister and ex didn't take advantage of her.

"So, let's see the chess board."

Obviously, she didn't want to talk about her stepsister anymore. He picked it up carefully, moved it to his worktable, and uncovered it.

"That's *gorgeous.*"

He'd been given plenty of compliments on his work over the years, but when Zara said it, he found himself looking at it with new eyes. "Thanks. Knowing my work is going to be part of a movie where people will continue to see it for years to come makes me stretch."

"If I were a card-carrying member of the Rory Sullivan Fan Club, I'm sure I'd know whose movies you're talking about. But since you're just some guy I work with who happens to have some really great moves in the sack, I'm clueless."

Though he was less than thrilled at being referred to as *just some guy I work with*, he was pleased that she thought his moves were great. "Smith Sullivan is my cousin."

Her eyebrows went up. "I thought you were going to name some obscure indie film actor, not one of the biggest movie stars in the world. Have you made things for Smith's movies before?"

"A couple of times."

He waited for her to ask what his famous cousin was like, but she seemed far more interested in his varnishing technique. He wasn't sure anyone had ever watched his hands so carefully before. If he'd known it would be this hot to be with another maker...

No, he still wouldn't have jumped into bed with any of them. Zara was the only one he wanted.

"I'm sure I can't afford you," she mused, "but on the off chance that I win the lottery, you wouldn't consider making up one of the eyeglasses designs that I've envisioned in wood, would you?"

"I'd rather show you how to make it yourself."

"Seriously?" When she looked at him as though she couldn't believe her luck, he wanted to kiss her senseless.

So he stopped varnishing and did just that.

When he finally released her, it was so she could catch her breath while he finished with the chessboard.

A few minutes later, he asked, "Ready to swim?"

Zara surprised him by taking off at a run and heading for the long staircase that led to the small cove in front of his house. As she ran, she pulled off one piece of clothing after another, waiting until she was at the shore to take off her glasses.

Rory might have been able to catch up with her had he not been so sucker-punched by Zara's glorious spontaneity...and by the sheer magnitude of the contrast to every other woman he'd been with.

It wasn't just Chelsea, but all of his ex-girlfriends. Where Zara was free and wild and reckless, the women he'd been with before her had been sweet, but restrained. As though they were afraid to step too far out of the box.

It suddenly struck him that he'd been looking at the

situation with Brittany all wrong. Only someone as strong as Zara could put aside the resentment and hurt of being cheated on and instead focus on a sisterly bond made as teenagers. She wasn't being walked over, she was helping someone she loved with one of the most important days of her life.

His admiration for Zara grew by leaps and bounds.

The fact that she was naked as she splashed in the waves didn't hurt either.

Pulling off his clothes and kicking his shoes away, he dived in and swam to her. They played chase in the water for a few minutes, before he caught her by an ankle and pulled her to him.

She was breathless and laughing as she wrapped her arms around his neck. "Took you long enough."

The only way to deal with sass like hers was to keep her mouth busy doing something else. Keeping one hand on her hip as she wound her legs around his waist, her breasts slipping and sliding against his chest, he threaded the other hand into her hair and crushed his mouth to hers.

She tasted like salt and sunshine…and joy.

Joy he'd never felt quite so keenly before.

She lifted her hips over him at the same moment that he drove into her, their kisses spiraling deeper with every thrust, every gasp of pleasure.

They were on the precipice of climax when he

pulled back to look at her. Though he loved her in glasses, it was a rare treat to see directly into her hazel eyes.

They'd made love several times during the past twenty-four hours, but it wasn't enough. He craved her in a way he'd never craved anything, or anyone, else.

"You're not going to call me *sweetheart* again, are you?"

He put his hand on her cheek, caressing her soft skin as he told her the truth. "I might."

The words were barely out of his mouth when her eyelids fluttered shut and her head fell back as she catapulted into orgasm. He buried his face in the crook of her neck as he followed her into ecstasy.

"Best wild swim ever." They were both panting as they clung to each other in the water, and Zara's voice was breathier than usual.

Of course he had to kiss her again, a kiss that would surely have brought them right back around to more lovemaking had she not begun to shiver in the cold water. "Come on," he said, "let's head back inside. I'll make you my world-famous hot chocolate."

As soon as she got to the shore, she put her glasses back on, then started running again, this time up the steep steps. He'd been laughing as he'd chased her all the way down, and now he was laughing again as he chased her back up.

No woman had ever grated on him the way Zara had for the past year. But that suddenly seemed a small price to pay for all the laughter.

It was amazing how natural it felt to walk naked into his house together, both of them holding their clothes, rather than putting them back on over wet skin. If Zara lived here with him, they could do this every day—jump into the water whenever the spirit took them.

His brain caught up several seconds later. *If Zara lived here with him?*

The odds that she would ever agree to give up her own space had to be nil. Then again...she'd agreed to more than one night, hadn't she, when he'd assumed such a thing would be an impossibility.

She tossed him a towel from the bathroom, the thick cotton smacking him in the face and yanking him out of his surprising musings.

"It doesn't count, you know."

He briskly rubbed his hair to dry it before moving on to his face, shoulders, and chest. "What doesn't?"

"The sex."

Maybe the water had been colder than he thought, because he didn't follow her. "The sex doesn't count for what?"

She rolled her eyes as though the answer was obvi-ous. "For our long-term couple compatibility. We are still a *terrible* fit, and by Saturday both of us will be dying to cut each other loose."

He almost laughed out loud at the irony of the fact that while he'd just been wondering about the odds of convincing her to live with him, she was doing her level best to add to her list of all the reasons they *shouldn't* be together.

Of course, he couldn't just agree with her and be done with it. Not because taking opposite sides on most topics was an integral part of their interactions, but because he wasn't sure he agreed that the sex they'd been having was just a feel-good way to pass a few hours.

"Sex might not be the be-all and end-all of a relationship," he said, "but it definitely counts. Especially when it's this good." Case in point: They'd had each other twice today, and he was already raring for more.

She wrapped her towel even more firmly around herself as though to lay that idea to rest. "I *knew* you'd end up thinking sex means more than it really does."

He was pretty sure it was the guy in a relationship who normally said that. It figured that the two of them would end up flipping things upside down. After all, their entire relationship to this point had been completely backward, given that they'd begun as enemies before becoming allies. "What do you think sex means?"

"It's fun. It's a good way to get some exercise. And, with the right person, I suppose it can also help bring you closer."

"So you *do* agree with me. What we're doing here—" He gestured between their naked bodies. "—counts."

"No." She shook her head, hard enough for little droplets of water to fly from the tips of her hair. "I said *with the right person* it counts."

Rory loved having sex with Zara. He'd need to have his head checked if he didn't. But the way she kept deliberately pointing out how sure she was that they could never have anything more than that pushed all his buttons.

He didn't expect her to turn into a big, emotional ball of mush after they made love. He wouldn't mind, however, if she could at least pretend to be a little more starry-eyed over what they'd just shared— especially given how many stars he kept seeing.

She'd seemed so emotional during their lovemaking. But was he seeing only what he wanted to see?

Ironic, wasn't it, that he now longed for the very thing he'd been so averse to in his past relationships. All of his previous girlfriends had been so starry-eyed around him that their emotional states had become stained by desperation.

Zara would never be desperate. Not in a million

years.

Maybe he should have left it. But everything inside of him felt churned up. All because of the breathtaking, infuriating, brilliant, and frustratingly unavailable woman who might as well be six miles away, rather than six feet.

So instead of letting her comment go, he decided to push her buttons just as hard as she was pushing his. "What if it turns out that I'm your right person? And you're mine?"

CHAPTER SIXTEEN

Zara stared at Rory with an expression he couldn't quite read—a mixture of what looked like panic, disbelief, and maybe even regret—before she threw back her head and laughed.

When she caught her breath again, she said, "I thought you were serious there for a second."

Rory had felt this way only twice in his life. The first time a challenge he couldn't ignore had been laid in front of him was when his mentor had accused him of stealing his designs. He'd vowed then to prove to both his mentor and the rest of the world that everything he created was totally original.

And now, with less than a dozen words, Zara had challenged him to prove to her that the two of them *were* the right people for each other.

Had he known it from the start? Had this been why she'd gotten under his skin so easily? Because he'd been fighting the inevitable loss of his heart to her? A heart he'd believed would be better kept under wraps, rather than risk hurting anyone else the way he'd hurt

Chelsea.

Only, he'd never counted on meeting a woman like Zara. Her strength on all fronts constantly stunned him, from her pursuit of her career to her relationship with Brittany.

Zara would never let Rory get away with hurting her. If he made a mistake, she would call him on it, and he would change. Because she was worth changing for.

Five and a half days.

He now had five and a half days left to convince her that come Saturday, the very *last* thing either of them would want to do was cut loose from each other.

He knew better than to push her further today on the "right person for each other" argument, however. She was wary enough of relationships that it would be far better to lull her, at least for a little while, into believing that she was safe from losing her heart to him...while he did everything in his power to make damned sure that she did.

Especially now that he had finally realized he was well on the way to losing his heart to her.

"Time for hot chocolate," he said. "I would say clothing optional, but I'd hate for any of the scalding liquid to spill on your skin." They dried off, then put on their clothes and headed into the kitchen.

He appreciated how comfortable she seemed in his home as she sat on the couch by the picture window, tucking her feet beneath her and opening a blanket over her lap. On Friday, when he'd brought her here to sleep off the Prosecco, he'd been surprised—and more than a little taken aback—by how much he liked having her in his space. Today, he simply let himself enjoy it.

"Why did you choose to live in a home attached to a lighthouse? I'm not knocking it," she clarified before he could respond. "This view is extraordinary, and I love unique houses like this. But you're quite a ways out of town, and it must feel like you're on the edge of the world during a storm."

He was about to respond when she took a sip of her drink. Her eyes closed in a look of ecstasy he was becoming familiar with. He now knew two things that made her look that way—orgasms and his hot chocolate. He hoped to find many more by Saturday.

"I hate to admit it, but you weren't overselling your hot chocolate-making skills." She took another sip. "I could happily bathe in this."

"And I could happily lick it off you," he offered.

She wagged her finger at him. "You're going to have to put your one-track mind back into your pants for a few minutes. At least until you tell me why you're so fascinated by lighthouses." She pointed to the right front leg of his coffee table, where he'd etched the outlines of a tiny lighthouse. "Everything you make has a lighthouse on it, doesn't it? It's your business logo too."

Rory had always been better at joking around with people than being serious. Off-the-cuff responses were his specialty. But that wouldn't be enough for Zara. "I was eight years old when I took out the Laser sailboat without asking my parents' permission. I thought I knew what I was doing, that nothing could swamp me. If you think I'm cocky now, you should have seen me at eight." He smiled, even though the memory of just how close death had come was chilling. "I didn't know to check for storm warnings. Especially not when the sky was blue and the wind was barely enough to set my sail fluttering. I'd never seen a storm blow in so fast. If I had been with my parents, or one of my siblings, I might have been able to keep my wits about me. But the truth is—and I'll deny it if you ever tell another soul—I lost it. I panicked and forgot everything I knew about sailing. I was certain that I was going to die as the storm swept me up and tossed me around in a boat that felt no bigger than a thimble. And then I saw it."

She was gripping her mug tightly enough for her knuckles to turn white. "A lighthouse."

"Yes. The Bass Harbor Head revolving lights were shining bright enough to be visible through driving rain and fog. Everything that's been said about what lighthouses symbolize—salvation, home, safety—is true. I found my way back to my family, to my friends, to my future, because of a light that showed me the way in rough waters."

"Your parents must have been frantic."

"*Frantic* is an understatement. They were beyond overjoyed that I made it home to them. And then I was grounded for the next decade."

Her face had paled as he'd recounted his narrow escape. He was glad to see her laugh again. "I can only imagine what a wild eighteen-year-old you were, making up for lost time after ten years' grounding."

"I'd say you already have a good sense of just how wild I can be," he said with a grin, just as his cell phone rang.

"Got a date you're standing up?" she quipped.

Once he picked up his phone, he realized she was almost perfectly on the mark. "It's my brothers and Flynn." Turner's text was quick and to the point.

Just finished playing hoops. Heading to pub. Should we save you a seat?

"I was supposed to meet them for a pickup game of basketball." He'd never forgotten before. Then again, he'd never known anyone as distracting as Zara. "They've just headed for a post-game drink at the pub."

Immediately, she shoved the blanket off her lap and stood.

He reached for her hand. "Where are you going?"

"I'm leaving so that you can go hang with your brothers. I'm sure you'd much rather do that than sit here and argue about what we're going to watch on TV."

Yet again, she had it wrong. Although it had driven Chelsea crazy that he was always wanting to do something or make something rather than waste time lounging around on the couch with her, tonight he wanted nothing more than to cuddle up under a blanket with Zara. Even if they fought over the remote the entire time.

Still, he didn't feel right about blowing the guys off. When Rory gave his word, he stuck by it.

"You could spend the night here, if you want." He liked the thought of Zara making herself at home in his kitchen. Of finding her asleep in his bed when he got home.

Judging by the firm shake of her head, she wasn't a fan of his suggestion. "I've already stayed too long."

"I like having you here. In my house. In my arms too." He kissed her, hoping that would help her see that he meant everything he'd just said.

But from her uncharacteristic silence on the drive back into town—for once, she didn't even complain about his music—he was pretty sure she hadn't.

★ ★ ★

Turner, Hudson, and Flynn were on their second pints of Guinness by the time Rory arrived at the pub.

Since Turner had returned from Los Angeles to continue growing his animation business from Maine, rather than California, Rory saw his younger brother at least once a week, whether on the basketball court, in the family café, or at their parents' house.

It was far rarer to see Hudson these days. The oldest at thirty-seven, he'd moved to Boston not long after marrying Larissa. Rory liked Hudson's wife. Unfortunately, he wasn't certain that Larissa and Hudson liked each other all that much anymore. Hudson was in town for a few days to work on a landscape-design commission at one of the big estates on Mount Desert Island.

Flynn was the most recent addition to the group. Six months ago, after becoming the legal guardian for his niece, the award-winning screenwriter had come to Bar Harbor from Hollywood to escape the paparazzi. Their cousin Smith had arranged with Cassie for Flynn and Ruby to stay in her cabin in the woods—at which point Rory's sister had fallen head over heels in love with both Flynn and the baby. Fortunately, Flynn was just as smitten with Cassie. Otherwise, Rory would have had to tear the guy apart with his bare hands. It helped that Flynn wasn't just some soft-handed zillionaire writer from California. He more than knew his way around a pile of wood and a saw and hammer. He wasn't bad with a basketball either.

"You're usually first one on the court," Turner said once Rory was settled into his seat with a beer. "Where were you?"

"It's been a pretty strange forty-eight hours."

Flynn's storyteller antenna went up. "How so?"

"You know Zara from the warehouse?"

When Hudson shook his head, Turner quickly filled him in. "Zara makes eyeglasses frames in an office down the hall from Rory's woodshop. They are always at each other's throats." Turner turned his focus back to Rory. "I'd guess that the two of you finally killed each other were it not for the fact that you're sitting here in one intact piece."

"Something happened on Friday morning," Rory explained. "It's her story, not mine, so I won't go into the details. But as a result, we've been together a great deal since, including an overnight trip to Camden last night and this morning."

"And by *together* you mean…" Hudson made a rude gesture with his hands.

Rory had never gotten angry with his brothers for doing something like that before. Now he was downright furious. "Don't *ever* talk about Zara like that again."

"Sorry, I won't," Hudson said. Then, turning to the others, he said, "That's a yes."

"Cassie told me she thinks your bickering is hiding a deeper passion," Flynn noted. "Those were her exact words."

When Rory didn't disagree, Turner's eyebrows went up. "Are you saying this isn't just a one-night stand?"

"That's what it was supposed to be. That's what Zara thinks it still is."

"Hold on a second. Are *you* the one gunning for more?" Hudson looked as surprised as Turner. "Even after what happened with Chelsea?"

"Zara isn't anything like Chelsea," Rory snapped.

"No," Turner agreed, "they don't seem to be similar at all."

Rory wasn't sure what Cassie had told Flynn about Chelsea's accident, so he quickly explained, "Chelsea and I dated for a couple of years, before I finally broke it off. This was before you came to town. She didn't have an easy time with the breakup and wound up in the hospital after drinking too much and falling outside a cocktail bar. She blamed me for nearly killing her." He took a sip of his beer to wet his dry throat. "I blamed myself too."

"That's the first time I've heard you say that in past tense," Turner noted.

"Talking with Zara has made me see things differently," Rory told them. "I thought I was always going to be crap at relationships, considering that Chelsea wasn't the first woman to crash and burn after we broke up. Even when I knew I wasn't feeling it with the women I dated, I still always felt like I needed to be their knight in shining armor—and that it would be cruel to revoke the invitation to be a part of our family when they all seemed to need it so badly."

"That's an impossible standard to live up to," Flynn commented. "Even if you could be a knight in shining armor once or twice, no one can live that way all the time. I'm still trying to accept that I'm going to fail Ruby and Cassie sometimes, no matter how much I want to be there for her every second of every day."

"I can't get my head around failure either," Hudson mused, frowning yet again. "Even when it seems inevitable."

If Rory hadn't been so twisted up over his situation with Zara, he would have pinned Hudson to the wall about the marital troubles he'd been hinting at for a while now. But if Rory couldn't figure out his own life, what kind of helpful advice could he give to his brother?

Turner was looking thoughtfully at Rory. "What

about Zara? Does she expect you to be perfect too?"

Rory couldn't hold back his laughter. "Zara doesn't expect *anything* from me. In fact, I've never been with anyone who has lower expectations of me than she does. Which, in an ironic twist, is making me want to do whatever it takes to prove to her that I'm someone she can count on. But I only have until Saturday to convince her that we should be together." Frustration roiled through him that he still hadn't come up with a foolproof plan.

"Why Saturday?" Flynn asked.

"That's the deadline we've given ourselves to break up." At the other men's confused expressions, Rory said, "Again, I can't explain why without breaking her confidence. Regardless, the clock is ticking down on our last five days together—unless I can figure out how to convince her to stay."

"Bring her chocolate," Hudson suggested. "That's always worked for me. At least it used to."

"Good tip," Rory said, though he knew it was going to take a heck of a lot more than chocolate to convince Zara to give her heart to him.

"If I had your talent," Flynn said, "I'd make her something tangible to show her what she means to you."

"Another good suggestion." If only Rory knew what to make that would strip away her wariness about being with him. He shifted his attention to Turner. "Got any brilliant ideas to add to the mix?"

"If I did, I wouldn't be going home to an empty house, unlike these two. Although I have to wonder, what are you doing here with us when you're on such a tight deadline with Zara?"

Turner was right. If Rory headed out now, he could make it to the grocery store to pick up some chocolate cake—she'd mentioned it was one of her weaknesses, after all—before it closed. And then he could beg Zara to let him share it with her tonight.

Despite the fact that his glass was still full, he stood. But before he left, he asked Flynn, "Am I still on to babysit Ruby tomorrow afternoon?"

"If you're sure you're up for it. She can be quite a handful now that she's mobile."

"Of course I'm up for it. Drop her by my wood-shop as early as you need to."

Rory headed straight for the grocery store. It wasn't until he was walking inside that he realized the song playing over the store's speakers was *Can't Fight This Feeling* by REO Speedwagon. He had to laugh at just how on point the cheesy pop song was. And before he knew it, he was channeling Zara by whistling along as he walked the aisles.

CHAPTER SEVENTEEN

As soon as Rory had dropped Zara off at her cottage, she'd decided to tackle the most difficult item on her to-do list: Call her stepmom and advocate for a change of wedding location for Brittany.

Margie wasn't an evil stepmother. Truthfully, she had never been anything but kind and patient with Zara. That didn't mean she was a pushover, however. And perhaps Zara would have had a more difficult time convincing her to switch wedding venues during their phone call had Margie not been so distracted by questions about Zara's unexpected party date.

Her stepmother wanted to know absolutely everything about Rory. Specifically, did Zara think Rory was *the one*?

Though she knew she had to keep pretending if she wanted everyone in her family to think they were an item, she should have laughed inwardly at the preposterous idea of Rory being *the one* for her.

But she hadn't laughed.

Instead, she'd stuttered and stumbled over her

words until Margie said in a delighted voice, "That's exactly how I was both times I fell in love—first with Brittany's father and then with yours. I was hardly able to string two words together. And I was glowing with happiness, just the way you were last night. I'm so happy you've been able to move on with someone so wonderful."

In love?

In love?

Was that how Zara and Rory had seemed to everyone last night? Yes, they were now friends. And they obviously had the hots for each other.

But had they been signaling something more in the way they'd looked at each other?

In the way they'd talked?

In the way they'd touched?

Zara had never come close to falling in love. Even with Cameron, her hurt feelings had far more to do with his cheating on her than with breaking her heart.

So how on earth could the guy she'd been bickering with day in and day out at work end up being the one to break through to her heart? Even if it turned out that Rory was a far nicer, sweeter, more thoughtful, and caring guy than she'd ever imagined.

No. She shook her head hard enough to make it ache.

Just *no*.

Still, even after she texted Brittany with the good news about the wedding location, she felt shaken up inside. Talking to Margie about the wedding had reminded Zara all too keenly that she would never be able to talk about weddings with her own mom. Nor would they be able to talk about all the things that came before a wedding, like meeting the guy of her dreams and falling in love.

Or being confused about whether or not she'd *already* met the guy of her dreams in the guise of the *last* person she'd ever thought to dream about...

On the nights when she most missed her mom, Zara always did the same thing—she pulled the hope chest from her closet and brought it into the living room.

Her mother had given her the wooden box when she was eight years old. The chest held precious memories and symbolized her wishes for Zara's life to be full of hope and dreams and love. As soon as Zara was born, her mother had begun to fill the chest with photo scrapbooks, favorite recipes, a baby quilt she'd used during the first few years of her life, a charm bracelet that had been passed down from her grandmother, and even silly things like Zara's favorite superhero Halloween outfit she'd worn three years in a row.

Though the thin wood chest hadn't weathered well

over the years, and the latch and hinges were on the verge of breaking, everything inside was in good shape. Sitting cross-legged on the couch, Zara opened the chest and carefully lifted out each of the items. Her first pair of baby shoes. Her first lost tooth at six. Her first-place swim ribbon from third grade. The family recipe book. The funny jokes on the notes her mom used to leave in Zara's lunchbox.

Her hand trembled as she lifted a picture her dad had taken of Zara and her mom during the Family Fun Day that the Kennebunkport town council put on each summer. They had their arms around each other, and they were laughing. So happy. So carefree.

And without a clue about the horrible thing that would happen just seven days later.

A knock at the door startled Zara so much that the picture fluttered from her hand. She quickly picked it up and put it back in the chest, then got up to see who was visiting her so late on a Sunday night. Most likely it was Ellen from down the street. Zara's neighbor was always doing late-night baking and running out of sugar or flour or chocolate chips. Zara had gotten in the habit of buying extra of those ingredients just in case.

But it wasn't Ellen at the door.

"Rory?" Zara was hit with the strangest feeling as she saw him standing on her front porch—she'd never been so glad to see anyone in her life. It was almost like her grief over missing her mother had triggered a telepathic message to Rory, letting him know how much she needed to be with a friend tonight. "What are you doing here?"

"I missed you." His simple answer landed right in the center of her heart. "And also..." He lifted the lid on a pink pastry box. "Chocolate cake."

She read the label. "Double dark chocolate fudge."

"I would have asked for triple, but the woman behind the counter was already giving me the stink eye for keeping the store open."

"Or she could have been giving you the stink eye because it's fun to see a big, brawny, know-it-all guy squirm."

"It's certainly possible," he agreed. And then, "Can I come in? Or should I just hand you the cake and head home?"

She feigned having to think about it. "That's a tough one..." Then she took the cake from him and stepped aside. "Of course you can come in, if only to make sure I don't eat the entire thing by myself."

"It's good to feel needed," he teased.

As she headed for the kitchen to cut the cake and put it on plates, she realized everything from her hope chest was still strewn on the couch and coffee table. Knowing he must be trying to figure out why she was looking at old pictures and scrapbooks and a kid-sized superhero outfit, she put the cake box down, then went to explain as she began to put things away.

"That's my hope chest. My mom gave it to me when I was eight." She tried to play it like it was no big deal, but the catch in her voice gave her away, as did the way her hands were shaking so hard she had to stop clearing up.

He reached for her hands and wrapped them in his. "You must miss her a great deal."

Not trusting her voice, she nodded.

"I'd love to hear more about your mom." He looked from the chest, then back to her face. "If you feel up to talking about her, that is."

Her stomach felt all twisted up. Zara's dad had always become so sad when she brought up the subject of her mom that she'd learned not to speak of her at all. And it had never seemed fair to talk about her with her stepmother.

Brittany was the only person Zara had ever really been able to talk to about her mother...and even then, she'd never been brave enough to tell her stepsister absolutely everything. Then, as they'd grown older and Brittany had stopped bringing up her father so much and seemed to have recovered from losing him, Zara had taken that as a cue to stop bringing up her mother too.

Even though she hadn't gotten over losing her mom at all.

Suddenly, she realized just how badly she wanted to talk with someone about her. No, not just *someone*.

Rory.

Zara wanted *Rory* to know how special her mother had been. How loving and smart. How she'd been brilliant at needlepoint. How her smile could light up a room. How she could never get into a kayak without tipping it over.

And how Zara still longed for her every single day.

"You would have loved her. Everyone did."

Rory led her over to an open spot on the couch. "Was your mom a firecracker like you?"

"She most definitely was." The thought made Zara smile. "She was really sweet and kind, but if you disappointed her, you were going to hear about it. And she could yell so loud it made your ears ring."

"That sounds a lot like my mom. Tell me more."

"She had a job in human resources at a manufacturing company in Kennebunkport and always swore that she was more comfortable behind a desk than out trying to sell people something or being bubbly and chatty. But one year, after a bad storm destroyed the playground equipment in the local park, she spearheaded the biggest fundraiser our town had ever seen. I hated having to go door to door asking for donations when the rest of my friends were goofing off, but she was right that our town needed that park rebuilt. We both went and talked with nearly every single person in town. If I hadn't done that with her, I'm not sure I would have had the nerve to ever start selling my eyeglasses frames." Zara was silent for a moment. "Looking back, it's easy to see how much we take our parents for granted. That they'll always be there for us and to teach us the things we'll need to know later in life. I wish I had been mature enough to tell her how special she was and how much I learned from her before she died."

"She would be really proud of you, Zara." He was still holding her hand. "I hope you know that."

Her chest tightened again as pain rammed her hard in the solar plexus. She'd tried so hard to bury her shame and her guilt over the years, but the truth was she'd never actually succeeded. And now, she couldn't keep it inside anymore. Couldn't keep secret the truth that she'd never told anyone—not her father, not Brittany, and certainly not any of her boyfriends.

Only with Rory was Zara compelled to finally admit, and to speak aloud, the terribly painful truth of the day her mother died.

"I was fourteen, and she had taken me to see the eye doctor. I was having trouble seeing both the board at school and the soccer ball, and the optometrist confirmed that I needed glasses. He recommended that I begin with glasses, then graduate to contacts down the road in college, because he said teenagers tend to have trouble keeping contact lenses clean and remembering to take them out at night. I was so upset about having to wear glasses and looking like a nerd. Mom tried to reason with me. She promised we would find some really pretty frames, and she knew I would totally pull them off."

Zara's next breath shook in her chest, and she instinctively reached for Rory's other hand, knowing she would never be able to get through her story without his grounding touch.

"I had a crush on the coolest boy in class, and I knew he would think I was the world's biggest loser if I came to school wearing glasses, so I yelled at her that I would *never* wear glasses, and if she made me, it would be her fault if no one wanted to be my friend anymore. She told me I would always be beautiful whether I wore glasses or not, and that if someone didn't want to be my friend for a dumb reason like that, they weren't worth being friends with in the first place."

Zara scrunched her eyes shut as her tears started to fall. "When we pulled into the driveway, I got out and slammed the door and said I would hate her forever if she made me wear glasses." Her words were blurring together in her tear-clogged throat. "A little while later, she came up to my room, which I had locked, and said through the door that she was going back to the optometrist to talk to him about getting contacts for me. I didn't open the door, didn't say thank you, didn't give her a hug or tell her I loved her." Eyes closed, she was fourteen again, hearing the police officer tell her the horrible news. "A car shot through a stop sign and hit her. I've never told anyone this before—I couldn't bear to admit it even to myself—but *she died because of me.*"

Somewhere in there, Rory had put his arms around her. She held tightly to him, her face buried against his neck, his hair.

"It was an accident," he said. "It wasn't your fault."

"It was," she said through her sobs. "If I hadn't been such a little jerk, if I'd just worn the glasses without making such a stupid fuss, she wouldn't have driven back to the office. She would have stayed home with me. And I would still—" Her throat tightened around the words. "I would still have my mom."

"You weren't the one driving the car that went through the stop sign. And you were no different from any other fourteen-year-old girl who didn't want to seem different, especially around a guy."

She wished she could believe him. "I swore I would never change myself for a guy again." She sniffled loudly. "And I swore I would never wear contacts either. That's why I got a degree in industrial and product design. So that I could devote my career to designing cool glasses. So that other kids—and adults—who needed them would never have to worry about being uncool again."

"After what you've been through," he said in a soft voice, "I think you're amazing."

"I'm not." She appreciated that he had her back, but he needed to understand one thing more. "The last words I ever spoke to my mom were that I hated her—and she got hit by that car because I made her feel she had to go back to the doctor's office." Fresh tears fell, drenching her cheeks. "I will never forgive myself for either of those things."

He gently brushed her tears away with their clasped hands. "Your mom would have never blamed you for what happened. Not in a million years. Not when she knew just how wonderful, how good, how generous you are. I guarantee that the only thing she ever wanted for you is happiness. And the very last thing she would have wanted was for you to spend fifteen years beating yourself up with guilt and blame."

But Zara could only hear his words as if through a haze. "I went through all the stages of grief—denial, anger, bargaining, depression—before making it to what I thought was acceptance. But the truth is I haven't accepted her death or my role in it. Even all these years later, grief sneaks up on me at the most unexpected times. Like tonight, while I was going through the hope chest. Or when I'm driving, if one of her favorite songs comes on the radio. Or if I see a mom and her teenage daughter fighting, I want to shake them both and tell them to appreciate each other because this might be the last fight they ever have. And then I hate myself all over again for being the reason Mom was in that intersection." She looked up at him through blurry eyes. "What if I can never accept that she's gone? And what if I go to my own grave hating myself?"

"You won't." He gathered her closer in his arms. "I won't let you."

It was exactly the kind of statement a guy who thought he could control the world would make. But helping Zara put her grief to rest—and the burden of guilt she'd carried around since she was fourteen—was surely an impossible task.

The ocean of tears she'd cried had drained her to the point where all she wanted was to keep her face buried against Rory's broad chest and sleep. He must have read her mind, because the next thing she knew, he was picking her up and carrying her into the bedroom.

He laid her down on the bed, but she didn't let go of him. "Stay." Her eyes still closed, she breathed him in. "I need you."

He brushed his lips across her cheek. "I'm not going anywhere," he promised.

A few minutes later, he had both of their clothes stripped away and the covers over them. Zara nestled into the crook of his arm, draped an arm and a leg over him, then dropped instantly to sleep.

CHAPTER EIGHTEEN

Zara was still sleeping when Rory woke on Monday morning. They were still holding tightly to each other.

And his heart was still breaking for her.

It absolutely gutted him to learn that she blamed herself for her mother's death. When they'd first connected over the engagement party on Friday, he'd thought her biggest problem was her stepsister stealing her boyfriend. And when he'd told her his story about Chelsea, Zara had clearly wanted to help him get over his guilty conscience and forgive himself for his inadvertent role in his ex-girlfriend's accident. Now, however, he realized that Zara was the one who truly needed to forgive herself. Losing her mom was a million times bigger than the problems he'd had with his ex.

At the party when she'd said she wanted one night where she knew how it felt to be wanted even if she didn't deserve it, he hadn't understood how she could possibly think she was undeserving. But where he'd struggled with his guilt for a year, Zara had struggled with it for half her life, to the point where she actually seemed to think she didn't deserve to be wanted, to be adored. To be happy.

Not forty-eight hours ago, he'd been certain that he had nothing real to offer her in the long term. But after talking with his brothers last night—and then again after Zara had shared her painful past with him—he had begun to see how wrong he'd been.

Zara sparked feelings inside Rory that no one else ever had. And he wanted nothing more than to do whatever he could to help her heal.

He wanted to hold her and kiss her.

He wanted to laugh with her and challenge her.

He wanted to protect her and help her.

He wanted to support her and learn from her.

He wanted to be there for her for as long as she would have him.

If what he felt for Zara wasn't magic, he didn't know what was.

He pressed a kiss to her temple, and as he turned the problem of how to help her over inside his head, Flynn's suggestion came back to him. *Make her something tangible to show her what she means to you.*

Suddenly, Rory knew exactly what to make. A new, strong, beautiful hope chest, made from a cedar log in his workshop, the same wood traditionally used for hope chests. This chest, however, would not only hold her memories of her mother and her mother's hopes for Zara, but also all the new memories, hopes, and dreams that Zara would make in the future with people she loved...if only she could heal.

As soon as they got into the warehouse this morning, he would contact his current clients to let them know he would need a short extension on his deadlines. He wanted to build Zara's hope chest immediately. It had to be ready by Saturday.

First, though, he would do his damnedest to bring her smile back this morning by returning to last night's chocolate cake plan, which they hadn't gotten around to.

Carefully sliding out from beneath Zara and the sheets, he went into the kitchen to brew coffee to drink with the cake. He was just pouring the fresh brew into mugs when he heard her footsteps.

"If I knew you would wake me up with coffee," she said in a slightly husky voice, "I would have slept with you a long time ago."

As upset as she'd been last night, he was glad she'd woken up her usual snarky self. Even if he now knew just how deep her river ran beneath that snark.

Happy just to be with her, he smiled as he handed her the mug, which she sipped from gratefully. She'd always secretly made him smile. Frankly, it was a relief not to have to hide it anymore.

Now if only he could find ways to keep her smiling...

"What would you say to chocolate cake with the coffee?" He held out a forkful of cake, studying her face for outward signs of the grief and guilt she'd let him see last night. But all he saw was a beautiful woman savoring cake, then sighing with obvious pleasure.

"I would say that you should marry me."

For a guy who had never considered marriage before, he was surprised by how much he liked the sound of that.

How had Zara managed to change so many things for him in such a short time?

"Although," she added as she ran her free hand down his naked torso, "any marriage proposals would surely be a result of losing my mind over your feeding me coffee and cake while naked. No question, this is my favorite breakfast of all time."

"Mine too. Although there is something wrong with this picture." He reached for the ties on her thick, fluffy robe and undid them. "You're overdressed."

She shrugged her shoulders to help him push the fabric off her body. "Feed me more cake so that I'll have the energy to jump you."

"Your demand is my command." He forked up another huge bite and put it to her lips. "You have a little chocolate icing right here." He leaned forward to lick the sweet cream from the corner of her mouth. "And here too." He licked the other corner. "And right here." He covered her mouth with his and slid his tongue against hers.

He was surprised when she used one hand flat on his chest to push him away. "This is *my* jumping, thank you very much." She pointed to an armchair in the corner by a window that looked out to the backyard. "Sit."

Though he wasn't at all happy about moving away from her when every cell in his body was urging him closer, he did as instructed. Of course, she had to further torment him by taking her sweet time finishing her coffee, all while standing naked, looking so damned beautiful in her cat-eye glasses.

At last, she put her mug down and brought over the cake. She put the open box on the side table beside the chair, then straddled him. "Have you had anything to eat yet?"

His mouth was suddenly too dry to respond. All he could do was shake his head.

There was a decidedly wicked glint in her eyes as she reached into the box and grabbed a chunk of cake. The next thing he knew, she was smearing it across her chest.

"Oh no," she exclaimed. "I have cake on myself."

Rory finally managed to find his voice. "I can help

with that."

"I'm very glad to hear it." The flirtatious smile she gave him had his excitement ratcheting up another dozen levels. "Start with my fingers."

He brought her fingers to his mouth, licking them clean, one at a time. As he laved her sensitive skin, her hips began to move restlessly over his.

God, she was gorgeous. And so wonderfully uninhibited. He'd never imagined a woman like her existed. A woman who challenged him at the same time as she tugged at his heartstrings.

And who was also shockingly sexy.

When he was done, she made a show of examining her fingers. "Excellent work. Your attention to detail has always impressed me." She threaded her hands into his hair, then pushed her breasts toward his mouth. "Impress me again, Rory."

He didn't need to be told twice before he ran his tongue over her soft skin. When she arched her back in an obvious bid to get even closer, he put his hands on her hips and pulled her flush against his erection.

She gasped at the delicious contact. Heat against heat. Hard against soft.

And both of them desperate for more.

He wanted nothing more than to drive up into her, but she'd made it clear that she wanted to be in charge this morning—and her happiness had become more important to him than anything else. Even his desperate need to take her.

Fortunately, the moment he finished licking the cake and icing off her naked skin, she rose over him...

And made him the happiest man alive.

Clinging tightly to each other, their breath coming in short pants, they rocked together in the chair, driving each other higher and higher. He was only barely holding himself back when she put her hands on his cheeks and stilled as she stared into his eyes.

"I like you so much," she said, and then she kissed him.

The kind of kiss that was insanely hot and passionate.

The kind of kiss that made his chest swell, and ache, and yearn in a way it never had before.

The kind of kiss that was all magic, from start to finish.

She gasped as pleasure took her over, her release explosive enough to tear his control completely away.

They sat wrapped around each other for a long while, her head resting on his shoulder, his hands still gripping her hips.

"I suppose we should head into work soon," she murmured, sighing as she sat back.

Rory was hugely tempted to convince her to chuck in her work ethic and spend the rest of the morning in his arms. But not only did he respect her career too much to keep her from her very busy daily schedule, he also wanted to get going on her hope chest. Plus, he had a very special little girl coming to spend the afternoon with him.

"We probably should. I have a new project to start this morning." He ran his hands up her back, delighting in touching her while they talked. "And I'm also going to be babysitting Ruby this afternoon to help Flynn and Cassie out. My mom usually watches her for a few hours each day, but with my parents away this week, each of us signed up to cover a day."

"Lucky you," Zara said, "getting to spend a whole day with that awesome little girl."

Zara had met Ruby last month when his sister Cassie had brought her along while she dropped off custom candy orders to the other makers in the building. While Ruby was certainly sweet, she'd become downright grizzly by the end of the delivery, letting out some eardrum-popping screams. It was telling that Zara had only been left with the impression of *awesome*—she clearly loved kids.

Again, it was strange how much that mattered to Rory. Especially when it wasn't as though he'd been sitting around all these years planning his personal extension on the Sullivan family tree.

"Honestly," he said, "I'm a little nervous about it.

Not because she isn't a totally cool kid, but because this is the first time they're trusting me to have her all alone."

"Look at you," Zara teased, "finally nervous about something for once in your life."

If only she knew just how nervous he was about how to be there for her, about getting it all wrong and losing her—

Zara reached up to stroke his cheek affectionately. "You're actually very sweet when you're vulnerable." She kissed him softly, then surprised him yet again by saying, "What would you say about my taking the afternoon off to babysit with you? As long as Flynn and Cassie are okay with it, of course."

"I would say you're the greatest girlfriend a guy could ever have." He didn't bother to contain his enthusiasm. Not only because Zara's being there really would take the edge off his solo baby-minding panic, but also because it meant spending another few hours with a woman he was coming to adore. "And I'm sure Flynn and Cassie will be glad to have two of us on duty. He told me last night that Ruby's become a bit of a handful lately."

"*Temporary* girlfriend." When he gave her a confused look, she explained, "When you said I'm the greatest girlfriend a guy could have, you forgot to use the all-important *temporary* tag."

He barely managed to hold back a scowl at her reminder.

"In fact," she added as she climbed off his lap and took the cake into the kitchen, "now that I'm thinking about it, babysitting Ruby together will be a great way to help us add to our incompatibility list for Saturday's breakup. I'm sure we'll have different ideas about how to best entertain her."

"What are you talking about?" Considering how great he'd felt minutes ago, the words came out extremely grumpy.

She frowned at him as though he were missing a few screws. "Our list of the reasons we could never work as a couple, obviously." She washed her hands, then put her robe back on before finally tidying away her hope chest.

He would have argued with her—complete with a bullet-point list of a dozen great reasons he now believed they belonged together—had he not been hit with just how vulnerable she looked as she carefully put away her mother's mementos.

"After everything we talked about last night," he said, "are you okay this morning?"

"I'm fine." She gave him a smile that was supposed to reassure him, then carried the hope chest to her closet. But since the smile hadn't reached her eyes, he was anything but reassured.

He tried again. "When I told you about my situation with Chelsea, the things you said to me helped a lot. But I'm not sure if anything I said last night helped you, so if you want to talk about it some more—"

"No." The word came out sharply. She shot him an apologetic look. "You were really great last night. But I'm totally okay now."

He wanted to believe her, wished she could magically get over fifteen years of pain overnight. But he knew better. Knew how hard it must be to always seem so bulletproof.

"Zara." Though she held herself stiffly as he drew her against him, he didn't let her go. "I'm here for you. If you need me, for anything, for any reason, whether we're dating or not, I'm on your side. You know that, right?"

But he couldn't read the expression in her eyes. He didn't know if she doubted him or believed him. He didn't know if she was ever going to open up to him again, or if last night was the furthest she'd ever let him into her heart. He didn't know if their talk had helped at all, or if she was just as racked with guilt and blame as ever.

And he didn't know if she was ever going to let herself fall for him the way he'd already fallen for her.

"I do know it," she finally said. "Although now that we're about to head into work—and will also see your sister and Flynn today—we should probably agree on how we're going to deal with our co-workers and your family for the rest of the week. I'm thinking that since Brittany and Cameron won't be there to witness us as a couple, we should just act the way we always have. I mean, if we're all over each other, it will only make things more confusing for the people around us after we split on Saturday."

Though he wasn't at all surprised by her suggestion, that didn't mean he liked it. Still, he'd already said he would never do anything to make her feel uncomfortable. "I'll follow your lead."

"Thanks for coming over last night, and for staying." She gave him a quick kiss. "I'll see you at the warehouse in a bit."

But as she went into her bedroom to shower and change, and he headed home to do the same, he couldn't stop wishing he knew exactly what to say, exactly what to do, to break through to Zara's heart.

With a groan, he realized he might have to cave and ask his sisters for advice on how to properly woo Zara.

Wouldn't they just love that?

CHAPTER NINETEEN

Zara was sluggish at the office all morning. Even though she never slept better than when she was in Rory's arms.

She knew why, of course. Knew that it was because she'd opened up her emotional floodgates by telling him about the day her mother died.

She still couldn't believe she'd told him the truth about the car crash. She'd never told *anyone* the things she'd said to her mom that afternoon—had barely even admitted them to herself.

Zara hadn't been surprised when he'd told her it wasn't her fault. What she was surprised by, however, was his vow to help her recover from her grief and shed her guilt.

No one but Rory Sullivan would have dared make such bold, confident claims. So bold and so confident that a part of her couldn't help but want to believe he might be able to pull it off.

The sound of a baby's laughter from down the hall had her pushing away from her drafting table with no small measure of relief. The last thing she wanted today was to be alone with her thoughts. And while she wasn't sure she was much more comfortable being with Rory—not when he now knew what a complete and total mess she was—she was very much looking forward to spending some time with Ruby.

Few things cheered Zara like time with little kids. Their sweetness, their innocence, their laughter were all a balm to her soul. Zara couldn't stand the thought of her sadness touching any part of Ruby, so she vowed to do whatever it took to tamp down the darkness rumbling around inside of her.

Rory was spinning Ruby around in the air while the little girl laughed. Flynn, Ruby's adoptive father, and Cassie, Flynn's girlfriend and Rory's sister, were laughing too.

"Zara, hi!" Cassie came over to give her a hug. "We just heard the news that you're going to join Rory and Ruby today."

"Only if it's okay with you and Flynn?" Zara shot the famous screenwriter a questioning glance.

Before he could reply, Ruby spotted Zara and held out her arms. Last month, when Cassie had brought her by to drop off some candy, they had played the mother of all peekaboo games. Of course Zara was more than happy to cuddle the sweet little girl again. And when Ruby covered her eyes in an obvious bid to play their favorite game, Zara said, "Peekaboo!" Then she gently lifted Ruby's hands from her eyes, while making a silly face that sent the baby into gales of giggles.

"You have the stamp of approval from the most important person in the room," Flynn noted.

"She's such a smarty-pants," Zara said as she cuddled Ruby closer. "I can't believe she not only remembers me, but also that this was the game we played last month."

"See?" Cassie looked triumphant as she turned to Flynn. "I told you Ruby's a genius."

Clearly proud of his little girl, he said, "I'm pretty sure *I'm* the one who's always saying that."

Rory leaned over to nuzzle Ruby's cheek, before looking out to the parking lot. "When does the delivery van arrive with all her things?"

Cassie made a face at her brother. "That would be funny if it weren't so true. We'll be right back."

A handful of minutes later, it seemed half of Rory's workshop was covered with Ruby's supplies. Everything from a portable crib to a vibrating seat to a portable mobile play station, not to mention enough diapers and baby food to supply a daycare center.

"If there's anything else you need, both of us will have our cell phones on," Flynn said.

"Ruby is going to be fine," Rory said as he gently

stroked her soft curls. While he'd expressed some nerves to Zara this morning, he seemed to know better than to let Ruby's father see them. "Better than fine— she's going to have the time of her life with Uncle Rory and Aunt Zara."

Zara's stomach flipped at the casual way he'd just linked them together. And how strangely right it seemed.

Flynn looked like he was going to say something more—maybe even change his mind at the last minute about leaving Ruby for the afternoon—when Cassie put her hand on his arm as though to forestall his panic, then moved to give Ruby a kiss and hug.

"Have fun, sweet girl. Love you to forever and back."

Flynn followed Cassie's lead, tucking a finger beneath Ruby's chin as he told her, "Cassie and I will see you tonight. Have fun today with Rory and Zara." From Ruby's serious expression, Zara felt that the one-year-old could fully understand what her daddy was saying. He kissed her on each cheek and then the tip of her nose. "Love you."

She kissed him back on his nose, then said, "Shmoo."

Zara's heart squeezed at Ruby's baby version of *love you*. Her heart was so innocent, so pure.

What Zara wouldn't give to feel that way again.

Flynn and Cassie went out to their car and were about to drive away when Flynn suddenly hit the brakes and Cassie threw open the passenger door to run back into the workshop.

"I can't believe I almost forgot to give you Ellie the Elephant." She handed Ruby a small stuffed elephant that was pink with purple polka dots. To Zara, Cassie explained, "It's Ruby's favorite toy."

Zara already knew about Ellie the Elephant, of course. Earlier that year, Flynn had transitioned from writing thriller screenplays to writing a children's story about a brother and sister named Joe and Alice. Having survived a rough past, the siblings met a girl named Cassie and her stuffed elephant, Ellie. Together, they went off to discover fantasy lands. It was both an audience and a critical hit.

Rory shook his head at his sister. "We would have been toast if you'd forgotten the elephant."

Seeing that Cassie was looking a little panicked about leaving Ruby, Zara said, "But now that we've got Ruby's favorite toy, everything is going to go great today."

"We'll drop her off at your cabin at six tonight." Rory waved his sister out of the workshop. "Bye-bye."

Ruby mirrored his movements, waving wildly at Cassie. "Bye-bye, Mommy!"

A laugh burst from Cassie's lips, and she couldn't

resist giving Ruby another smooch. Finally, she returned to Flynn's car, and they managed to drive all the way out of the lot this time.

Zara admitted to Rory, "I'm already on cuteness overload with this one." She lifted Ruby up so that she could blow raspberries against her tummy. Ruby laughed, delighted with their new game. Of course, Rory had to get in on it, leaning over to blow his own raspberries.

This time when Ruby giggled, however, a powerful smell permeated the air.

Rory wrinkled his nose. "I was hoping she had already done that today."

Zara laughed. "Even if she had, I'm pretty sure it wouldn't guarantee that you'd be out of the diaper-changing zone until tonight."

"You wouldn't happen to have done this before, would you?"

Zara had babysat quite a bit as a teenager, but she wasn't about to let him off the hook so easily. "Are you saying you *haven't*?"

"I have." He grimaced. "I wouldn't say I'm great at it, though."

"How *not great* are you?"

"Suffice it to say that full-body wipe-downs and changes of clothes have been involved. And not just for the baby."

Ruby mimicked Rory's grimace, looking less than thrilled about the fact that neither of them was rushing to clean her up.

Zara couldn't stand it anymore. "Fine, I'll do it." She took the changing mat out of the bag, then a clean diaper and wipes, and laid them on the worktable. "But just to be clear, if I didn't owe you for being so great about coming to the engagement party and—" No, she couldn't bring up her mom again unless she wanted to risk her hastily rebuilt emotional dam breaking. "Well, just everything, I wouldn't be saving your butt like this."

"Isn't it Ruby's butt you're saving?" he quipped.

Though she rolled her eyes, she otherwise ignored him as she laid Ruby down and set to work getting her all cleaned up. Fortunately, the baby was perfectly happy to have a virtual stranger tend to her, singing a nonsensical song to her stuffed elephant as Zara made short work of her dirty diaper, then snapped her back into her pretty romper.

As she picked Ruby up, Zara realized that the big cedar log Rory'd had in his woodshop for the past few weeks was no longer in the middle of the room. "Did you figure out what you're going to use the cedar for?"

A strange look came over his face. One that reminded her of a little boy caught sneaking candy out of a sweet shop.

He tried to cover it with a smile and a nod. "It's the new project I was telling you about this morning. I'm not ready to show it to anybody, though."

She raised her eyebrows, a little surprised by how proprietary he was over this project when she'd never noticed him being that way before. "Okay."

Ruby grabbed her hair just then, and when Zara shifted her attention to untangle it from the baby's fingers, Rory threw a big sheet over a table in the corner.

Seriously, he was acting really weird.

"Why don't we get Ruby's things packed into my truck?" he suggested. "Then we can head out for our big adventure."

"Oooh, hear that, little miss? We're going on a big adventure!" Zara rubbed her cheek on the top of the baby's head, letting the simple sweetness of the gesture soothe her.

It took several trips to get everything into his truck, then a few minutes of his cursing a blue streak under his breath as he worked to get Ruby's car seat strapped into the extended backseat.

"And here I thought you were good at fitting things together."

He ran a hand through his hair. "That was worse than the diaper change."

She was midway through getting Ruby buckled

into her car seat when she stopped to shoot him an incredulous look. "The diaper change you didn't have anything to do with, you mean?"

"Just being in the same room was bad enough."

She shouldn't laugh and encourage him. Of course, she did anyway. "Next diaper change is all you." She gave him a sinister grin. "I hope it's *really* messy."

She had just finished getting Ruby settled into the car, her elephant clasped tightly to her chest, when Rory put his hand on Zara's hip and pulled her into him for a kiss.

It wasn't until she was breathless and her knees were weak that she remembered where they were. "Someone will see." Though they hadn't completely ruled out PDAs at work, they had agreed they wouldn't flaunt their temporary relationship.

He didn't look at all remorseful, however. "Let them." And then he kissed her again, making her head spin so much that she was still a little dizzy when she got into the car and they headed off.

As a solo business owner, Zara rarely took time off work. If she didn't put in the hours, her business paid the price. Fortunately, despite her sluggishness this morning, she was well prepared for her big photo shoot tomorrow, so she wasn't particularly worried about bunking off early for once. Especially when a grand adventure with two of her favorite people was on the docket.

She caught her thought a few beats after it passed through her brain. When had Rory become one of her favorite people? And why was it impossible to deny that it was true?

The sweet sound of Ruby singing in the backseat snapped Zara out of her stunned musings. "Where to first?"

"How about we pick up lobster rolls for lunch," Rory said, "then head into the park to have a picnic and play with some of the eighty-seven toys that Flynn and Cassie packed for Ruby?"

"Sounds like the perfect plan." One of the best parts of moving to Bar Harbor was being able to hike and bike ride in Acadia National Park. Zara had traveled extensively after college, but Acadia remained one of the most beautiful places she'd seen.

"Say that again."

She turned to Rory. "Say what again?"

"How perfect I am."

She snorted, glad he was being his usual silly self. The last thing she wanted was for him to feel sorry for her, to be constantly checking whether she was going to crumble again. "I said your *plan* is perfect, not that you are." She hated to think how insufferable he'd be if he ever guessed just how perfect she was beginning to think he was.

He still looked extremely pleased with himself. "Close enough."

"It's not even the tiniest bit close," she argued, which only made him laugh.

Again, she probably shouldn't have joined in, but she couldn't help herself. Especially when he reached over to hold her hand.

His warmth, and the steadiness of his grip, helped ground her further. Clearly, for all her protestations that she was *fine* and *okay*, he knew how much she needed his touch and reassurance.

Soon, they reached the small deli on the corner of the green. And, of course, when Rory carried Ruby into the store, all of the women inside went absolutely gaga over the handsome man and his baby. Honestly, Zara wasn't sure that she could blame them.

He was so gentle with Ruby. So sweet. And funny too, when he crossed his perfect eyes to make her laugh, or made silly sounds, or kissed her little rosebud mouth when she puckered up. Some might even call him the perfect dad-to-be.

Of all the crazy thoughts she'd had about Rory since Friday, Zara couldn't believe she was suddenly picturing him as the perfect father. It was one thing to appreciate him as a sex god and to realize just how kind he could be.

But it was another entirely to frame him as the man

she'd want by her side raising a family.

When they'd made their one-week dating plan on Saturday, Zara had assumed this week would be about nothing more than having a few laughs and great sex while proving that they could never work as a couple. Only, what had begun as a fairly lighthearted plan to show each other that they could both manage a clean breakup had quickly morphed into something much bigger.

Big enough that she had shared the deepest, darkest depths of her soul with him last night.

And he'd held her tight through every second of it.

The woman behind the deli counter finally got Zara's attention, making her realize belatedly that she'd been woolgathering at the front of the line. Pulling herself together, she ordered their picnic lunch. Two lobster rolls, a container of potato salad, a big bag of chips, and two lemonades. She wavered over adding chocolate cake—after all, they'd already had cake for breakfast—but if ever there was a double chocolate cake day, this was it.

After she paid for lunch, she hoisted the rather heavy reusable fabric bag over her shoulder, then went to look for her companions. All she had to do was follow the sound of Ruby's laughter.

Zara found them over by a table of local artisan cookies, where Rory was pretending to be an elephant like Ruby's precious stuffed animal. He was cracking up nearly as hard as the baby as he swung his right arm like a trunk.

She might have stood watching them forever had Rory not noticed her. "Got everything?"

Zara nodded, reaching deep for the sassy self she'd always been with him, rather than this new version of herself who felt all mushy inside every time she looked at him. "It smells so good I'm about to sit down and have my picnic right here."

"If you can hold out another ten minutes, I promise your patience will be richly rewarded." They headed out to the car, and he buckled Ruby back into her car seat. "I worked summers in college as a seasonal ranger in the park, so I know all the secret spots."

"I can so see you in a forest-green ranger's uniform." As they got into the front seat, she asked, "You wouldn't happen to have it still, would you?"

"If you're asking because you've got a thing for men in uniform, the answer is yes."

"I might," she said, hugely relieved that she was able to stuff the darkness away to flirt with him. Though she'd managed to keep her emotions at bay this morning while they'd been making love, she'd been worried about how the rest of the day would go. "I'll bet you got up to plenty of naughty things during those summers, didn't you?"

He shot her a wicked grin, one that made her toes curl. "You know me so well."

Amazingly, he was right. Between Friday morning and Monday afternoon, she'd come to know Rory better than she'd known Cameron after two months.

Just then, Ruby started to make disgruntled noises from her car seat. Figuring she must be hungry for lunch, Zara turned around to entertain her until they got to their picnic spot.

Ten minutes later, Rory pulled into a small dirt lot surrounded by a thick grove of pine trees. The setting didn't look particularly remarkable from the parking lot, but she decided to have faith in his secret spot. After all, he had yet to let her down on any front. Amazingly.

"I'll take Ruby," Zara offered, "and you can bring everything else."

She hoisted Ruby onto her hip, making sure that she had her elephant, while he slung the food bag over his shoulder. "What did you buy?" he grumbled. "A dozen coconuts?"

"What can I say? When I'm hungry, my eyes are way bigger than my stomach."

He added an enormous baby bag to his load, along with a blanket for them to sit on and a bag of Ruby's toys, then said, "Follow me."

Zara had to take a moment to appreciate how well

he wore a pair of faded jeans before finally getting a move on. They hiked a narrow path between tree trunks...and then she got the shock of her life.

"You're kidding me." She gaped at the wide stretch of green grass that overlooked the ocean. It was breathtaking. "It should be illegal to keep a place like this a secret!"

He was grinning as he laid down the blanket. "I had to pinkie swear with the rangers that I'd never tell another soul." He lifted his gaze to hers. "You're the first person I've brought here."

Her eyes went wide. "Are you saying that even your family doesn't know about this place?"

"Nope." He brushed a lock of hair away from her mouth. "Only you." He tickled Ruby's tummy. "And you, little girl."

"Are you going to make me pinkie swear too?" Zara asked.

"I have a better idea. You can swear your loyalty to me with a kiss."

His request shouldn't have made Zara catch her breath. He was simply asking her, in his usual teasing way, to keep secret this area of the park. And yet as she said, "I swear," then leaned forward to press her lips to his, it didn't feel like teasing.

Not even close.

CHAPTER TWENTY

With her heart racing at how *big* everything suddenly seemed between them, Zara abruptly pulled back from the far-too-meaningful kiss, even though putting three feet of space between them wouldn't make any difference.

Whether she was kissing Rory or not, he had an undeniable pull over her.

For a few seconds, she thought he might reach for her and kiss her again. Instead, he turned and smiled at Ruby.

"Your turn now, sweet pea." As soon as the little girl saw him pucker his lips, she did the same, and he smacked a kiss on her mouth.

Zara's heart had gone completely to mush by the time she sat on the blanket.

Settling Ruby between her spread legs, she reached into the baby's bag. As soon as Ruby saw her containers of food, she grabbed them, managing to get the top off a bright green bowl. Thankfully, dried apple pieces spilled onto the blanket rather than pea puree. Ruby gobbled up her treats, using both hands to stuff the food into her mouth.

"Looks like you have a kindred spirit there," Rory said with a laugh.

Zara nodded her agreement as she ripped open the bag of chips. "I'm all for double-fisting these right now." When Rory's stomach audibly growled, though, she took pity on him and fed him the chips from her right hand while she devoured the ones in her left.

"God, I love it when you do things like this," he said with his mouth half full. He looked from where Ruby was sitting between Zara's legs munching her food, to where Zara was picking up potato chip crumbs to do the same. "I never knew spending time with a woman could be so good."

She didn't know how to respond. The air between them felt far too charged given the tenuous hold she had on her own emotions at the moment. Which was why she deliberately moved the conversation in a different direction.

"How'd you get into woodworking?" Surely that topic couldn't go any deeper than she was comfortable with, or set off another emotional bomb.

Rory unwrapped the lobster rolls and handed her one. "My earliest memories are of my dad and two of my uncles building together. Decks, planter boxes, sheds—even a house for a neighbor. As soon as I was big enough to hold a hammer, I wanted in. Evidently, I was underfoot so often that they had no choice but to let me help. It wasn't really about woodworking back then—it was more that I wanted to hang out with the guys. My dad's brothers seemed so much larger than life when I was a kid." He grinned. "Still do, even though I don't see them nearly as much as I'd like to."

Zara should have known better than to think she could skirt emotional land mines by asking Rory about his livelihood. He was so close to his family that it made perfect sense that his initial love for woodworking had come from spending time with his father and uncles. Why wouldn't he want to do that when his family sounded absolutely perfect?

She was obviously a glutton for punishment, because she couldn't resist asking him for more. "Where do they live?"

"They're all over the country. Uncle William lives on a lake in the Adirondacks. He and his wife, who passed away more than thirty years ago, raised their four kids in New York City, and my cousins all still live in New York state. Uncle Max and Aunt Claudia live in Seattle, and my five cousins are all near each other in Washington. Unfortunately, Uncle Jack from San Francisco passed away from an aneurism when his youngest kids were two, leaving my Aunt Mary to raise their eight kids by herself."

"She raised eight children by herself?" Zara couldn't have been more wrong about the Sullivans' perfect lives. She felt her own loss of her mother so keenly that she sometimes forgot she wasn't the only one who had experienced that kind of pain. "I can't imagine how hard that must have been." Not only for Rory's aunt, but for his eight cousins who had lost their father.

"Aunt Mary is a superstar," he agreed. "And my San Francisco cousins are all really close, probably because they had to help raise each other."

It was all too similar to the way Zara and Brittany had helped get each other through their teenage years. Which brought her back full circle to last night, when she'd lost it.

Zara kept her gaze firmly on the jar of apple puree that she was opening for Ruby, lest Rory notice she was getting emotional again. He'd already had to deal with her tears last night. He didn't need to be drenched by the waterworks again.

But she should have known that she couldn't hide anything from him. He reached for her hand, and Ruby—who was shockingly in tune with emotions, given that she was only one—mirrored his action by putting her little hand over Zara's too.

"I didn't mean to bring up something that hurts you," he said in a gentle voice.

"You didn't," she protested.

Of course he saw through her. "I can't imagine how much it must have hurt to lose your mom. How much it must still hurt. I wish I could take away your pain." He reached out to cup her cheek with his free hand. "I'm so damned sorry I don't know how to do that, sweetheart."

Tears burned behind her eyes. At his empathy. At his wishes. At the way he'd called her *sweetheart* again.

Seven days together should have been so short, so easy to sail through without any problems. Instead, everything was continually changing between them. First friends, then lovers, then...

Well, she wasn't sure what they were to each other now. Only that it wasn't at all easy, or simple, or clear-cut. Instead, being with Rory was sweet, and fun, and sexy—but also extremely emotional.

Fortunately, that was when Ruby decided to pick up a spoon, plunge it into the applesauce, and fling the contents *and* the plastic spoon at Zara's face.

"You silly bunny," she said to the baby. And then to Rory, she added, half-joking, "You're not supposed to call me that."

His gaze was intense. "I've never been good at doing what I'm told."

"It's one of the things I like best about you," she said as she squeezed his hand to let him know she appreciated his support even if she was terrible at accepting it, then freed her hand to wipe her face. "And you're great to care so much. But..."

"Back off?" he guessed.

Though she didn't want to hurt his feelings when he was clearly going out of his way to be nice to her, she said, "I was hoping we could have a nice afternoon with Ruby."

"Of course we can."

Fortunately, the awkward moment was broken by Ruby flinging more applesauce all over them, which made them both laugh.

Hoping again to move them into safer territory, Zara asked, "Are there any other famous cousins you've been hiding in the woodwork?" Surely, talking about celebrities would be totally innocuous.

"Good thing you're sitting down already," Rory said. "This might take a while."

She thought he must be exaggerating...until he started to list them all.

"Chase is a brilliant photographer. Marcus's wife, Nicola, is a pop star—you would know her as Nico. Zach is a race car driver. Ryan has won the World Series multiple times. His wife, Vicki, is a sculptor. I've already told you about Smith, and his wife, Valentina, runs their film studio with him. Lori is a big-deal choreographer. My Aunt Mary was a supermodel before she had the kids. Mia's husband, Ford, is a rock star. Ian is a billionaire, and his wife, Tatiana, is an Academy Award-winning actress, who also happens to be Valentina's younger sister. Drake is a renowned painter, like my Uncle William, and Drake's fiancée, Rosa, was an international reality-TV star. Suzanne owns a major software company. And Alec hangs out in the billionaire's club with Ian, courtesy of his private plane business."

Zara was momentarily speechless. "No one can be related to that many rich and famous people."

"I haven't even gotten to my cousins in Europe and beyond." He smiled at her reaction. "It sounds worse than it is, though. You'd be surprised by how normal they all are."

"Oh sure, all the billionaires I know are *totally* normal."

He laughed. "It's true, they are. Plus, there are plenty of regular Jills and Joes in the mix."

She scoffed, saying, "I doubt that," as he found the bag of baby wipes and made short work of cleaning off Ruby's face and hands. Clearly, he had more experience with kids than he'd shown during the diaper change. Zara had the feeling she'd been played. Big-time. "So, who are all these 'normal' Sullivans you claim to be related to?"

"Chase's wife, Chloe, makes quilts. And Marcus

owns a winery."

"Owning a winery is not *regular*," she pointed out.

"I guess not, but doing accounting like Gabe's wife, Megan, or running a dog daycare business like Zach's wife, Heather, is down to earth."

"I suppose so," Zara grudgingly agreed. "Although after hearing that insanely long list of mega-achievers, I feel like I should head straight back to my office and work around the clock for a decade straight." And here she'd thought it was bad enough to compare herself to Brittany. "Good thing you're super successful so that you don't have to worry about trying to keep up."

"I'm happy with where I am," he agreed, "but I've never wanted to be a billionaire or win an Oscar or sing onstage in front of a hundred thousand people. All I've ever wanted is to build things with my hands and know that I've been able to make a few people happy with the things I've made." He pulled a ball out of Ruby's toy bag and lightly tossed it to her. When she caught it, he cheered like she'd just won the World Series. "Hanging with my family is right up there too," he told Zara. "It's the most important thing of all, actually."

He was right that it wasn't about how much money you made, or how many fans you had. It was about fulfilling your passion—and if you could make people happy while you were at it, that was an amazing bonus. A picnic with a laughing little girl and her gorgeous babysitter on a beautiful day wasn't bad either.

As for family being the most important thing of all…

Of course Zara agreed. But if she talked about family right now, she was bound to fall apart all over again. And even though Rory had a truly great shoulder to cry on, she really didn't want to end up a sniveling mess.

"Confucius had it right," she said as she deliberately turned their focus from family to work. "Choose a job you love, and you will never have to work a day in your life."

"Did you hear that?" he asked.

She listened carefully for any strange sounds, but all she could hear was the wind through the trees, the crash of the ocean waves, and Ruby batting the ball with her little hands. "What am I supposed to be hearing?"

"The sound of my heart going pitter-patter." He laughed at her confusion. "As if it isn't already enough that you're beautiful and talented and sexy as hell, you've just quoted Confucius." He leaned in closer. "Give me more."

She shouldn't be so pleased by his compliment. Nor should she offer to entertain him like a trained quote-spouting monkey. Then again, why shouldn't she have some fun with it? After all, she was the one insisting on having fun today, rather than going anywhere deep.

"Okay, here's one that I've wanted to say to you every day for the past year whenever you annoyed me. 'Waste no more time arguing about what a good man should be. Be one.'" Though it had turned out that he was the *best* kind of man beneath all his swagger, she still gave him a *wicked* smile. "So says Marcus Aurelius, Emperor of Rome."

"God, that's hot. Don't stop."

"Most guys would be begging me to let up already, not begging me to continue. You're really weird. Isn't he, Ruby?"

She rubbed her hand over Ruby's full tummy, and the little girl closed her eyes, looking perfectly at peace. Zara felt momentarily at peace too, sitting in this beautiful park, spouting esoteric quotes. Cameron had hated it when she did that, unlike Rory, who was going gaga for it.

"How about a few more seconds of your brilliance in exchange for a hit of chocolate cake?" he suggested.

"Now you're the one who knows me all too well." It was easy for him to buy her cooperation as he opened the container holding the cake and presented her with a forkful.

After she'd swallowed the delicious dessert, she hit

him with another quote that fit his loquacious tendencies perfectly: "'Do not say a little in many words, but a great deal in few.'"

He threw back his head and laughed. "Only you would know how to hit me right where it hurts with classic Pythagoras."

"I was hoping you wouldn't know that one."

"Who wouldn't know the wisdom of the great Ionian Greek mathematician and philosopher?" he asked. "Also, there's a really similar saying in Gaelic."

"You know Gaelic?" Yet again, she was impressed.

"My mom is the only one of us who knows Gaelic well, although she tried really hard to teach it to us when we were kids. She did have a phrase for each of us, though. Mine was *Beagán a rá agus é a rá go maith.* Which translates more or less to 'Say little, but say it well.'"

Though Zara's already mushy heart had gone completely to goo as he spoke in the super-sexy foreign tongue, she teased him with, "Has she ever stopped saying it to you?"

"Nope."

Ruby broke into their conversation with an excited yelp. She pointed at a falcon flying above them, clearly far more interested in the park's wildlife than in eating—or in listening to them chatter.

"If you've had your fill of lunch," Rory said, "why

don't we pick up some bikes and a kid trailer from the rental place in the park? I've already run it by Flynn, and he's on board if you're up for a ride."

"I'd love that."

And amazingly, when he smiled, she felt warm from head to toe...even in the innermost parts of her heart that she'd been afraid would always feel cold.

CHAPTER TWENTY-ONE

After a great bike ride and a stop for ice cream in town, they drove to Cassie and Flynn's cabin. Zara hadn't had a chance to explore Bar Harbor nearly as much as she wanted to during the past year, and as they drove through the forest, she was wowed yet again.

From the backseat, Ruby's snores were surprisingly loud considering her size, and Zara and Rory shared a smile as they drove.

"Thanks for spending the day with us." Rory spoke softly so he wouldn't wake the baby.

"I had a lot of fun." Zara turned to look back at Ruby's sleeping face. "What a great kid, huh?"

"Ruby's the best. My nephew, Kevin, is a really cool kid too. Have you met him?"

"Your sister—Ashley, right?—brought him to the last warehouse art show. Remind me how old he is."

"He'll be eleven soon."

"Let me guess—he idolizes his Uncle Rory, doesn't he?"

"What kid wouldn't?" Rory joked. "Seriously,

though, we all spent so much time with him when he was little that he's super close to everyone in our family." Before she could ask why, he explained, "Ashley got pregnant as a senior in high school. Kevin's dad—" Anger flashed across Rory's face, and his hands tightened on the steering wheel. "The guy is a total waste of space. Anyway, we all pitched in with babysitting when he was little."

"I knew it!" Zara poked him in the shoulder. "You *were* playing me earlier when you acted like you didn't know how to change a diaper."

Rory had the nerve to grin. "Hook, line, and sinker."

She poked him harder. "What else have you been faking?"

He pulled off the road into the cabin's driveway, then hit the brakes, though they were still at least three hundred yards from the house. "Nothing." He reached for her hand. "Everything I've said, everything I've done, since Friday—it's all real, Zara."

She couldn't look away from his intense gaze...and didn't know what to say apart from, "Okay," in a voice that made it clear just how difficult she was suddenly finding it to catch her breath.

Ruby woke up with a mini-roar, and Zara let go of Rory's hand to tend to her while he drove the final stretch of the long driveway. Flynn and Cassie, who were waiting for them on the front steps, jogged out to the car. But when Flynn opened the back passenger door to get Ruby out, Zara was surprised when the little girl turned to look for her, then reached out.

As Flynn obligingly put Ruby into Zara's arms, Cassie said, "I was going to ask how she did, but I can see that the answer is absolutely fantastic."

Zara nuzzled the top of Ruby's head. "She's such a sweetheart—so much fun, and so happy. We laughed nonstop today." It was exactly what Zara had needed. To giggle with a sweet little girl, and her equally sweet babysitter. And as she walked toward the house with Ruby on her hip, Zara knew she'd miss the baby's soft weight, her fresh scent, and her innate joy.

"Come inside," Flynn said. "Cassie has made you both special thank-you baskets."

"You're giving us candy?" Zara asked in a hopeful voice.

Cassie smiled. "What better way is there to say thank you?"

"Chocolate cake can be a pretty good way," Rory suggested with a slow smile meant only for Zara.

Zara couldn't prevent a blush. Because despite the wild careening of her emotions since last night's confession, she'd never forget the super-sexy way they'd eaten chocolate cake for breakfast this morning.

What's more, even though her hair was tangled

from the bike ride and her clothes were stained with a mixture of Ruby's soft food and Zara's own meal, Rory was looking at her not only with heat in his eyes—but also with so much affection.

She'd been sure he was a shallow, self-obsessed player.

How much more wrong could she have been?

Cassie and Flynn's cabin was gorgeous inside and out, from the flower boxes beside the front door, to the brightly colored cushions and rugs and artwork inside, to the beautifully varnished wood walls, ceiling, and floorboards. "I love your home."

"Thanks so much. We love it too." Cassie shot Rory a fond smile. "Rory is far too modest to admit it, but he's the one who did most of the renovation work on it."

"Modest?" Though Zara now knew just how big his heart was, she couldn't resist asking, "Are we talking about the same person?"

Cassie's peals of laughter bounced off the walls as Rory said, "You may protest about my ego, but I know you secretly love it." He stroked her cheek with the back of his hand. "And I'm sure you'll agree that it's *exactly* the right size."

Zara couldn't miss the look Cassie and Flynn shared at Rory's obvious double entendre, especially coming on the heels of his not-so-subtle chocolate cake comment. Their look told Zara they were under the misapprehension that he wasn't just teasing her about hot sex, but that she and Rory were together for real.

Only…was it really a misapprehension? Because regardless of how sure Zara had been on Saturday that they could never make it as a real couple—the very subject she had continued to stubbornly bang on about this morning, even though she hadn't truly believed it—if she was being completely honest with herself, weren't they already more a couple than she'd ever been with anyone else?

Okay, so they weren't on the same page about plenty of likes and dislikes. But she wasn't sure any of that mattered anymore.

At last, Ruby reached for Cassie. "Mommy!"

Cassie's face lit up, and she dropped a kiss on Ruby's cheek as she took her into her arms. "I'm so happy you had such a fun day with Rory and Zara."

"Eeeee." Ruby looked around, clearly searching for something. "Eeeee."

Rory rooted around in the baby's bags. "Looking for this?" He held out the stuffed elephant.

Ruby grabbed it, then made it dance in the air and sing a song. Though the words she sang were unintelligible to the rest of them, she cracked all of them up anyway.

Flynn held up a bottle of wine labeled Sullivan

Winery, Napa Valley. "How about we say thank you with a glass of wine along with the candy?"

Any other evening, Zara would have loved to. But tonight, she felt too close to the edge of so many enormous emotions. She didn't want to be rude, though, and wasn't sure how to decline gracefully.

Before she could reply, however, Rory said, "I'm afraid I need to head out now."

Zara hadn't realized he had somewhere else to be tonight. She tried not to let her heart sink at the thought of being without him for a few hours. After all, she'd been boyfriendless for most of her life, so this was nothing new.

But that was before she knew how good it was to have the support of a friend—and a lover—like Rory.

Ruby yawned and rubbed her eyes, prompting Cassie to say, "It's probably for the best if we give Ruby a bath and dinner straightaway after her fun day with Uncle Rory and Aunt Zara."

Yet again, conflicting emotions hit Zara. On the one hand, it was lovely to be so warmly welcomed into the Sullivan fold. On the other, she was wary of letting herself get too attached to Rory's family when she knew just how quickly she could lose the people she cared about. Especially when there was every chance she might still lose Rory—and not just because they hadn't actually modified their Saturday breakup plan yet.

When he'd signed on to date her for the week, he hadn't had a clue just how messed up she was. And despite how close they'd become, she wouldn't blame him for cutting and running.

As she'd told him their first night together, you couldn't force yourself to love someone back, just because they'd gone and fallen in love with you. So she couldn't expect him to fall in love with her just because—

Her thoughts skidded to a halt.

Oh God.

She'd fallen in love with Rory.

The shock of it nearly felled her, and she had to reach out to steady herself on the back of the couch. Her brain scrabbled desperately to refute the realization that their relationship had very quickly gone deeper than she'd ever thought it could.

Deep enough to fall head over heels in love.

Every part of her was reeling. But there was no point in trying to deny it—heck, even her stepmother had seen the truth that night in Camden.

Then she realized Cassie was speaking to her. "I hope we'll see you again soon, Zara. Maybe at dinner with our parents on Friday night?"

"I'm not sure about my schedule for the rest of the week," Zara fumbled.

The only thing she was absolutely sure of was that her heart was one hundred percent Rory's.

Oh God.

She hoped Rory's sister didn't notice her hands shaking as Cassie gave them their goody bags, along with a big hug.

Flynn shook Zara's hand and then Rory's. "Thanks again for giving Ruby such a great afternoon."

"Anytime," Zara said in what she hoped was a normal voice. "Your little girl is a delight in every way."

Normally on the way out to the car, Zara would have shoved several of Cassie's homemade marmalades into her mouth. But she was so stunned by her realization that she was in love with Rory that she could barely walk a straight line, let alone multitask by chewing and swallowing hard candy too.

She could feel Rory's eyes on her, but he didn't speak until he had turned on the ignition and was heading down the driveway. "Your place or mine?"

Zara shot him a confused look. "I thought you had to get back to your workshop—or take care of something at home."

"Nope. I just wanted some alone time with you. I was hoping you want that too."

Of course she did. But after last night, she already knew that she was incapable of keeping anything from him. If she spent tonight with him—and especially if they made love, which they surely would, given that they couldn't keep their hands off each other—she might blurt out how she felt.

"Zara?" He took his eyes off the road long enough to give her a concerned glance. "What's wrong?"

Oh God.

She couldn't just up and make such a reckless declaration to him, could she?

Shouldn't she take some time—take a step back—analyze her feelings more carefully?

Shouldn't she make sure she'd looked at things from all angles before she went and handed over her heart on a silver platter?

But she realized she couldn't do it. Couldn't keep it from him.

Not when he had come to mean so much to her.

Not when he had come to mean *everything* to her.

"I'm in love with you."

He pulled over and hit the brakes so hard, Zara's seat belt barely held her in her seat.

"Say that again."

Baring her soul to him in a way she'd never thought she would with anyone, yet again she said, "I'm in love with you. I just realized it when—"

Before she could finish her sentence, the wonderful, sweet press of his lips stopped her words. And then his hands were unbuckling her seat belt and then his too so that he could put his arms around her and pull her against him.

"I love you too."

The relief—and the joy—in his voice poured into her, filling all the shadowy cracks with light.

"You do?" she asked.

"Of course I do."

"But I never thought we would—"

He kissed away whatever list of reasons she might have tried to put up against the odds of this ever happening. It wasn't until a car honked as it drove past that he drew back.

"I want to take you home and make love to you, Zara."

"I want that too." She truly did—more than she'd ever wanted anything in her entire life.

And as he held tightly to her hand for the rest of their drive, it felt as though all her dreams were coming true.

Even the ones she hadn't dared to ask for.

CHAPTER TWENTY-TWO

This was the best day of Rory's life. No monetary prize or career award could ever compete with hearing Zara say *I love you.*

Once they arrived at his house, in one smooth move, he pushed his seat back as far as it would go while pulling Zara onto his lap. She laughed as she straddled him, and he loved the way her laughter filled his entire body.

In the blink of an eye, the passion sparking between them as they kissed ignited into full-blown flames. As he ran kisses from her mouth down her neck and then over the upper swell of her breasts exposed in her tank top, she ground against him. Gripping her hips to increase the delicious friction, he drank in her gasp of pleasure.

Most other couples, on the eve of declaring their love for each other, would surely celebrate with rose petals and champagne and soft whispers. But making out in his car struck Rory as exactly right for them. Nothing about their relationship had been ordinary—

and something told him it never would be, thank God.

As they broke their kiss to yank off each other's shirts, he needed her to know something else. "You make me so damned happy."

"You make me happy too." She pressed her palms flat over his chest, then slowly trailed her fingers down toward his abdominal muscles. "And not just because I can't get enough of your hot bod." She lifted her eyes to meet his. "Your heart—" She leaned forward to press a kiss to his chest. "—is so big. Big enough that I couldn't fight my feelings for you, no matter what I did."

"It was so cute watching you try," he said in a teasing voice.

Of course she whacked him lightly on the chest. "Don't act like you weren't fighting too."

"I wasn't." He was dead serious. "Our first night together, I knew you were the one for me."

She paused in her unfastening of his jeans. "Don't mess with me, Rory."

"I'm not." Although he *was* perfectly game for messing with the satin straps of her sexy red lace bra so that they fell down her shoulders. "As soon as you kissed me, I was a goner."

"That was just sex," she said, exactly the way she'd said it so many times during the past few days.

"Nope." He yanked her bra cups down to expose

her beautiful breasts. "It was *never* just sex." Moving his hands from her hips, he cupped her breasts. "Even now, in the front seat of my car, what we're doing is so much more than just sex." He blew lightly across the aroused tips of her breasts, then brushed the callused pads of his thumbs over her as he said, "I adore you, Zara. Every inch of your body, every thought in your mind, every emotion in your heart."

"*Rory.*" His name was a whisper of heat, and tenderness, on her lips. "You're right, damn it. It was never just sex." Even her love for him—and the fact that she obviously adored the way he was caressing her—didn't lessen her irritation at his being right.

"You know what else I'm going to be right about?" he said.

Though she made a show of rolling her eyes, the flush on her cheeks spoke to her intense arousal as she asked, "What?"

He grinned wickedly. "How fast you're going to come for me."

Before she could reply, he slid one hand into her jeans and panties...then over the gorgeously slick heat between her thighs.

Her head fell back as she pushed against his hand, her inner muscles already working against his fingers as his touch sent her spiraling into climax within seconds. As aftershocks continued to rock through her, she laid her head on his shoulder, and he stroked her hair with his free hand.

"Now let's go inside so I can *really* rock your world," he whispered in her ear.

She gave a gratifying shiver as he lightly sank his teeth into her lobe. Finally, she managed to reply. "Setting some pretty high expectations, aren't we?"

"Not just setting them—swearing by them. I'm never going to let you down, Zara."

She lifted her head from his shoulder. "Only you would make a promise that big."

"What can I say?" he said. "Everything about me is big."

She cupped him through denim. "I'll say."

Knowing he would take her in the car if they didn't get out of it in the next five seconds, he popped open the door and swung them out. He practically sprinted into his house with her in his arms, making a beeline for his bedroom while Zara laughed, tightly gripping his hips with her legs and his neck with her arms.

They'd made love in the ocean outside his house, but not only had they never spent the night there, he'd never had her in his bed.

Putting her down on top of the navy and white striped duvet, he stepped back to take in the way her hair flowed across his pillow, the rosy flush of her cheeks and bare chest, the beautiful—

Lightning fast, she reached out and yanked him on top of her, cutting off his train of thought.

"That's more like it," she said with evident satisfaction as his heavy weight pushed her into the down of the duvet, even though the movement had knocked off her glasses. "Everything is better when you're close to me."

"*Everything,*" he agreed, his voice made hoarse with emotion. "You're everything I could ever want in a woman."

The first time he'd complimented her, she'd told him he didn't need to shower her with pretty—and false—compliments. Which only made the smile on her lips tonight, and the light in her eyes, all the sweeter.

Placing her hands on either side of his face, she drew him into the sweetest kiss he'd ever experienced. Emotion coursed alongside arousal as, in perfect sync, they stripped away the rest of their clothes. Rory threaded his fingers through hers, and without breaking their kiss, in one long thrust he made her his—just as she made him hers.

"I swear," he said in a raw voice as he stilled above her, "I'm going to make you the happiest woman alive." On all fronts, from the hot sex they'd keep having, to doing everything he could to help her heal from her mother's death, to the amazing future he couldn't wait for. "You'll never regret loving me."

"How could I ever regret loving you?" Emotion throbbed in her voice. "For the first time in so long, I'm happy. Truly happy. And you're the reason why."

They found each other's lips in the same moment, passion and love driving them higher and higher, flying together, soaring in each other's arms.

They were still catching their breath when Zara said, "You know that park ranger outfit you mentioned earlier?" She smiled the kind of soft, post-great-orgasm smile he hoped to see a million times more. "I sure would love to see it."

"Wait here."

She put her glasses back on as he walked into his bedroom closet. Fortunately, it didn't take him long to find what he was looking for. He'd considered throwing the uniform out several times over the years, but something had always held him back. Now he knew what it was—he'd been waiting to wear it again for Zara.

Five minutes later, though he felt like a bit of an idiot, he walked back out. When Zara saw him, her eyes went wide, and her mouth dropped open.

"Oh. My. God." She started to laugh so hard that she actually started snorting. "You must have been *so* scrawny back then." She lifted her glasses to wipe away her tears of laughter.

She was right—the uniform was several sizes too small. His quadriceps were hugely straining the fabric across the legs. As for the long-sleeved, button-up shirt, while he'd managed to get his arms into it, there wasn't a chance of doing up the buttons. He hadn't even bothered with the regulation tie.

"I look like a bad parody of an exotic dancer."

"I know I sound like a broken record after our night in Camden, but you've got to dance again for me now."

There wasn't another soul he would consider doing this for. But he'd do anything to see Zara's eyes light up this way.

"I'll provide the music by whistling," she offered.

She couldn't be serious, could she? "Your whistling is the opposite of music."

But she clearly didn't care what he thought of the atonal wheezing from her lips. Not only that, but he was almost certain she was trying to whistle *Pour Some Sugar on Me* by Def Leppard.

The sooner he started dancing, the sooner he'd be done with it. Rory opened with a few bicep pumps and rolls of his hips. Fifteen seconds into his routine, the seam at his shoulder ripped open. Then, as if the dam had been about to burst all along, the rest of the seams tore—the center back of the shirt, the inseam of the pants, and the back seam between his glutes.

Zara was unable to keep whistling around her extreme fit of the giggles. "You look like an apocalyptic zombie stripper!"

He lifted his arms and zombied toward the bed, saying in a bad Transylvanian accent, "I vant to eat your brains."

Both of them were laughing as they rolled together onto the bed. And as their lips met, Rory knew he could search the whole world over and never find anyone as right for him as Zara. For so long, she'd been right under his nose, but it wasn't until she'd let her walls fall—and he did too—that they both realized what had been right there all along.

Not only magic...but true love.

CHAPTER TWENTY-THREE

Zara woke to the sound of the waves crashing on the shore outside Rory's bedroom window. The sun was starting to rise. And Rory was fast asleep beside her.

More accurately, he was sleeping *beneath* her. She'd never instinctively wrapped her arms and legs around a lover and held on for dear life all night long. Not until Rory.

It had been an absolutely perfect night. Emotional and deep. Sexy and funny.

And most of all, *happy*.

She hadn't felt this happy since before her mother passed away. She'd felt pleased and proud and excited. But never full to the brim with joy.

Miraculously, at some point last night, Rory had managed to blow away the dark clouds that had hovered on the edge of her consciousness these past fifteen years. Clouds she'd assumed would always be there. And despite how shaky she'd felt in the aftermath of spilling her guts to him about her mother, for the first time in a very long time, Zara felt hopeful.

Hopeful that maybe, just maybe, she had finally moved beyond her mother's death—and could start living her life anew.

"I know you have to get into work soon for your photo shoot..." Rory said, his voice still a little gravelly with sleep as he stroked his big hand across her bare hip, then rested it over her stomach. "But I'm okay with quick if you are."

She grinned at him over her shoulder as she said, "I went to bed with Rory Sullivan...and woke up with Mr. Speedy." But she followed up her teasing by pressing her hips into his.

And while it was definitely quick—all it took was the barest touch of his lips against her breasts and his fingers between her thighs for her to be more than ready for him—their lovemaking was no less emotional than the night before. Nor was it any less explosive as he gave her not just one orgasm, but two in rapid succession, before he finally let himself go with a groan of pleasure.

Zara had never felt this solid with anyone. Though they both could be total firecrackers, what they were creating with each other felt so right. No question, he was exactly the kind of man her mother would have wanted for her.

For the first time, thinking about her mother didn't rend Zara's heart.

Fifteen minutes later, after she'd showered and put on one of Rory's long-sleeved shirts as a temporary dress until she could change at her cottage, they sat down to a breakfast of cereal and orange juice at his kitchen table.

Normally, she wolfed down breakfast, but she was so busy gaping at the morning sun glinting off the water that her shredded wheat started to get soggy. "I could get used to having breakfast here," she mused. "This view is incredible."

"Any other reasons?" he said, obviously fishing for compliments.

For once, she didn't feel like making a show of teasing him. "The fact that we love each other is the biggest one," she said simply. And then, "Who would ever have thought the two of us would fall in love?"

"Cassie said she knew all along."

"She did?"

He nodded. "She thinks our bickering hid *a deeper passion*."

Zara digested that information for a few moments. "If your sister saw it even before we did, then maybe it isn't so crazy after all."

"Even if it is," he replied, "there's no one I'd rather be crazy with."

Of course she had to push her cereal bowl aside to kiss him. Which meant that Zara was breathless with desire by the time he reluctantly pulled away.

"You can't be late for your photo shoot," he reminded her.

It took her brain several long moments to accept that there was more to her life than making love with Rory as often as possible. "Right." She gave one last longing look at his lips, before checking the clock and verifying that they really did need to get a move on. "We should go."

They swung by her cottage so that she could change, then headed into the warehouse. Zara was just leaning across the stick shift to kiss Rory good-bye in the warehouse parking lot when her phone rang.

She was on such a high that seeing Brittany's name on caller ID—and knowing her stepsister was surely about to press her case for help with wedding planning—couldn't even bring her down. "Hey, Britt, what's up?"

"Z, I have bad news." A tiny pinprick pierced Zara's joy bubble. "Both James and Angel have come down with chicken pox."

"Both of them? How is that possible?"

"Well, they're dating," Brittany explained, "so I'm assuming that's how. I can try to find two more models, but I doubt they'll be able to do the shoot today."

This photo shoot was Zara's biggest to date. The

two models were a large expense, but nothing compared to the cost of the advertising spots Zara had booked for the promotions they would be starring in. She'd never spent this much money to advertise her glasses before, but she believed she finally had enough customer data and previous sales to warrant making her first really big business investment.

In the early days, Brittany had been nice enough to model the frames. Once Zara had earned enough from selling her glasses to invest in upgrading her branding, Brittany had come through for her again by connecting her with up-and-coming models in Maine. The Instagram feed of the man who had been booked for the day—James Bellings—was one women drooled over. Zara might have been tempted to do a little drooling herself, but even before she'd started sleeping with Rory, she hadn't been able to stop herself from comparing the model to him...and finding the stranger coming up short on all fronts compared to her woodworking colleague. The female model—Angel Davalos—was an absolutely gorgeous woman. Her eyes told Zara that she'd lived life, rather than just sailed through it. Brittany had told her the woman was getting her master's in education, as well, which Zara appreciated.

Rather than pay for a photographer and a studio every time she had a new launch, over the past few years, Zara had taken enough photography classes to feel comfortable behind the camera. She'd also taken classes in graphic design so that she could confidently manipulate photos for print and online advertisements, along with posts for her blog, website, and social media channels.

Only, none of that mattered now that her models couldn't come to the shoot. Zara had prepaid for most of her ad space. She was going to lose a ton of money. Money she couldn't afford to lose.

"What do you want me to do?" Britt asked. "Should I make some calls to the agencies to see if they can offer anyone on super-short notice?"

"Thanks, Britt, but I really need to get the shots today. I'll have to figure something else out."

"What about Rory? I'm sure he'd do whatever he could to help you out. And," her stepsister added with a giggle, "he's certainly good-looking enough to be a model."

Zara wasn't at all surprised by Brittany's reaction to Rory. Even at her stepsister's own engagement party, she'd clearly been wowed by him. But Zara didn't have time to deal with worrying about Brittany trying to steal him away right now. Not when this photo shoot—and losing ridiculous sums of money on the advertisements—would put her business at serious risk if she didn't come up with a solution, and fast.

"Thanks for the heads-up, Britt." She was trying not to panic. "I'll figure something out."

But before she could disconnect, Brittany called out, "Wait! Have you decided whether you're going to help me plan the wedding?"

Having guessed this was coming, Zara replied, "I've got to figure out my photo shoot first. I'll call you later, and we can talk more about it."

She had only just disconnected when Rory said, "I'll do it."

It was the same thing he'd said on Friday morning when he'd found her getting drunk on Prosecco. She hadn't even needed to give him the full details of how screwed she would be if she couldn't do the shoot this morning.

He'd simply offered.

Because he was amazing.

Yet again, she could hardly believe her luck not only that she'd found a man like him—but that he actually loved her too.

"I promise it won't take too long to photograph you in my frames." She wouldn't have a female model in her ads, but Rory would make all of her unisex frames look good. "I'll make it really easy for you. And—"

He put his hands over hers, stilling her wild gesticulations. "I'm happy to help." As he spoke, he stroked the backs of her hands with his thumbs. Just that one tiny touch was enough to set her on fire. "Anything you need, I'm game."

The list of things she needed from him went so far beyond modeling her frames it boggled the mind.

"Where do you want me?" he asked.

Anywhere. Everywhere. All the freaking time.

And not just for sex. But for laughs. And hugs. And cuddling up under a blanket watching a bad movie together.

"I've got everything set up in the other room."

After she made sure her office windows were completely covered so that she could control the light with her rig, he asked, "Am I okay in this?" He gestured to his long-sleeved blue flannel shirt, black T-shirt, and faded jeans. "Or do you need me to grab something else from Turner's house?"

"You look great."

He let his eyes run over her, head to toe. "So do you."

Even after all the intimate things they'd done together, his compliment made her blush. "Thank you."

In an effort to look extra professional while shooting her models, instead of grabbing overalls or baggy jeans, she'd put on a print dress that Brittany had brought her from Thailand. More fitted than her usual outfits, the soft linen was at once incredibly comfortable and attractive. She'd paired the dress with one of her favorite frames—a rainbow color combination that made her smile every time she looked at herself in the mirror.

Fifteen minutes later, she was holding the professional camera at the ready. "Let's shoot this pair first." She handed Rory a forest-green frame, and when he slipped them on, her heart flip-flopped in her chest, practically doing a full somersault.

"How do I look?"

She lifted the camera and began shooting. "You know damn well how good you look."

In fact, she was pretty sure there was nothing sexier than Rory wearing her glasses frames. It helped that he was perfectly comfortable in front of the camera. And when his lips curved up at the corners, her hands actually started to shake from the lust curling through her.

"You're a natural, considering this is your first time modeling."

"Actually, it was an easy way to pay off my loans in college," he told her, looking a little sheepish. "Don't hold it against me."

"It's not your fault you're exceptional-looking. Same with Brittany—there's no point in people like me being upset that you've got more than your fair share of the good genes in the pool."

"What does *people like me* mean?"

The intense look he was giving her made for great photos, so she kept shooting as she said, "It means normal people."

"Normal?" He looked at her as though she were crazy, which wasn't nearly as good a look for her ad campaign, so she lowered her camera. "You are anything but normal, Zara. You're *exceptional*. In every way."

Figuring his comments were a result of being blinded by all the shockingly good sex—and possibly also the fact that he was in love with her, a thought that sent another burst of joy through her—she insisted, "I'm totally okay with not being a traditional beauty queen. Everyone, regardless of whether or not they fit traditional patterns of beauty, should get to feel special and sparkly every day. And that's what I hope my glasses do for people."

She was about to lift her camera to shoot again, when he asked, "Your camera has burst mode, right?" When she nodded, he reached into her box of new frames and pulled out two, handing the blue frames to her and taking the pink for himself. "Set it so it keeps taking pictures, and come get in the shot with me. Let's make some magic together."

Magic was what he had told her his parents had— the reason he believed they had such a strong marriage, even after so many years. And as she set the camera to automatically shoot a new picture every five seconds, then pulled off her glasses to put on the blue ones, Zara wondered, was it possible that she could bring the same kind of magic to his life that he had already brought to hers?

The lenses were clear glass, and without her prescription lenses, everything was fuzzy.

"I'm right here," he teased, waving his arms in an exaggerated motion.

Though she absolutely *hated* having her picture taken—she couldn't think of a time she'd managed to be anything other than stiff as a board in front of the camera—instead of seizing up as she heard the shutter open and close, she found herself playfully smacking his chest. "You're incorrigible."

"Only for you, *baby*."

Just as it always did, his *baby* had her laughing. She was pretty sure she was never going to be able to hear that word again without cracking up. She prayed Brittany and Cameron wouldn't say it during their vows, or Zara was going to embarrass herself during the wedding.

Less than a week ago, her stomach would have twisted up when she thought about the two of them saying their vows. This morning, however, she felt totally fine about it.

Amazing.

"You look happy." Rory brushed a lock of hair from her face before directing her. "Now turn to face the camera so that the rest of the world can see it too."

Feeling a million times more comfortable in front of the camera than she ever had before, instead of fighting him on it, she did as directed. "I am happy." Because when she was laughing with Rory like this, she truly did feel happier than she'd ever thought she could be.

"So...what are you thinking about that's made you so happy? Or should I ask, *who* are you thinking about?"

She poked him in the side. "Fishing for compliments much?"

"I love you too."

Hearing him say the words melted her heart all over again. So she kissed him. Once, then again, and again, and again. She was amazed that when they were kissing, all her fears, her worries, even the dark clouds of guilt and grief from losing her mom, stayed away.

"Seriously, though," he said, "what were you thinking about?"

"For the first time, I feel completely free of the whole Brittany and Cameron thing."

"I'm glad to hear it."

"I am too. Especially since she just asked again if I'd help plan the wedding."

He didn't look surprised. "I thought as much. I take it that means you're still considering doing it?"

"It's going to be one of the most important days of her life," Zara explained. "I know she must really be missing having her father here to celebrate it with her. I can't fill his shoes, but at the very least I can be there to give her support when she needs it most."

Rory was silent for a few moments. "I would feel the same way with any of my siblings, no matter what they had done to hurt me. And I'm amazed by how strong you are. Strong enough to support Brittany despite everything."

"But?" She could hear the word hanging silently in the air between them.

"I hate that she hasn't apologized to you for seeing Cameron behind your back. When I think about how she lied to you..." His hands clenched. "I wish I had been there to protect you, Zara. And I wish I could make sure she never hurts you like that again. That *no one* ever hurts you."

Zara had to kiss him—he could be cocky and over-bearing and had terrible taste in music. But he was also *wonderful*.

"I feel the same way about you," Zara said softly. "I wish I could turn back time to protect you from the way Chelsea and her friend blamed you for her accident, when all along you had tried to be nothing but kind."

They reached for each other's hands at the same time.

"From here on out," he said in a low voice that rumbled with warmth across the surface of her skin, "I promise I'm going to be there for you. No matter what."

"Me too." She smiled into his eyes. "You won't be able to escape me. I'm going to be constantly hovering over you in my superhero cape."

He leaned forward to press his lips to hers, then whispered, "Now I can't stop thinking about how hot you'd look in a skintight superhero outfit. If I bought one online, would you wear it for me?"

She laughed as she said, "Perv," then whacked him lightly in the gut—aka his rock-hard six-pack.

"There's no point in pretending you don't love it."

"I really do," she admitted, before forcing herself to get back to business rather than tearing his clothes off and making love to him again. "I also need at least one great picture of you wearing each frame before I can cut you loose."

For the next two hours, they knocked out pictures of Rory in a dozen different frames. Of course, he looked fantastic in all of them. Fortunately, by the time he started to look a little weary of posing, they were done. She made them each a hazelnut latte, then quickly copied the digital photos onto her computer.

Wow. He hadn't only given her a handful of good ones—she had her pick of great pictures.

"Anything you can use?" He had a faint foam mustache on his upper lip. Zara was glad she didn't have to exercise restraint anymore—she leaned forward to lick it off.

"A better question is whether there will be any I *can't* use." She looked at one where they were both laughing. She doubted she had ever looked that happy before. That alive. "If the frames fly off my shelves as quickly as I think they're going to with these photos, I'd be crazy not to beg you to model for my next set of ads."

"Let me see what you've got."

She waved him away. "There's no time for comments from the peanut gallery." Amazingly, he found a peanut in her office to throw at her, making her laugh as she batted it away. "You can see the pictures once I've put together the best ones for the ads."

"Before this weekend, I'd have been worried about you using the ones where I'm cross-eyed. But now…"

"You'd *still* better be extra nice to me until the ads go live—just in case I switch the pictures out," she joked.

"I'm *more* than happy to be nice to you, Zara."

"Your mind really is always in the gutter, isn't it?"

He put his hands on her hips and pulled her close. "Isn't yours?"

There was no point in denying it. Not when her greedy mouth was already on his, and she was shoving his flannel shirt off his shoulders. "Always," she confessed. "In fact, in the hotel in Camden, I believe you said you were wondering what kind of underwear I wear at the office. Do you still want to know?"

His eyes were full of heat as he said, "Hell yes."

And as she did a sexy little striptease for him in her office—after which he made her see the most blissfully bright stars in the universe as he loved her up against her office door—she was amazed at how Rory was always there just when she needed him.

For so long, her blind faith in life going her way had died along with her mother on Washington Street in Camden. She hadn't thought she would ever be able to embrace joy without the fear of losing the person she loved always hovering in the dark clouds above her.

But Rory had an amazing way of filling up her life with so much sunlight that, for once, the storm clouds didn't dare rain all over her happiness.

CHAPTER TWENTY-FOUR

When Rory headed into his woodshop that afternoon, he was drawn like a magnet to his secret hope chest project. After pulling off the cover, he ran his hands over the shell. His own hopes were in every nail and dowel and joint of the cedar box.

The construction of the frame was fairly simple, but the inlay he had worked out for the top of the box would take every ounce of his concentration.

One hour passed into the next, the lunch he'd missed long forgotten as he worked. He was so deep in his work that he nearly dropped a heavy metal clamp on his foot when he heard a familiar voice say, "Uncle Rory, want to see the new magic trick I just learned?"

Rory tossed a sheet over the hope chest before turning to his nephew with a grin. "Hey, Kev." He did the bro handshake with his nephew, then hugged his sister Ashley, before turning back to Kevin. "Show me."

Kevin put on a top hat, then did the classic spoon-bend trick by pressing down on a spoon and appearing to bend it, then lifting it up a few moments later to show that it was still straight.

"That was awesome. Where'd you learn to do that?"

"Caleb showed me at school. We've started a magic club."

"Can anyone join the club, or do you have to be ten?"

Kevin thought about it for a second. "We can probably make an exception for you. I'll ask the guys."

"Rory, I just realized I never fed you, and you must be starved. I ran out to get some sandwiches and chocolate cake." Zara skidded to a stop in the middle of his workshop when she realized he wasn't alone. "Hi, Ashley. Hi, Kevin. I didn't mean to interrupt. I just wanted to bring Rory lunch since I made him work through it today."

"You didn't interrupt, Zara," Ashley assured her. "And it's great to see you again."

Rory's sisters clearly had a soft spot for Zara. Probably because they loved knowing she was always taking him down a peg.

"I hope my brother has been behaving lately?"

"He's been really great, actually." Zara's blush told him she hadn't forgotten what they'd been up to in her office only hours earlier.

And when she reached for his hand, he wanted to

pump his fist and yell *hallelujah*. Because he knew this public display of affection—something she had been so opposed to before now—was another way of saying how much she wanted to be with him.

Pulling Zara closer, he turned to grin like a fool at his sister.

Ashley should have looked more surprised by their PDA. But clearly, Turner and Hudson had left the pub on Sunday night and spread the word that Rory was falling for Zara. Not that Rory had expected anything less, when being a part of his big family was like living life on a permanent speakerphone.

Still blushing, Zara turned her attention to Kevin. "I like your top hat."

Rory was pretty sure his nephew had a crush on Zara, and this was confirmed by his stammering response to her compliment. Good to know Kevin had good taste in women. It would hopefully be one less thing for them to worry about as he got older. Though he wasn't Rory's kid, he'd always tried to look out for him as though he were.

"Kevin just did a killer magic trick," Rory told her.

"I love magic," Zara exclaimed. "Could you do the trick again for me?"

"Sure," Kevin mumbled, looking embarrassed by all the attention. But by the way he recentered his top hat and cleared his throat, he was pleased by Zara's interest nonetheless.

He did the spoon-bend trick again, finishing with, *"Abracadabra."*

Zara clapped. "That was amazing!"

Kevin mumbled, "Thanks."

Ashley's phone rang, and her face paled when she saw who it was. "Hello." Her voice was flat. "Really?" Her irritation seemed to mount at whatever the other person said. A person whose identity Rory could easily guess. "I'll see what he thinks." She put on a smile that didn't read entirely true as she looked at Kevin. "It's your dad. Do you want to talk to him?"

"Yes!"

She handed Kevin the phone, and he was already talking a mile a minute as he went to sit on the couch in the far corner of Rory's workshop.

"His dad doesn't call for weeks," Ashley said in a low voice ripe with frustration, "and then suddenly, from out of the blue, he wants to be Kevin's best friend. I'm sick of it." She sighed. "Sorry, Zara, I don't mean to air my dirty laundry in front of you."

"It's okay," Zara said. "I've got heaps of dirty laundry myself, if you ever want to see it."

Rory was glad to see his sister smile at Zara's comment.

"I love your glasses, by the way. Whenever I see you," Ashley continued, "I always regret not needing to wear any."

"I love that you wish you had bad eyesight so that you could wear my glasses." Zara was now beaming as much as Kevin. "Don't tell Cassie, but you're officially my favorite Sullivan now."

Rory couldn't resist saying, "I thought *I* was your favorite Sullivan."

Zara leaned in to kiss him, which was good enough confirmation for him. He'd thought it was pretty damn great when she'd reached for his hand in front of his sister—but kissing him in front of Ashley felt like a straight-up public declaration of love.

"Sorry to toss you a sandwich and run," Zara said, "but I've got to get back to work. Great to see you, Ashley. Tell Kevin I'd love to see more magic sometime. And, Rory, if you want to save some of the chocolate cake for later, I'll share it with you."

He couldn't take his eyes from her as she left the room. And it wasn't the fact that she'd just put the most glorious chocolate-cake-licking fantasies into his mind that made it impossible for him to look away.

No, the reason had absolutely everything to do with *magic*.

"I thought Turner and Hudson had to be pulling my leg," Ashley said once he finally turned back to his sister. "But they're right—you're falling big-time for Zara, aren't you?"

"I'm not falling, Ash. I'm already all the way there."

"Wow." She was silent for a long moment as she absorbed the big news. "You and Zara have always set off sparks when you're together. It's just that after what happened with Chelsea, I was worried you wouldn't let yourself try with anyone else, even though it was obvious that she was never going to be the right one for you."

"It was? I thought everyone loved Chelsea and wanted her to be a part of the family."

"We did love her, but that doesn't mean we loved her *with* you. Whereas Zara never takes any of your nonsense. She challenges you in all the best ways." He was surprised to see Ashley frown. "How have you been able to do it?" she asked. "How have you been able to trust again after what happened with Chelsea? How have you been able to risk going to that scary place for Zara? Because as far as my experience goes, people putting their hearts on the line is a very rare thing."

Rory had always taken his duty to look after his younger sister seriously. It killed him that during the years he'd been away at college, she'd hooked up with Kevin's father. Though Rory knew he couldn't rewind time, he still wished there was something he could have done to protect her. Everyone in their family felt the same way. Still, if she hadn't hooked up with the scumbag, she wouldn't have had Kevin. And the world would have been a much sorrier place without his nephew.

"Honestly, I never saw Zara coming." Rory hadn't always felt able to speak so openly to his siblings about his feelings. But Zara had opened him up in more ways than one. "For so long, I told myself that I couldn't stop thinking about her because of how annoying it was when she whistled cheesy pop songs off-key, or left half-finished cups of coffee all over the warehouse, or argued with every word out of my mouth." He shook his head at what an idiot he'd been. "Turns out I was just as blind a fool as you, Lola, and Cassie always say I am."

"You're not *that* bad," his sister teased. But then she grew serious again. "I really am happy for you, Rory. And selfishly, it gives me hope. Because if you can find real love after what you went through, then maybe I can too, one day."

"You made a mistake and trusted the wrong person, Ash. But you can't beat yourself up for it forever. I'm absolutely positive that Prince Charming is out there for you."

"I'm not looking for a hero—a nice, normal guy would be just fine. Although I probably wouldn't kick the actor who plays Thor out of my bed for eating crackers."

"That is *not* the kind of picture a guy needs his sister to put in his head," he grumbled.

"You're welcome," she said with a laugh. "And thanks. I never thought I'd be coming to you for advice about love, but you're actually pretty good at giving it."

"Pretty ironic considering that just a couple of days ago, I was planning to ask you for suggestions on how to woo Zara."

"Really?" Ashley's eyes grew big. "Not only did I not think I'd ever see you all mushy and turned inside-out over a woman—but now you're telling me you almost asked me for my advice rather than barking at me like a know-it-all. Wonders truly will never cease." She still looked a little stunned as she said, "Well, if you ever do need my advice, you know where to find me."

"Sounds like you think I'm going to screw things up." The slightly aggressive words were out of his mouth before he realized they were coming.

She looked at him as though he were crazy. "Of course that's not what I'm saying."

"Sorry, Ash. I don't know where that came from. Forget it."

But she knew him well enough not to let it go just yet. "If you're secretly worried that you're going to make a wrong step and lose Zara—you're wrong. The one thing I know for sure about you is that when you love someone, even if you *do* mess things up for a little while, you always work to find a way to fix it." She looked around his woodshop at the intricate, detailed projects he'd completed, even the ones that had seemed impossible at first. "If anyone has the determination not to give up, it's you."

Kevin ran over, beaming from ear to ear. "Dad was *mega* impressed with my magic trick!"

"Of course he was." Ashley smiled at her son as she slipped her phone back into her pocket. "What else did you guys talk about?" Rory could hear the wariness in her voice, though she was doing her best to disguise it.

"Stuff," Kevin said with a shrug. He turned to Rory. "Hey, can you show me how to use the lathe again? We're making a birdhouse at school, and my teacher said if I know how to use the lathe, I can be in charge of turning the dowel for the perch of the birdhouse."

"Sure." While Rory worked with his nephew, Ashley went over to the couch to send increasingly agitated texts, her mouth pinched and her eyes narrowed as she glared at the screen. She looked like that only when she was dealing with Kevin's father.

"Everything okay?" he called over to her.

She smiled and nodded, but he knew it was entirely for her son's benefit. When it came to Kevin's dad, nothing was ever truly okay. Rory wished there was something he could do to help, but unfortunately, rearranging the guy's face with his fists wouldn't help either Kevin or Ashley.

"Okay," she said forty-five minutes later. "It's time for us to head home and get homework done. Thanks for letting us barge in."

"Anytime," he said, meaning it. "See you guys Friday night."

Which reminded him—he needed Zara's confirmation that she would come to family dinner with him. No doubt they were all dying to know her better.

Once Ashley and Kevin left, he took the sheet off the hope chest and poured everything he felt for Zara, every single one of his hopes and dreams, into it.

Hitting his stride, he worked with pure focus past sundown, stopping only to order pizza to be delivered for dinner and telling them to bring a second, fully loaded pizza to Zara's office, along with a chocolate chip cookie pie for dessert and enough soda to fuel a major league sports team. Having prepaid for the pizza and tip on the phone, he barely looked up when the teenager delivered it. He ate a couple of slices while he waited for the individual inlay pieces on the chest's lid to dry.

By the time he'd cut, sanded, and glued each piece, it was pitch black outside. A sliver of moon was high in the sky, and there were only two cars left in the parking lot—Zara's and his.

Rory uttered a low groan as he stretched his back. He knew better than to hold one position for so long without moving away from his workbench and walking around to keep limber. But he'd been totally in the zone.

He not only hoped the chest would be one more way for Zara to see how much she meant to him—he also hoped that it would be another way for him to help her heal from losing her mother.

He put the sheet over the chest, then headed for Zara's office. If she was still racing against the clock to put her ads together, he would pitch in to help her in any way he could.

From the doorway, he smiled as he took in the scene. She was asleep at her desk, her hand clasping the computer mouse. The pizza box was open and empty, save for half a piece, and she'd demolished both her huge drink and dessert.

He squatted beside her office chair and put his hand on her arm, saying her name several times before she stirred. When her hand holding the mouse shifted, the computer screen came to life on one of the photos from this morning's shoot.

It was a picture of the two of them staring into each other's eyes. Not like a man and woman did when they were just friends. Not like temporary lovers either.

When he looked at that picture, all he saw was pure love.

"Rory? What time is it?" Her voice was slurred with sleep.

He looked at his watch. "Five past one in the morning." He brushed the hair away from her face. "Did you get your ads done?"

She nodded, and her eyes closed again.

"Let's get you home."

Taking her hands in his, he helped her out to his car, where she dozed off again until he guided her from the car to the bedroom in her cottage. With great care, he stripped away her clothes. And though it was tempting to kiss every inch of skin that he bared, he knew she needed sleep more than anything else.

It felt so right to climb into bed with her and wrap his arms around her. Especially when she whispered, "I love you," to him right before she fell asleep.

CHAPTER TWENTY-FIVE

"You're looking particularly smug this morning," Zara noted as they drove to work together on Wednesday.

He grinned at her. "So are you."

It had been the perfect morning. Not only had they had hot morning sex—they'd had it twice, first in bed and then in the shower.

Even better, he hadn't yet seen any storm clouds appear in Zara's eyes. He hoped like hell that they never returned. After battling them for half her life, Zara deserved to know only joy from here on out.

Joy that he was determined to give her in any way he possibly could, both in and out of bed.

"What's on tap for you today?" she asked. "Still working on that secret project?"

He nodded, then deliberately diverted her attention by saying, "I don't need to ask what you'll be doing. I already know you're going be filling orders all day for your new glasses line."

"Pretty confident about the effectiveness of my new model, aren't you?"

"I hear he's pretty special."

He expected her to come back with good-natured snark. Instead, she reached for his hand. "He really is."

Rory turned into the warehouse parking lot, planning to kiss her breathless as soon as he turned off the car. That was when he saw them.

Both Brittany *and* Chelsea were standing outside the building. And they were talking. Though he had no idea why Chelsea was here, he had a bad feeling about it.

As soon as Zara saw her stepsister, she said, "Oh no. I forgot to call Britt back about her wedding. I wonder if that's someone she brought along to help convince me?"

"I very much doubt they've met before," Rory told her. "That's Chelsea."

Zara spun to face him in the passenger seat. "Chelsea? I thought she was in California."

"I thought she was too."

Zara undid her seat belt, and before he could stop her, she was striding toward his ex and her stepsister. "Hey, Britt, we'll talk about your wedding in a minute." With that, she turned to Chelsea and bared her teeth in a faint approximation of a smile. "I'm Zara. Rory's colleague here at the warehouse. And," she said pointedly, "his girlfriend. I'm surprised to see you here."

Chelsea lifted her chin defiantly. "We have a few unresolved issues to discuss."

"You sure as hell do," Zara agreed.

Rory heeded the alarm bells ringing in his head by reaching forward to take Zara's hand before she could deck his ex with it.

Chelsea had the same delicate look about her, as though she might blow away in a strong wind. The only difference a year had made was her California tan. A glance between his ex and Zara confirmed what Rory had finally realized this week: Only a truly strong woman like Zara could ever have rocked his world...and broken through to his stubborn heart.

He focused on his ex. "I've been wanting to talk to you too, Chelsea." He had never had a chance to apologize to her, and as he'd said to Zara, he believed expressing honest remorse was important. And though he no longer believed he was fully to blame for Chelsea's accident, he would always wish he had been kinder to her during their breakup. "Come in, and I'll make you a cup of coffee."

"Make it three," Zara said after he decided it was safe to let go of her hand to unlock and open his garage-style door.

"Four," Brittany said as she led the way into his woodshop. "If my sister is staying, I'm staying too."

"First of all, I don't drink caffeine," Chelsea said to

Rory. "I'd have thought we were together long enough for you to remember that." The implied blame in her words was easily evident. "And this conversation—" Chelsea was looking at Zara and Brittany now. "—is only between me and Rory. So I would appreciate it if you would both leave."

He almost laughed at her assumption that Zara would back off. Zara, on the other hand, actually *did* laugh, a sound of disbelief tinged with fury.

"Once you and your friend put that massive guilt trip on Rory's shoulders after your accident outside the bar," Zara said in a lethal voice, "you involved every person who loves him. Which is why I'm not going anywhere."

"It *was* his fault." Chelsea's cheeks held two blotches of color. "I never would have hurt myself that night if he hadn't been so cruel."

"Cruel?" Zara took a menacing step toward Chelsea before Rory could intervene again. "How dare you say that? How dare you even think it?"

Growing up, Rory's mother had been the ultimate protective mama bear for her seven kids. In this moment, when he should have been working to diffuse the situation, he couldn't stop thinking what a great mother Zara would be to her kids one day. To *their* kids. She wouldn't put up with anyone hurting them.

Unfortunately, while he marveled over Zara, his ex

was busy baring her claws. "You think he loves you?" Chelsea was the one laughing now, a sound as bitter as nails screeching down a blackboard. "Well, let me tell you—he's great at making you think that. Great at making sure you keep hanging on. Until one day, it's over." She snapped her fingers. "Just like that."

"Chelsea—" Rory tried to get between the women, but Zara stepped around him.

"I get how much breakups can hurt. I really do." Zara nodded at Brittany. "My sister stole my boyfriend earlier this year."

Brittany gasped. "You and Cameron only went on a couple of dates!"

Zara turned a look on her stepsister. "We went out for two months. One-sixth of a year. Sixty days. However you want to calculate it, it was a hell of a lot more than a couple of dates." Her point made, Zara refocused on Chelsea. "Being cheated on sucked and hurt, and I was furious with them both."

"You were?" Brittany interjected again.

"Of course I was!" Zara told her stepsister. "Which I promise we are finally going to get into after this." Again, she turned to Chelsea. "But even in my lowest moments, I knew lashing out at them, hurting them the way they'd hurt me, wouldn't bring him back to me. And when I really looked at the situation—when I made myself push away the pain of betrayal and was completely honest with myself—I realized he was never going to be my right person."

Chelsea looked at Rory, tears making her eyes glassy. "I thought you *were* my right person." Her voice was smaller now. All of her looked smaller, actually.

He moved so that his back shielded Zara from Chelsea's line of sight, then took Zara's hands in his. "I love you," he said softly. Then he kissed her and said, "I've got it from here."

Zara stared into his eyes for a long moment before nodding. "You know where I'll be if you need me— getting that long-overdue apology from my sister. Come on, Britt, let's go up to my office."

For once, Brittany looked less than wholly confident as she followed Zara out of his woodshop.

Zara was nearly out of the room when she stopped. "I'm glad you recovered from your accident, Chelsea. Really glad."

Once Rory and Chelsea were alone, it was up to him to come clean with her in a way he never had before. "I'm sorry I did so many things wrong in our relationship. I'm sorry I didn't know how to be honest about my feelings. If I could turn back time and do it all differently, I would. I never wanted to hurt you."

"What's the point in turning back time when I can see now that you never loved me? Not enough. Not the way you love *her*."

He couldn't argue with that, but he still needed Chelsea to know something. "I always cared about you. I was always your friend. And I will forever regret the part I played in your accident. I hope you can find a way to forgive me one day."

Suddenly, she sat on one of his stools, dropping her head into her hands. "This wasn't how this conversation was supposed to go." Her tears started to fall in earnest. "I had this confrontation all planned out. I was going to be brave and tough and put you in your place. You were going to see that I don't need you anymore and how much happier I am without you."

"I can't tell you how glad I am to hear that you're happy, Chelsea. But I already knew how brave you are. And far tougher than you've ever given yourself credit for. I've always admired the way you rose above your childhood and created a new life for yourself. You never needed me."

She lifted her head, tears spiking her eyelashes as she stared at him. He could almost see her synapses making connections, ones she'd never realized had been there all along. "Oh my God…you're right. I *did* do all of that on my own. And more since then. So much more."

He smiled at her. "I'm glad you came to see me. I'm glad we've finally talked."

But she didn't smile back. "I shouldn't have done

it," she said, her voice trembling again. "It wasn't fair to make you feel as though my accident was entirely your fault. I know the things Alexa said were really harsh..." She looked at him anxiously. "Will you forgive me?"

"Of course. You never even had to ask."

She sighed. "Stop reminding me why I fell in love with you in the first place." Then she shook her head as if to dislodge the thought while she slid off the stool. "Good luck with everything, Rory."

And as she drove out of the lot, the guilt that Rory had been carrying around for the past year finally fell completely away. Were it not for Zara opening up his heart—and having his back, no matter what—he likely would never have been able to speak so honestly and openly with Chelsea.

Speaking of having each other's backs...he strained his ears toward Zara's office. There didn't seem to be any yelling.

Though he was tempted to check on them, growing up with three sisters had taught him to tread carefully when it came to getting between women who needed to hash things out. Zara and Brittany's heart-to-heart was long overdue.

Luckily for Brittany, Zara had the biggest heart in the world.

CHAPTER TWENTY-SIX

Zara meant what she'd just said to Chelsea about not wanting to lash out at her stepsister and ruin her happiness, and also that Brittany and Cameron were far better suited. But there was another reason that she hadn't yet admitted. The biggest reason of all.

Zara was afraid she'd lose Brittany if she confronted her.

Since the age of fifteen, her stepsister had been one of the most important people in her life. If not for Brittany, Zara might never have recovered from losing her mom. She couldn't bear the thought of losing her stepsister too.

Only, she hadn't given Brittany nearly enough credit, had she? Because if their relationship was as strong as Zara had always believed, then talking through a messy emotional situation wouldn't make her stepsister run.

Plus, once Zara had seen Chelsea standing outside the warehouse—and had been unable to stop herself from jumping into the fray to protect the man she loved—she now fully understood why he so badly wanted Brittany to apologize for her behavior.

There was nothing worse than knowing someone you loved had been hurt.

She dearly hoped that Chelsea had finally seen the light and apologized to Rory. Zara knew he was hoping for the same for her from her stepsister.

So as soon as Zara shut the office door behind them, she asked the question that had been on the tip of her tongue for a year. "Why did you do it? Why couldn't you have at least waited until we broke up to date Cameron?"

As always, Brittany didn't have a hair out of place, nor was there a single wrinkle in her expensive dress. The look in her eyes, however, was far from self-assured. For the first time in recent memory, she looked nervous and upset. "I know this is going to sound crazy, but I swear I was just trying to show you that you deserved better, that you deserved to be a guy's absolute number one."

Zara folded her arms across her chest. "You're right, that does sound *completely* crazy."

"Let me explain," Brittany begged. "I didn't mean to fall in love with Cameron—"

"Your explanation sucks so far. But go ahead, I'm still listening."

"At first," Brittany continued, "my goal was to

show you that any guy who didn't put you first wasn't worthy of you. I wanted you to hold out for a guy like Rory, who would *never* stray from your side, not in a million years." Brittany scowled. "You should know that once his ex-girlfriend found out you two were an item out there, she tried to give me an earful about all the ways he had wronged her. Clearly, she wanted me to try to break you up. But I didn't buy anything she was saying for a second."

"Why didn't you? You've only spent an hour or so with Rory, so it's not like you know much about him at all."

"Zara, he didn't even *look* at me when you were in Camden. Or here, for that matter."

"That's how you knew? Because he didn't ogle you?"

"I don't want to sound vain—" Brittany ignored Zara's raised eyebrows. "—but every other guy you've been with undressed me with his eyes the moment we met. Only Rory was different. He didn't even seem to notice I was female. Trust me when I say that you've *definitely* found your one in a million with Rory."

One in a million. Zara had never wanted anything more than she wanted her stepsister to be right.

"Just so I'm perfectly clear here," Zara said as she returned her focus to their discussion, "are you saying that you betrayed me with Cameron to *help* me?"

"Yes."

Zara couldn't hold back her laughter at such a classic Brittany move. Her stepsister always wanted to be thanked for whatever she did—even stealing Zara's boyfriend! In some strange way, though, she supposed it was nice to know that she could always count on Brittany to be Brittany.

"I don't know what to say, Britt."

"I do." Her stepsister had never looked so contrite. "I'm an idiot. I can see that now. All this time, I've been trying to convince myself that I only had your best interests at heart, and I swear that I did..." She fell silent for a few moments. "But the truth is that I'm also really envious of you and your career and talent and style."

Zara held up a hand. "We both know I can't touch your style, which then puts everything else you said into question."

"You have more style in your pinkie finger than I have in my entire body. You couldn't pick me out of a lineup of blondes in PR—but you've never been afraid to be unique." Brittany reached for Zara's hand. "I should have found another way to show you how important you are to me." Her eyes filled with tears. "You saved me after I lost my dad, when I thought the whole world had ended."

"You saved me too." Zara's own tears had started

to spill over. She wiped them away with the back of her free hand. "But honestly, Britt, there have to be a *zillion* better ways to show me you love me."

"I know," Britt said with a rueful shake of her perfect hair. "You have *no idea* how guilty I've felt all year about my misguided attempt to take care of you. So guilty that I've only made it worse by trying to pretend I didn't do anything wrong."

"It wasn't losing Cameron that hurt," Zara told her. "What hurt most of all was worrying that I had lost *you*."

"You would *never* lose me!" Brittany threw her arms around Zara, and it was such a relief to hold her stepsister tight. "Does this mean you forgive me?" Brittany said into her hair a few beats later.

Zara smiled at her irrepressible hope and confidence. "Of course I forgive you. Although...you aren't the only one who didn't tell the complete truth."

Brittany cocked her head. "About what?"

"At your party on Saturday, Rory and I weren't a real couple." At Brittany's incredulous look, she explained, "He found me freaking out over your engagement the day before, and he offered to go as my pretend date to show you that I was doing just fine."

"But..." Brittany looked toward Rory's workshop. "He just told you he loves you. And you were sure as heck acting like you love him too. I can't believe that was just an act for his ex's benefit—or for mine."

"It wasn't." Zara was glad that she could finally talk about this with her stepsister. She'd missed their heart-to-hearts this year. "Something changed for us during your engagement party. And even though none of it was supposed to be real—"

"You couldn't keep your hands off each other."

"Do you blame me?" But Zara needed her stepsister to know one more thing. "What we have is so much more than just chemistry. I really love him, and he really loves me." She ran a hand through her hair. "Honestly, I'm still more than a little surprised by how everything changed so fast for us."

"Falling in love is pretty epic, isn't it?"

"It is." Before she could think better of it, Zara added, "And terrifying."

"I know the sky fell for both of us once," Brittany said, "but we can't live every moment worrying that it will fall again. You deserve to be happy, Z. We both do."

It was exactly what Zara had been telling herself since joy had finally broken through. That it was okay to be happy. That it was okay to embrace contentment. That it was okay to lose herself in the delight of being with Rory. She couldn't express just how helpful it was to hear her stepsister confirm that all of those things were true.

"I'll do it," Zara said abruptly. "I'll help with your wedding."

"Fantastic!" Brittany was grinning from ear to ear. "I actually brought my folder of ideas, if you've got some time to go over them now."

"Good to know I'm not a sure thing," Zara joked.

"You're my sister." Brittany gave her a kiss on the cheek. "I knew you'd agree to help. And I have a feeling it won't be too long before I help *you* plan the wedding of the century to that gorgeous woodworker of yours."

"Whoa!" Zara tried to laugh off her suddenly racing heart. "We're only at the beginning."

Brittany rolled her eyes. "You're so adorable when you're in denial." Then she pulled the world's fattest folder out of her bag, pieces of lace and silk falling out onto Zara's desk. "We've got a million decisions to make, so we'd better get started."

★ ★ ★

Three hours later, Zara's head spun from her crash course in wedding planning. Brittany had, not unexpectedly, left the folder behind so that Zara could continue to make headway on the details.

She went to find Rory just as he was coming to find her. They were in the middle of the hallway between their workspaces when he threaded his hands into her hair and gave her one of the best kisses of her life. Even when one of their co-workers walked past, they didn't let each other go.

At last, he asked, "Everything go okay with Brittany?"

Wondering how on earth he could talk when she was still trying to get her breath back, she nodded. "Everything's great. Although you'll never believe her crazy reasoning for what she did. But before I tell you about that, I need to know—how did things go between you and Chelsea after we left?"

"Thank you for being my own personal superhero," he said first. And then, "We cleared the air. It was good to finally get a chance to talk things through. We both needed to say we were sorry."

"Britt and I did too."

"So I made the right decision in leaving you alone with her for so long?"

"Absolutely. You would only have ended up smothered in napkin samples if you'd made the mistake of walking into my office."

"After attending more than a dozen weddings for my cousins the past few years, there's a good chance that I know more about putting one on than either of you."

"You really shouldn't have told me that," Zara said. "Because now I know *exactly* how to keep you in line.

One call to Britt to drop that little nugget her way, and you're toast."

"Actually..." He pulled her close. "I have a *much* better idea for how you can keep me in line."

"I haven't checked my email yet today to deal with all those orders you claim are going to be pouring in," she said. But of course that didn't stop her from taking his hand and leading him into her office to see if they were on the same page.

And after they'd torn each other's clothes off and had a glorious quickie, she could confirm that they most definitely were.

CHAPTER TWENTY-SEVEN

The next twenty-four hours were a blur. Once Zara had finally logged on to email and checked her voice mail Wednesday afternoon, she'd learned that her new ads had been a bigger hit than even Rory had anticipated. Orders were through the roof, and she'd spent nearly every second since packaging and mailing her frames to buyers from around the world.

Joyce from the post office was cracking jokes about Zara spending more hours on the premises than most of the full-time employees, she had bought out all the packing supplies from the local stores, and her inventory was down to the bare bones.

She'd just gotten off the phone with her materials supplier to let them know she needed a rush on her next order to meet the increased demand when she felt two strong hands massaging her shoulders.

"Mmmm, that feels so good."

"Tell me how I can help." He spun her chair around so that they were face-to-face, then resumed massaging her shoulders from the front. "I'm done for the day, so I'm all yours."

Zara had long thought that one of the biggest bene-fits to starting her own business was that it kept her too busy to stew about everything she wanted to avoid. But even she knew when she'd hit her work-hour limits. Fortunately, she had an idea about another good way to make sure the storm clouds couldn't possibly return to ruin her newfound happiness.

"And remember," he added, "nothing's off-limits." He put on his best lecherous look. "No matter how filthy."

"Perv." But she had to pull him down for a kiss an-yway. She was loved and in love. She'd made up with her stepsister. And her business was growing like gangbusters. Surely there was no way the darkness could get back in now. "I want to turn it up to eleven."

"Tell me more, baby."

They both laughed at his faux-smarmy *baby*.

"Well, I am pretty impressed by the armadillo in your pants."

"Armadillo?" He looked confused...and then the light bulb went on. "Are you trying to tell me that D minor is the saddest of all keys?"

"Ding ding ding!" She grinned. "The Criterion Theatre is playing *This Is Spinal Tap* this week between new releases. What do you say we go annoy everyone at the showing by quoting all the best lines and making out during the rest of the movie?"

"I know I keep saying this—" He pulled her up out of her seat. "—but you really are the perfect girlfriend."

★ ★ ★

For two hours, they fed each other candy, competed over who could yell out the classic lines louder—it was part of the *This Is Spinal Tap* experience, so they didn't feel bad about disturbing the other attendees—and laughed their heads off at one of the best mockumentaries ever made.

Oh yeah, and making out with Zara in the dark theater was pretty damned awesome too.

By the time they left the movie, the sun had set. A food truck was parked in front of the theater, pumping out the smell of fries and bratwurst.

"Perfect," Zara said. "I'm *starved*."

She acted like she hadn't eaten in days, and this was after they'd already polished off an extra-large popcorn, huge red Slushies, and several boxes of candy. Rory was confident that his mother was going to *love* Zara—but given that few things made Beth Sullivan happier than feeding people, she was going to be even more over the moon about Zara and her appetite at the dinner table every Friday night.

Which reminded him… "You're in for dinner with my family tomorrow night, right?"

"Of course. But only if you're sure that your parents won't be thrown off by having to add another person on short notice."

"We're Sullivans. The more the merrier."

"What should I bring?"

"Just your beautiful self. My mom always cooks for a thousand. And I'm sure she'll be pulling out the red carpet for you, so if you happen to have any favorite Irish dishes, I'll let her know."

"Why would she want to roll anything out for me?"

"She knows I wouldn't bring you to dinner if you weren't important to me. And I'm sure my brothers and sisters have been singing your praises to my parents this week. Plus," he added with a smug grin that he guessed would push her buttons, "now that you've finally done the impossible by taming the biggest prize in the family, who wouldn't be impressed by you?"

"I've certainly won the biggest—"

He kissed away the rest of her sentence, which surely would have been stuffed full of expletives and insults.

The woman taking orders in the food truck cleared her throat to get their attention. "What would you like to eat tonight?"

Zara pinched him before he could give one of his

inappropriate,   fourteen-year-old-worthy   responses. "Two bratwurst with everything, an extra-large fries, and a chocolate shake." She turned to him. "Your turn."

"I'll have the same." After he paid, he said to Zara, "We are going to have one heck of a grocery bill."

"We've only just started dating," she was quick to point out. "It's not like we're moving in together."

Their shakes came up in the pickup window, and she had just put her hands around the cups when he said, "Move in with me."

"What?" Zara fumbled the cups, and they tipped. Rory set them back to rights before they fell and splatted all over the sidewalk.

Though he knew she'd heard him perfectly the first time, he repeated himself. "Move in with me."

But from the stunned look on her face, she was still wildly thrown off by his proposition. "You're serious, aren't you?"

"If you moved in, we could swim wild together every single day. I'd make sure there was always chocolate cake in the house." He leaned in to whisper, "We could alternate whose body we eat it from. Monday, Wednesday, and Friday, I'll lick it off you. Tuesday, Thursday, and Saturday, you can lick it off me. As for Sundays…" He let her see everything he felt for her as he said, "Sundays will be for staying in bed all day long. Even after we've polished off the cake."

Their orders were called, and he was almost positive that her legs and arms were shaking as she took the tray over to the plastic tables and chairs on the sidewalk.

"If someone told me a year ago that I was going to fall for you," she said in a voice that was notably breathless from the erotic picture he had just painted, "I would never have believed it."

"Is that a yes?"

She rolled her eyes. "You really are a piece of work."

"A maybe, then?"

She shoved a French fry between his lips. "Maybe this will keep your mouth busy."

Knowing it would be better to give her time to see the light, instead of continuing to push her on moving in with him, he made her laugh instead with stories about the scrapes he and his siblings had gotten into when they were kids. Then she regaled him with the tale of how her first attempt at making glasses frames had been such a disaster that they'd melted while she was wearing them on the beach, leaving her with orange and red circles around her eyes for a month.

The easy conversation and laughter didn't stop the sparks from flaring between them, however. Fortunately, after they walked back to her cottage and Zara closed the door behind him, she said, "Oh look, there's some cake left. And since it's Thursday, that must mean it's my turn to lick it off *you*."

Just hearing her say the words was nearly enough to make him lose it. That didn't stop him, however, from racing her to the cake box in the fridge. He beat her by a hair, grabbing the box and holding it over his head.

She went onto her tippy-toes to reach for it, deliberately rubbing her body against his. "You don't play fair, do you?"

"All's fair in love and who gets to eat chocolate cake off who first. Besides, that was just a hypothetical weekly schedule. And since you haven't agreed to move in with me yet..." He shrugged as though their little kitchen tussle couldn't be helped.

"If you think I'm going to agree *now*, you've got your head even farther up your—"

He covered her mouth with his, kissing away the rest of her snarky sentence. But it wasn't enough just to kiss her. He needed to touch her, to hold her, to show her exactly how much he loved her.

He put the cake box down and lifted her onto the counter beside it. She wrapped her legs around his waist, and when her billowy skirt lifted to bare her legs, he ran his hands over her thighs before pulling her dress up and off her body. Lucky him—she was wearing another incendiary lingerie set, this one bright green and gorgeously sheer.

He reached into the cake box, smeared cake onto the tip of one breast, then lowered his mouth to lave her aroused flesh through the fabric. Her head fell back as she arched into his mouth and threaded her fingers into his hair to hold him to her. As he turned his attention to her other breast, he danced his fingertips up her thigh to the heated core of her arousal. Covering her fabric-covered sex with his palm, he pressed the heel of his hand against her as she rocked into it.

"Damn you." She lifted her head to look into his eyes. "Damn you for putting that insanely sexy picture of living together into my head. Damn you for being so irresistible. Damn you for stealing my heart when I didn't think it would ever happen."

Yet again, Rory was amazed that even in the midst of the sexiest possible moments, making love with Zara was exactly that—*love*.

"You stole mine too," he whispered against her lips, then kissed her at the same moment he slid his hand beneath the fabric and entered her with his fingers.

He swallowed her cries of pleasure as she climaxed so unexpectedly, and so beautifully. He could spend every moment of his life making her happy and never want for another thing.

"My turn," she said once her tremors finally subsided.

Before he fully realized her intent, she grabbed a fistful of his shirt in each hand and yanked it open. Buttons went flying, but neither of them cared as she scooped up some cake and spread it onto his chest and stomach.

"Time to switch places," she said. And when she hopped off the counter, he was more than happy to take her place. "Mmm," she said when his chest and abs were at eye level. "Now you're the perfect height to be my very sweet treat." Leaning forward, she lightly licked the right side of his chest. His muscles jumped in response, making her smile. "This is *fun*." She ran her tongue over his left side, and when those muscles jumped, she laughed. "I could do this all day."

Now it was his turn to groan. The power was entirely in her hands—and mouth—now. She could so easily keep teasing him like this.

And he would love every single second of it.

Every sweet press of her lips, her tongue, even her teeth, over his chest and abs, made the fire inside him burn hotter and hotter. He was so lost to the feel of her tongue running the ridges between his abdominal muscles that he didn't realize she'd unbuttoned his jeans until she was reaching into denim and cotton to wrap one hand around him.

"Not just a pretty face," she murmured as she lowered her lips to his erection. "You're pretty *everywhere*."

And then she was taking him inside her mouth, and it was only through sheer force of will that he held it together. But his self-control could hold out only for so long, so before she could send him all the way over with another long, slow lick of her tongue, he pulled her up onto the counter with him.

She laughed as she straddled him, the sound quickly changing to a gasp as he gripped her hips and drove up into her.

"*Rory.*" She braced herself on his chest with her hands. Her gaze held his as she stilled over him. "Yes, I'll move in with you."

He pulled her mouth down to his and kissed her with all the love in his heart...then gave her that same love not only with his body, but with his soul too.

CHAPTER TWENTY-EIGHT

Every part of Zara's life was gunning happily ahead at a hundred miles an hour. She was slammed with another wonderful rush of orders on Friday. Brittany was extremely chipper over having her stepsister as her wedding-planning partner. And Zara's body and heart had never felt more alive.

The person responsible for her massive turn of fortune on all fronts?

Rory Sullivan.

She should have guessed that pictures of him wearing her frames would send orders pouring in so fast that she'd have to put a note on her website changing her shipping timeline from twenty-four hours to two weeks, so that she could build more frames in the interim.

But how could she have predicted that, when she hadn't been able to predict that she would not only fall in love with Rory—but agree to move in with him as well?

It was just that when Rory was loving her, or making her laugh, or spouting off his far-too-smart mouth—and especially when he was making her breathless, and boneless, with his sexy kisses and caresses—it felt like the storm clouds that had been ever present in Zara's heart for the past fifteen years disappeared completely.

Even tonight, on the verge of meeting nearly everyone in his family, she wasn't nervous. On the contrary, she couldn't wait to learn more about the people who had helped shape the extraordinary man she'd fallen in love with.

At six p.m., they took his car from the warehouse, parking outside his parents' home. But as they went up the front walk, Rory stopped them before they reached the door. "My family can be a bit much the first time you're surrounded by all of us. If you start freaking out for any reason, don't forget our secret code." He stuck out his tongue and crossed his eyes.

Had she been at all nervous, Rory making her laugh at his silly face would have been the perfect remedy. "I already know how great your family is," she reassured him. "So there will be no need for this." She crossed her own eyes and hung her tongue out of the side of her mouth.

He leaned in to nip at it, which spun into a kiss, of course. One so hot that it temporarily made her forget they were standing in front of his parents' home.

The front door swung open midsnog. "Yuck!"

Zara broke away from Rory to see Kevin standing in the doorway, looking *horrified* to find his uncle sucking face with her.

"Hey, dude." Rory kept his arm around Zara's waist as they walked inside. "Got any new magic tricks to show me?"

It was exactly the right way to wipe the disgust off the ten-year-old's face. "Sure. I'll go get my bag."

"Well, hello there." A drop-dead-gorgeous woman close to Zara's age walked into the room, her hand outstretched. "I'm Lola, and it is *fabulous* to finally meet you." She grinned as she added, "Nice kiss, by the way. We were all debating whether we'd need the fire extinguisher to make sure the house didn't burn down."

Zara should have been embarrassed. After all, Rory's sister had just confirmed that his entire family had seen them making out. But she couldn't get over the vision in front of her.

Lola looked as though she had walked off the pages of a fifties pinup calendar. From her hair to her makeup to her bountiful curves, she was breathtaking. Even Rory's looks couldn't compete with his sister's—and that was really saying something, considering he was easily one of the best-looking men on the planet.

Zara spoke without thinking. "What would it take

to convince you to model my eyeglasses frames for my next set of ads?"

"What's on offer if I agree to do it?" Lola playfully responded.

Belatedly, Zara realized she should have waited at least a few more minutes before propositioning Rory's sister. Especially considering that Lola surely had to deal with people drooling over her stunning looks all the time. "Sorry, I shouldn't have just blurted that out. Can we both forget I suggested it?"

But before Lola could respond, Rory bragged, "Zara sold out of her inventory this week after putting *my* face on her ads."

The spark of sibling rivalry between them was palpable as Lola shot back, "I guarantee sales from my ads would *crush* yours." She turned to Zara. "I'd love to model your frames. Just let me know when you need me." She nodded toward the kitchen. "Now come into the kitchen and meet everyone."

Zara was surprised by the way her heart began to race. She told herself it was simply because she'd been caught kissing Rory and then narrowly avoided a misstep with Lola. Though Rory had said people often felt overwhelmed by meeting his entire family for the first time, Zara had been sure that she would be totally fine with it.

As soon as they walked into the crowded kitchen,

little Ruby grinned and held out her arms. "Zzzzz!"

"Hello, Zara." Flynn handed Ruby into Zara's waiting arms. "It's nice to see you again so soon."

"It's great to see you again too, Flynn." Zara nuzzled Ruby's cheek, closing her eyes as she breathed in her clean baby smell.

"Mom, Dad," Rory said, "this is Zara."

"Thank you so much for inviting me to dinner tonight."

"We're very glad you're here." His mother wiped her hands on a kitchen towel, then came around the kitchen island and took Zara's free hand in both of hers. "I'm Beth, and I'm not sure how we've managed to go this long without meeting each other, but it is our sincere pleasure to have you here tonight."

"It sure is." A man with salt-and-pepper hair took Zara's hand and shook it. Zara's heart skipped a beat as she realized she was looking at Rory thirty years from now. He was still handsome as sin, but his father's strength was not in the least diminished by the years. "I'm Ethan." He winked. "Welcome to the madhouse."

It turned out that he wasn't exaggerating. Over the course of the next few minutes, she met Rory's brother Hudson, said hello to Turner, whom she'd met briefly at the warehouse earlier that year, gave Cassie and Ashley hugs, and even scratched behind the ears of the dog lying beneath the kitchen table. Meanwhile, Ruby never let go of her, almost as though the little girl thought she needed the support.

Fortunately, it was easy to be swept into the chatter, and laughter, and food being passed around. At one point or another, each of Beth's children, her husband, Flynn—even the dog—asked Beth for an opinion, or assistance, or simply wanted her attention. She made it seem so effortless, juggling final dinner preparations along with the needs of her big family. And throughout, she went out of her way to include Zara in the conversation.

Everything Rory had told Zara about his mother made it clear just how much he loved and respected her. But now that Zara had finally met her, she realized it wasn't just this meal that revolved around Beth Sullivan.

The entire family revolved around her.

"Uncle Rory! Uncle Hudson! Uncle Turner! Grandpa! Mr. Flynn!" Kevin skidded back into the room. "I've set up my magic table outside! Come on." At the last second, Ashley's son turned to Zara. "You can come too if you want."

"Thanks," she said with a smile. "How about I catch the second round?" She didn't want to take Rory away from his time with the guys. And she wanted to get to know his mother and sisters better.

Rory dropped a kiss on the top of Zara's head before he left.

Ashley looked fondly after her son as the men all followed him into the backyard, then sent Zara a wry smile. "Thank God Kevin has his uncles and grandpa to make up for his worthless burnout of a dad."

Zara wasn't sure what to say to that. Which Lola clearly picked up on, saying, "It isn't Friday night dinner if at least one of us doesn't air our dirty laundry." She leaned forward with clear anticipation. "Got anything juicy to share with us, Zara?"

There was no way to keep her cheeks from flaming as Zara thought about all the extremely *juicy* things she and Rory had done together this week.

"Well, then..." Lola looked impressed. And also a little grossed out. "I'd ask you for details if it wasn't my brother making you blush like that."

"Lola!" Cassie called out her sister with a shake of her head. "It's also not Friday night dinner," she said to Zara, "if we don't horribly embarrass someone."

"True," Lola agreed, "and I promise I'll stop as soon as I tell you that I'm *really* glad Rory managed to convince you to go out with him."

Ruby beat Zara to a reply by grunting and filling her diaper in a very impressive way. They all laughed as Cassie hurried over to take her into a back bedroom for a diaper change.

At last, Zara said to Lola, "That's nice of you to say,

even if I'm not sure exactly why you feel that way."

"Well, first of all, your glasses are killer. I design textiles, and I hope you don't mind if I steal the look for a new line of girls-with-glasses fabrics."

Zara's frames were oversized tortoiseshell today. She'd worn them for an extra confidence boost. "I'd be honored."

"Great," Lola said. And then, "Second, you're clearly one of Ruby's favorite people—and that kid has some serious BS radar. I was babysitting her this week, and when my smarmy studio landlord bent down to pretend he was interested in playing with her, she nearly walloped his head off with her stuffed elephant."

"I would have liked to see that," Zara said, grinning at the picture of Warrior Ruby protecting her aunt from one of the many guys who likely wanted only one thing from her.

"And the biggest reason," Lola said, "is because I've never seen Rory look like this before—like he's found the missing piece of his heart. I'm not sure I even thought he was capable of it."

"It's true," Cassie agreed as she and Ruby returned to the kitchen. Rory's sister was clearly a master of diaper changes to have done it that quickly. "Now that he's with you, Rory is glowing so brightly with happiness he's practically neon."

Ashley, whom Zara noticed was quieter than her

sisters, nodded. "Not that we're saying any of this to put pressure on you not to dump him—"

"Speak for yourself," Lola interjected. She looked totally serious as she said to Zara, "As much as I enjoy seeing Rory knocked off his pedestal from time to time, I really hope you're going to stick around."

At last, Beth stepped in. "Ashley, Lola, Cassie— since I'll be opening up the café early tomorrow morning, and your brothers did the cooking last Friday night, I'm going to bow out now and let the three of you finish dinner." Beth handed Zara a Dublin Irish Cocktail, which was a mixture of whiskey, sour apple schnapps, and cranberry juice, then led her to a couch on the patio just outside the kitchen door.

"I'm sorry about that." Beth's Irish accent made her voice seem especially gentle. At the same time, there was undeniable strength to her. "I'm afraid we're all terribly excited about spending time with the woman who has stolen Rory's heart."

"Please, don't apologize. I love the way everyone feels comfortable saying whatever's on their mind. As I'm sure Rory will confirm for you, if he hasn't already, that's my usual MO too."

"I'm glad to hear it. I've always known it would take a very strong woman to capture his heart." Beth took a sip of her drink. "I understand that you make eyeglasses frames. It's such a clever way to combine art and design with a practical purpose. Are the lovely pair you're wearing one of your creations?"

"They are." Zara was warmed by Beth's compliment. It was exactly the way she would have wanted her own mother to feel about the work she poured her heart into. "I've been making frames for nearly eight years. The business has been a slow build—until just this week, when Rory volunteered to model frames for a new set of ads. Now I can't keep them in stock." She looked out into the backyard at the same moment he turned to look for her. She couldn't keep from smiling as their eyes met. "As you can imagine, he's quite pleased with himself."

"That sounds like my son," Beth said, laughing. "I also understand that you're a recent transplant to Bar Harbor?"

"Yes, I moved here a year ago from Camden, but I grew up in Kennebunkport."

"Both lovely towns," his mother remarked. "The breakwater beside Colony Beach is one of my favorite spots in Maine."

It had been Zara and her mom's special place. Though it was sheer coincidence for Beth to mention it, it wasn't easy for Zara to respond in a normal voice. "Mine too."

Just then, Lola stuck her head out of the kitchen door. "Mom, Ashley's going to ruin the colcannon.

She's putting too many scallions in it."

Ashley popped her head out next. "I'm the one who's in the café every day. Lola doesn't know what she's talking about."

"Yes, I do."

"No, you don't."

Beth regarded her daughters with raised eyebrows. "I suggest the two of you resolve things before I get out *The Forgiving Tree* and make you sit together and read it."

Both women groaned. "Anything but that," Lola said at the same time as Ashley said, "Forget we said anything."

Beth laughed as the door closed behind them. "All seven kids can recite that Berenstain Bears book by heart. As you can imagine, they've read it many, many times after getting in loads of scrapes when they were little. They all still get into plenty of scrapes, come to think of it. Of course, as their mum, I love them no matter what."

It was Zara's turn to respond...but the force of the blow to her heart was so sudden, and so enormous, that it was all she could do not to utter a keening cry of pain and double over.

And as the storm clouds came rushing back, thicker and darker than ever, Zara had the fleeting thought that she should have seen this coming. Not only was she still desperate to be forgiven for the last words she'd said to her mother—but sitting here with Beth, and watching her interact with her daughters, made Zara long with every piece of her heart for her own mother.

"Zara?" Beth's voice seemed to be coming from a distance. "Is everything okay?" A hand covered hers. "Tell me what's wrong, and I'll do whatever I can to help."

But Beth couldn't help her. Not when Zara's grief, and her guilty conscience, would forever steal her chances for true happiness.

Because even if the Sullivans weren't as perfect as she'd once assumed, the more time she spent around Rory's family, the more she longed for what they had.

Unwavering support.

Unconditional love.

And, most of all, a great mom whom they all clearly adored.

Zara had so desperately wanted to bury her head in the sand. And when she'd been floating on a love cloud with Rory, she'd managed to stuff the pain away for a little while. But Brittany had been right when she'd said that the longer she tried to pretend she hadn't screwed up, the guiltier she ended up feeling.

Now, at the worst possible moment, with nearly Rory's entire family present to witness Zara's breakdown, she finally understood that she would never again be able to pretend the way she had for fifteen years. She'd never be able to stuff her guilt, her pain, her regrets, down deep. She'd never be able to go about her daily life without being stabbed in the chest by the painful memories.

Not when all it had taken was a few minutes with Rory's mom for Zara to completely fall apart.

"I'm sorry." She abruptly pulled away from Beth's touch. "I need to go."

The silly face Rory had asked her to warn him with if she started freaking out was the last thing on Zara's mind as she jumped up from the outdoor couch, ran through the kitchen, then out the front door.

As she dashed through the square, a bolt of lightning struck the town hall's tower out of a sky that had been blue only minutes before. By the time she reached her cottage, it was pouring. She fumbled for her keys, let herself in, and slammed the door shut behind her.

But though she was now safe from the storm raging outside, she'd never be safe from the one raging inside of her.

CHAPTER TWENTY-NINE

From the moment Zara walked into his parents' kitchen, it was obvious to Rory just how much everyone in his family liked her. In fact, Turner and Hudson had both commented on how impressed they were that Rory had managed to snare her.

He felt exactly the same way—whatever lucky star he'd been under the day she walked into his life, he'd be forever grateful.

Just a few minutes ago, Rory had been pleased to see Zara chatting with his mother on the backyard patio. If anyone knew how to make sure his girlfriend felt welcome, it was Beth Sullivan. No one was immune to her Irish charm.

Still, Rory wished he and Zara had had a chance to talk more before coming to dinner tonight. The last thing he wanted was for her to feel like his family was coming on too strong—even if Zara had given him every assurance that she was well up to meeting most of them at once. Work had been crazy today, though. She had been slammed with orders, and he'd been working against the clock to finish the hope chest. He planned to give it to her later tonight, when they were alone.

Kevin had just finished showing them a new trick, saying, *"Abracadabra!"* with a flourish, when lightning flashed. The sky had been blue all day, but it wasn't odd for Maine weather to turn on a dime.

Rain was starting to fall as they helped Kevin gather up his bag of tricks. But as he turned to head into the house, Rory was surprised to see his mother standing alone on the outdoor brick patio with an alarmed look on her face.

He was at her side a moment later. "What happened? Where's Zara?"

"We were talking when she suddenly looked upset." His mother couldn't hide her concern. "Then she apologized and said she couldn't stay."

Rory's chest tightened as the fear of losing Zara gripped him hard and wouldn't let go. They'd declared their love for each other, though that didn't automatically mean everything was perfect. He'd tried to convince himself that any hesitation on Zara's part—like when he'd asked her to move in with him—was perfectly natural. After all, who wouldn't be a little wary about things moving so fast?

But deep in his heart, he'd known that what was eating away at her was far bigger than just the speed, or unexpectedness, of their relationship.

"I've got to find her. I've got to get her to talk to me."

His mother put a hand on his arm. "Please tell her that I didn't mean to upset her in any way. And promise me you'll remember that just because love isn't always easy, that doesn't mean it isn't right."

"I'm not going to give up on her," he reassured his Mom. "Not when I know that Zara is the one I've been waiting for my whole life—and that I'm the one she's been waiting for too."

★ ★ ★

Though he could cover the distance to Zara's cottage on foot in fifteen minutes, he drove to get there faster. Pure instinct had him taking the hope chest out of the backseat and jogging up her front walk. His heart was in his throat as he knocked on her door.

The good news was that she opened it immediately. The bad news was that there was not only no smile or snarky comment or kiss hello...there was no light in her eyes either.

Rory, frankly, had never imagined a world in which Zara's spark blew out.

"You're probably wondering why I left," she said as she stepped aside to let him in out of the storm.

Even her voice was flat, and fear squeezed his chest

as she walked over to the couch and sat. He sat too, putting the hope chest on the floor beside the coffee table, but she didn't seem to notice it as she looked down at her clasped hands.

"I was so sure…" When she paused, he thought emotion might finally break through. But she quickly bottled it up. "I thought we could date each other without drama, then break up without problems or hurt feelings. But I was wrong." She looked like she was reciting a page from the encyclopedia. "Our relationship did go all pear-shaped. Just like you were worried it might."

He put out his hand for hers, but she shifted just out of reach. His voice wasn't entirely steady as he said, "Nothing has gone pear-shaped. I still love you, and you love me." He would never believe otherwise. "Talk to me, Zara. Tell me what's wrong. Even if you think I don't want to hear it, you know you can always tell me the truth."

She was silent for a long moment. Finally, she said, "I was supposed to help you get over what happened with your ex. But how can I do that when I'm just like her?"

Of all the things he'd thought she might say, this was nowhere on the list. For all that she was perfectly calm and detached, he was getting more riled by the second. "You're *nothing* like Chelsea! Until the night we broke up, she did whatever I wanted. She thought the sun rose and set on me. She never argued with me about anything. She always played by the rules. You're her *exact* opposite."

"Actually," Zara replied in that same too-calm voice, "we're the same in the only way that counts. You didn't break things off with her for two years because you knew how badly she needed your family. Well, that's exactly how I feel." She looked away, as though she couldn't bear to face him. "Do you have any idea how much I want to be a part of your family? How much I want to spend time with your mom so that she can fill the hole inside of me that losing my mom left?" A tiny spark flickered in Zara's eyes—but it came from emotions he never wanted to see on her face again. Shame. Guilt. Fear. "One day, when you want to break up with me—which we both know will happen sooner or later, because I'm still such a mess— you'll think you need to let things linger the way you did with your previous girlfriends. Which is the opposite of everything I wanted for you when we embarked on this week together. I can't do that to you, Rory."

Everything she'd just said was gut-wrenching. And yet, unlike the night when she'd told him about her mom, she seemed totally shut down and matter-of-fact. Rory had always been able to get a rise out of her—

whether good or bad. For the first time, he couldn't get anything from her at all.

But as he'd told his mother, he would never give up on Zara. *Never.*

"Thank you for being honest with me and baring your heart to me the way you just did," he said softly. "Now I'm going to do the same for you, because I love you, and that's what love is all about. Sharing the good *and* the bad, no matter how hard or scary." Though he didn't reach for her hand, he scooted closer, needing to erase as much distance between them as he possibly could. "I screwed up, Zara, by wanting so badly to believe that falling in love and agreeing to move in together meant everything was resolved. I knew that you couldn't simply shake off the guilt and grief you feel over losing your mom, but I still hoped that if I just kept loving you with everything I am, and if I made sure you were always laughing, that I could heal your pain. I also hoped that after you spent time with my family, you'd see that not only do *I* have your back, but *all* of the Sullivans are now on your team as well. Because the truth is that instead of freaking out about how much you like my family, few things could make me happier. At the very least," he added with a smile that was difficult to muster when everything that mattered was at stake and he was horribly afraid that he was blowing it, "it will make fifty years of Friday night dinners so much easier for all of us."

At last, Zara couldn't restrain her response. *"Fifty years?"*

"At least." Though he was as scared as he'd ever been—absolutely terrified that he would lose her if he didn't get this right—he smiled into her beautiful eyes. "Do you remember when we were listing the reasons we'd fallen for each other on the drive to Camden? We might have tried to act like we were pretending, but both of us were telling the truth all along. I meant every word I said about admiring your fierce determination to pursue your dreams without letting anyone, or anything, get in your way. And I know that if anyone is strong enough to heal from the pain of losing her mother—if anyone can forgive herself for what she said and did on the day her mom passed away—it's you."

When the silence stretched between them, he racked his brain for another way to convince her to let him past the emotional walls she'd thrown up to protect herself. And then he remembered the hope chest on the floor beside them.

"I made you something." He picked up the chest and held it out, but she didn't take it. Praying he wasn't making things even worse, he told her, "I know how much the hope chest your mother gave you means to you. I want you to have one that will last forever. And I want you to know that your mom isn't the only one who wanted all of your hopes and dreams to come true—I want that too. I would give up everything I have, if only I could give that to you." And he would always look out for her the way her mother had obviously intended to.

"Rory…" She heaved in a breath, and when she let it go, her entire frame shook. "It's beautiful." But the hint of a spark in her eyes had gone out by the time she said, "It's too beautiful for me. I can't take it. I don't deserve it." She closed her eyes, looking utterly defeated. "Please, I need to be alone."

The very last thing he wanted to do was leave her. But he knew he couldn't force her to change her mind. All he could do right now was let her know one more thing. "The night you told me about your mother, I promised you I wasn't going anywhere. And I have no intention of being any less bullheaded and stubborn than I've always been. I'm not giving up on you, Zara, and I'm not giving up on us either. I'm going to keep loving you, whether you want me to or not, whether you think I should or not. I'm going to hold faith that you still love me too. And every single day, I'm going to show up at your house with a chocolate cake and tell you I love you."

With that, though it was the hardest thing he'd ever done, he made himself walk out into the raging storm.

* * *

Beth and Ethan Sullivan were getting ready for bed when he moved behind his wife and put his arms around her waist at the bathroom sink. "Everything is going to be okay with Rory and Zara."

Beth laid her head back against his chest. Looking at the two of them together in the mirror, she gave silent thanks for the millionth time that he'd traveled to her sleepy Irish town nearly forty years ago. She couldn't imagine what her life would have been like without her amazing Sullivan hero and the family they'd created together that was absolutely everything to her.

But then she sighed as she thought again about the distraught expressions on Rory's and Zara's faces before dinner. "I hope it will be."

Gently, Ethan turned her to face him. "We might not have done everything right as parents, but the one thing I know we nailed was teaching our kids how to fight for what really counts. Even," he added, "if it's going to take some of them longer to figure it out than we'd like it to."

She knew Ethan had shifted to talking about Hudson now. Their eldest son and his marriage woes had kept Beth up many, many nights. Unfortunately, he'd come to Bar Harbor without his other half again. And he definitely hadn't looked happy about it.

"Moms should be given magic wands," Beth noted, "like the one Kevin was playing with tonight, so that we can fix whatever our kids need fixed."

"Don't you know?" Ethan asked as he put his hands on either side of her face. "You've never needed a wand to bring magic into our lives. You do it every single day, simply by being you."

And as he kissed her, the magic between them was even stronger now than it had ever been.

CHAPTER THIRTY

12:01 a.m.

It was Saturday. The day Zara and Rory had agreed to break up.

For a while there, it had looked like they were going to go back on their agreement—and that true love might prevail in the end.

Only for their relationship to fall completely apart because Zara didn't deserve him.

When she had first climbed into bed, she'd been too numb to think about everything Rory had said to her before she asked him to leave. Too numb to rewind back to the moment when she'd freaked out in front of Beth Sullivan and fled dinner. Too numb to do anything but stare at the ceiling, which was blurry without her glasses, and listen to the loud sound of her own breathing in the too-silent room.

Even though she knew there no chance of sleeping without Rory there to be her full-body pillow.

After her mother had died, Zara had tried to drown

her grief and guilty conscience by pouring herself into her schoolwork and then her career. But at two a.m., when she finally gave up on sleep and went out to the kitchen table to try to get some work done on her laptop, she not only couldn't focus on the content of the new emails in her inbox, she also couldn't stop herself from opening the folder containing the pictures she'd taken for her ads.

Each photo broke her heart a little bit more. The ones where she and Rory were laughing. The ones where they were staring into each other's eyes. And especially the ones where he had his hands threaded into her hair and was kissing her.

She remembered the way she'd felt that day. As though she'd been riding on a wave of bliss so sweet she'd been sure she would never come down.

No fall had ever been more brutal.

So brutal that she had barely been able to function hours ago when he'd come to find out why she had freaked out at his parents' house.

She had seen how alarmed he'd been by her calm, matter-of-fact responses to his questions. If only he knew that she'd had to shut down absolutely every bit of her feelings. Otherwise, she would have crumbled completely. Crumbled into so many pieces that no one, and nothing, would ever be able to put her together.

Yet again, Zara wished she could talk to her mom.

Because she'd never needed her help more.

A bright flash of lightning lit up the room. Having grown up in Maine, Zara had seen plenty of storms. But none had ever seemed as fierce as this one. Almost as though the heavens were directly connected to the dark storm of her emotions.

It wasn't until a second bolt of lightning flashed that she finally saw it: The hope chest Rory had made for her was sitting on the coffee table.

Zara's heart beat unsteadily as she walked across the open-plan room to pick it up. *My God.* It was a thing of beauty, with stunning inlay forming a lighthouse on top and a hand-hammered latch.

But there was more. Rory had also carved a phrase into the side: *Tá mo chroí istigh ionat.*

Zara felt like her heart was about to leap out of her chest as she typed the Gaelic phrase into her web browser. The translation sent a sob breaking free from her chest.

My heart is in you.

As she brushed aside her tears to read further, she learned that *Tá mo chroí istigh ionat* was not only a way to say *I love you* in a romantic sense, but that it could also be used to encapsulate a parent's love for their child.

Trust Rory to know exactly what her hope chest meant to her—that it wasn't only about her mother's love, but that Zara's own heart was in it too. And still, there was more. Because hours ago, when he'd tried to give the chest to her, he'd said, *Your mom isn't the only one who wanted all of your hopes and dreams to come true— I want that too.*

He'd been trying to tell her that his heart was in the chest too, but she hadn't been able to hear him.

She ran her fingers over the carving. *My heart is in you.*

Her mother would have loved that. And she would have loved Rory for understanding Zara better, almost, than she knew herself.

She went to the closet and brought out the old, cracked hope chest she'd treasured for so many years. But it wasn't the cheap wooden box that had mattered, it was everything inside. And as she went through the silly photos, the sweet postcards with inspirational sayings, the delicious recipes, the small watercolors they'd painted together, and an old, well-worn copy of *The Forgiving Tree*—Zara finally understood that everything Rory had said to her the night she'd told him the story of her mother's accident was right.

Zara's mother had wanted only happiness, joy, hope, and optimism for her daughter. She wouldn't have wanted her to beat herself up for fifteen minutes, let alone fifteen years.

Carefully laying the book in her new hope chest,

along with all the other memories, Zara closed and latched the top. Inside the chest was room for more hopes, more dreams, more love—if only she could be brave enough to let herself have them. If only she could finally push herself out of the self-imposed exile from happiness where she'd lived for so many years.

Finally ready to break the chains she'd locked herself in at fourteen, Zara was tempted to rush through the storm to Rory's lighthouse to beg him to keep showing her the way.

But now that she was finally being honest with herself, she knew it wasn't that easy. There was something she needed to do first—someone she needed to talk to—before she could be ready to ask him to give her another chance.

Picking up her new hope chest, she brought it into bed with her. And even as she fell asleep, her hand remained over the lighthouse inlay.

★ ★ ★

By six thirty Saturday morning, the rain was coming down even harder than it had during the night. The wind was whipping through the treetops and sending white caps racing across the ocean's surface, as well.

As Zara approached the Sullivan Café, she hoped Beth hadn't changed her morning schedule at the last second. Fortunately, she'd barely knocked when Rory's mother opened the door.

"I'm so happy to see you." Beth's relief was obvious. "Come in. Can I make you something to eat or drink, or both?"

Zara was about to shake her head when her stomach growled at the delicious smells coming from the kitchen. She hadn't had anything to eat or drink since lunch the day before.

"That would be lovely. Thank you. I'd like to help, if that's okay."

Beth nodded. "I'd love that."

While Beth brewed two hazelnut lattes, Zara toasted bagels and laid out smoked salmon, cream cheese, and capers. When they were both settled in a booth with breakfast, Zara took a deep breath and began.

"I'm sorry for the way I behaved last night. You were so gracious to invite me into your home. I never should have run off the way I did."

"No apologies are necessary." Beth was kind and full of warmth. "We're all entitled to a good freak-out every now and then."

Zara nearly apologized again before she realized that she needed to begin as she meant to go on. And that meant not blaming herself every time she messed up. Instead, she would start trying to forgive herself, then move forward.

Still, she wanted Beth to know something im-

portant. "You have raised a wonderful man. Rory is..."
Her heart lodged in her throat. "He's unlike anyone
I've ever known. Not only loving, but also brave
enough to see that we were meant to be together—and
to stand behind it even when I wasn't sure I knew how
to do that. If my mom were here..." She needed to
pause to collect herself again. "I'd ask her how to make
things right with him. But since she isn't, I was hoping..." She looked into Beth's eyes. "I was hoping you
could help me. After all, you've raised seven great
children. Surely you know everything by now. Surely
you can tell me what to do."

"I'd be happy to help in any way I can." Beth
reached across the table to put her hand over Zara's.
"But first, I'd love it if you could tell me about your
mum."

Tears sprang to Zara's eyes as she told Rory's
mother about how much she'd loved her own. Beth
held her hand while she spoke, squeezing her fingers
tightly as she recalled the day of the car crash.

"I certainly don't know everything," Beth said
when Zara had finally finished speaking. "Not even
close, I'm afraid. What I do know for sure, however, is
that love is capable of healing even the deepest
wounds—but only if we let it." Beth smiled. "It's easy
for me to say I believe that you and my son were
meant to find each other, meant to heal each other,
meant to love each other. But the truth is that the only

thing that matters is what *you* believe…and how much you're willing to stand behind those beliefs."

From the moment her mother died, Zara hadn't believed that she was worthy of a future full of love and happiness. Not when her mother didn't have a future. Zara had stood behind that belief with fierce determination for half her life.

Only now, as she sat with Beth, did she fully understand what Rory had meant when he'd said that he believed she could be just as fiercely determined to allow herself to be happy, and to love and be loved, as she had been determined to remain in happiness exile.

"Thank you, Beth. For everything." Zara might never fully get over her mother's death, but with help from Rory, his family—and the strong, capable, loving woman it had taken Zara three decades to become— right here, right now, she was going to stop hating herself. "I've got to talk to Rory."

She knew exactly where she'd find him. At the top of his lighthouse, standing watch over the storm the way he'd stood watch over her heart.

Zara was just heading out the door when Kevin and Ashley came into the café. That was when it hit her—there was one more thing she could do to make absolutely sure that Rory would never doubt how much she loved him.

"Kevin," she said, "could I ask you a *huge* favor?"

CHAPTER THIRTY-ONE

In the time Rory had lived in the lighthouse, he'd never seen a storm like this.

All night long as he stood in the watch room, the sky and the sea had raged. Only the revolving light was powerful enough to pierce the darkness and guide home sailors who had been caught unawares by the storm.

As the clock ticked slowly on, Rory held on to his faith. Faith that everyone on the ocean would escape the storm unscathed.

And faith that Zara would find a way to break through her own storm too.

Three in the morning rolled around. Then four. Five. Six. Seven. And still there was no sunrise, not so much as a hint of light on the horizon.

Until, suddenly, a ray of sunlight miraculously broke through.

But what caught Rory's attention even more was the sound of footsteps on the metal, circular stairs that led up to the watch room.

He would know those footsteps anywhere—the purpose, the determination in every step. The hat was the first thing he saw rising out of the stairwell.

A magician's hat.

He wanted to throw back his head and laugh. He wanted to dance one of the Irish jigs his mother had taught them all when they were kids. He wanted to sing every cheesy pop song ever written.

Because Zara wearing a magician's hat could mean only one thing.

Thank God.

"I knew you'd be here." With her glasses all wet and steaming up, in mismatched sweatpants and sweatshirt, wearing Kevin's hat and holding his wand, Zara was the most beautiful sight in the world. "Guiding lost sailors home."

He wanted to pull her into his arms and kiss her. The only thing that could possibly stop him was the knowledge of how much they needed to say to each other first.

Still, he couldn't resist telling her, "That's because you know me so well."

She smiled, although it fell away too quickly. "I wish I had known myself better. Then I might have realized that once my mother died, and I blamed myself for it, I no longer liked myself. That's why I chose to go out with guys who didn't like me very much either. Guys like Cameron. It's also why I let Brittany get away with so much over the years—I thought being her doormat was no better than I deserved. It wasn't until you came along, and were such a force of nature, that you yanked me out of my happiness exile, whether I was willing to leave it or not."

"You yanked me out too, Zara. Just reached right into the heart I was planning to keep locked away forever and made me love you. Although I have a confession about last Saturday night: I never wanted to break up. I planned to wow you so much with my moves that you'd change your mind about ending things today."

"I don't know why I'm surprised to find out how sneaky you are," she said with an upward quirk of her lips. "Although now that we're coming completely clean, I should confess that the real reason *sweetheart* bothered me was because I didn't think I deserved a future full of love and promise when my mom couldn't have either of those things." At last, he put his arms around her as she said, "It took me until now to realize that there's no point in covering myself with heavy amour to protect myself from feeling pain that severe ever again. Not when you're so stubborn that you will just keep yanking down my walls until there are none left."

"You're welcome," he said, glad that he could make her smile with his faux-cocky response. "Seriously, though, I don't want to keep making the same mistake—not having the guts to get you to talk to me. Really talk to me about everything you're feeling, no matter how difficult. I shouldn't have secretly hoped that I could heal you with my love and that you'd find solace with my family—only for the opposite to happen when being around my parents, and especially my mother, triggered a fresh onslaught of grief."

"Your family is amazing, Rory. It's not your fault that when I met them, it all spun back around on me. Being loved by an amazing guy like you, who also happens to have a fantastic family...I felt like I had won the love lottery. But I didn't believe that I deserved it."

"What do you believe now?"

"I believe that when I'm with you, I feel safe. I believe that knowing you love me—and loving you right back—makes me able to get down off the thirty-stories-high tightrope I've been teetering on since I was fourteen. I believe that I'm finally ready to do what my mother would have wanted for me all along and let myself laugh again, and have fun, and dream, and hope for the future. I believe that you're the only person who could have been sure enough of himself to prove to me that I *am* lovable. And...I also believe that the two of us are magic."

"Go ahead," he teased. "I know you've been dying to say it from the moment you climbed up here."

Grinning, she stepped out of his arms to wave the wand. *"Abracadabra!"*

"Only the best damned magician in the world would have been able to steal my heart every single day since we first met."

She stepped back into his arms and wound her own around his neck. "I also believe that I need to be realistic this time. Like you, I wanted so badly for our love, and the joy I feel with you, to make everything better. To heal every broken part of me. But I've finally realized that it's not going to be that easy. I've been stuck with these storm clouds for long enough that I'm not going to be able to shake them off overnight. And maybe it isn't fair of me to ask you to stick with me through the inevitable ups and downs, but—"

"There's no one I'd rather be stuck with."

And as she leaned in to kiss him—and sunlight finally made the clouds outside vanish—she whispered, *"Tá mo chroí istigh ionat."*

EPILOGUE

Ruby was the cutest birthday girl ever. Though she had been showered with gifts for her first birthday, the little girl was far more enamored of the boxes the presents had come in than any of the fancy dolls or shiny toys.

"It's great to see Cassie so happy," Hudson commented as he watched his sister play with Ruby inside an enormous cardboard box. Yet again, Hudson's wife, Larissa, hadn't been able to make the trip to Bar Harbor for the weekend. "She deserves it."

"We all do," Lola said. She, Hudson, Turner, and Ashley relaxed in the shade of their parents' backyard. Rory and Zara were playing horseshoes against the back fence. At least, they would be playing if they could stop kissing for longer than five seconds. "If Rory can land a woman like Zara, there's hope for all of us."

Ashley laughed. "I said almost exactly the same thing to him. Good to know we're on the same wavelength."

Only Turner remained silent, looking lost in his thoughts. Lola nudged him. "What's going on in that animated brain of yours?"

"Nothing much," he said with a shrug.

But Lola didn't buy it. "You're a dark horse, Turner. I wouldn't be surprised to find out that you've been moonlighting as a secret agent, or something equally mysterious."

In an obvious bid to shift his sister's focus, Turner looked at his watch. "Brandon should have been here by now. His flight from Singapore landed an hour ago."

"Hopefully, he'll get here before Ruby goes down for her nap." Hudson couldn't quite hide the wistful note in his voice as he watched the little girl.

"I know Brandon loves to travel," Ashley put in, "but it seems like he's always on the road lately."

Then Lola said what they were all thinking: "It's almost like he's running from something...or someone."

Turner grabbed four beers from the cooler beside his seat and handed one to each sibling. "Here's to always knowing where we stand with each other, even if the rest of the world can be a total mystery." They clinked their bottles together and drank. "Now let's go show Rory and Zara how horseshoes should be played."

And as the four siblings walked across the lawn, they each let the question of true love—and whether it would ever be theirs—go.

For now...

ABOUT THE AUTHOR

Having sold more than 8 million books, Bella Andre's novels have been #1 bestsellers around the world and have appeared on the *New York Times* and *USA Today* bestseller lists 88 times. She has been the #1 Ranked Author on a top 10 list that included Nora Roberts, JK Rowling, James Patterson and Steven King, and Publishers Weekly named Oak Press (the publishing company she created to publish her own books) the Fastest-Growing Independent Publisher in the US. After signing a groundbreaking 7-figure print-only deal with Harlequin MIRA, Bella's "The Sullivans" series has been released in paperback in the US, Canada, and Australia.

Known for "sensual, empowered stories enveloped in heady romance" (Publishers Weekly), her books have been Cosmopolitan Magazine "Red Hot Reads" twice and have been translated into ten languages. Winner of the Award of Excellence, The Washington Post called her "One of the top writers in America" and she has been featured by Entertainment Weekly, NPR, USA Today, Forbes, The Wall Street Journal, and TIME Magazine. A graduate of Stanford University, she has given keynote speeches at publishing conferences from Copenhagen to Berlin to San Francisco, including a standing-room-only keynote at Book Expo America in New York City.

Bella also writes the *New York Times* bestselling "Four Weddings and a Fiasco" series as Lucy Kevin. Her sweet contemporary romances also include the USA Today bestselling Walker Island and Married in Malibu series written as Lucy Kevin.

If not behind her computer, you can find her reading her favorite authors, hiking, swimming or laughing. Married with two children, Bella splits her time between the Northern California wine country, a 100 year old log cabin in the Adirondacks, and a flat in London overlooking the Thames.

For a complete listing of books, as well as excerpts and contests, and to connect with Bella:

Sign up for Bella's newsletter:
BellaAndre.com/Newsletter

Visit Bella's website at:
www.BellaAndre.com

Follow Bella on Twitter at:
twitter.com/bellaandre

Join Bella on Facebook at:
facebook.com/bellaandrefans

Follow Bella on Instagram:
instagram.com/bellaandrebooks

Made in the USA
San Bernardino, CA
03 July 2019